When A

Light

Stripped

Away

When All The Lights Are Stripped Away

SUNIL NAIR

Marshall Cavendish
Editions

© 2012 Sunil Nair

Published by Marshall Cavendish Editions
An imprint of Marshall Cavendish International
1 New Industrial Road, Singapore 536196

Cover art by Opal Works Co. Ltd

Other Marshall Cavendish Offices:
Marshall Cavendish Ltd. PO Box 65829, London EC1P INY, UK • Marshall Cavendish Corporation.
99 White Plains Road, Tarrytown NY 10591-9001, USA • Marshall Cavendish International (Thailand)
Co Ltd. 253 Asoke, 12th Flr, Sukhumvit 21 Road, Klongtoey Nua, Wattana, Bangkok 10110, Thailand •
Marshall Cavendish (Malaysia) Sdn Bhd, Times Subang, Lot 46, Subang Hi-Tech Industrial Park, Batu
Tiga, 40000 Shah Alam, Selangor Darul Ehsan, Malaysia

Marshall Cavendish is a trademark of Times Publishing Limited

National Library Board, Singapore Cataloguing-in-Publication Data
Nair, Sunil, 1965-
When all the lights are stripped away / Sunil Nair. – Singapore : Marshall Cavendish Editions, c2012.
p. cm.
ISBN : 978-981-4361-44-6

1. Fathers and sons – Fiction. 2. Mothers and sons – Fiction.
3. Malaysia – Politics and government – Fiction. I. Title.

PR9530.9
M823 -- dc22 OCN770822193

Printed in Singapore by Markono Print Media Pte Ltd

To Tita

In memory of Amma and Acha,
who were nothing like
the Amma and Acha in the book

The Palace on Stilts

The letter summoning him home arrived in an airmail envelope bordered blue and red. There was no return address on the envelope but he knew Aini's writing well enough. The message, laid out squarely in the middle of the page in a coiled and unsteady hand, read:

> *Come home. I am dying.*
> *Acha*

Anil expected to feel something, but he was empty and numb, as if this sudden announcement from his father did not concern him in any way.

Santhia was standing at the far end of the room, leaning out of the waist-high window. The dusklight was dull and faint and her shadow draped thickly over the chair behind her. He called out to her. The orchestra of sounds streaming in through the window drowned his voice out. He called out to her again and this time she heard him above the rising din.

"What is it?" she asked.

"I have to go home. My father is dying."

Turning away from him she leaned out of the window again and said, "There is nothing left there for you."

She was right. But a month later he travelled south to his hometown, his only companions an old lady and a cockroach. The lady, dressed in the traditional Malay *baju kurung* and headscarf, impressed him with her silence. She sat perfectly still and stared at the never changing landscape of gentle slopes, rubber and oil palm plantations, mesmerised by the stroboscopic effect created by the perfectly aligned rows of trees and the slow movement of the train. She looked as if she was waiting for the land to speak to her, but it remained as silent as she was. The cockroach darted this way and that, unafraid of human presence and broad daylight. It appeared to him that everything was not the way it should have been. On an ordinary day the old lady would have spoken to him and offered him a *goreng pisang* or a piece of *kuih lapis*, and the cockroach would have waited and watched before coming out to play.

There is a knock on the door.

Aini walks into the room, not waiting for him to answer. She chases the dream away with her energy and presence. When he was a child he needed this little ritual with their maid to face the day. Aini would come in and hold him close for a while, his head cradled between her chin and breasts, his mouth pressed against the base of her throat, breathing in the smell of the food she had just prepared on her skin: *puttu, dhosa, idiapam*, the traditional South Indian breakfast dishes she had learned to cook from his mother, Amma. He would remain in this pose long enough for the last traces of the dream-filled night to vanish. He wants to repeat the ritual but Aini hovers above him, playing the air-spirit.

"He's awake and wants to see you."

"Why didn't he want to last night?"

"He was feeling a little weak and he didn't want you to see him that way. At least not the first time. You know how he is."

An image of his father drifts across his mind.

He walks with Aini down the corridor with only a sarong tied around his waist, his face unwashed. He does not want to stand on ceremony during his first meeting with his father. The house is a maze. He allows Aini to walk ahead and lead him to his father's study and bedroom, afraid that he might lose his way and take a wrong turn.

The house was modelled after Jim Thompson's in Bangkok. Acha first saw it in a book five years earlier. He immediately set about building a copy, put together from village houses transported from the nine states with sultanates, connected by elaborate passageways. Acha called it his palace on stilts. Amma said, "This monstrosity will be the death of me."

Through the palace on stilts he now walks thinking of the time when Amma exiled herself to a desk in a spare room and Acha was on fire with an architectural dream and Aini was busy running an unfamiliar, rented house and he was left neither here nor there. As he walks behind Aini he looks at her hips which have filled out since the last time he saw her. He runs the palm of his right hand gently along the walls, tracing the grain of the wood planks. Their footsteps echo through the passageway. He expects Acha to be standing erect, dressed in a cream linen suit and tapping his fingers to the tune of some Malay or Indonesian pop song playing on the radio. The sight that greets him as he turns the corner into the study is of a man he does not know.

"Surprised, aren't you?"

The voice comes from the man buried in the rattan chair, but he imagines a ventriloquist in action in some corner of the room, giving speech to the body that doesn't seem capable of generating sound. He moves closer to the chair and stares harder.

"No matter how hard you stare you won't be able to come to terms with how I look and what has become of me. This is what I am now. You won't change me with your eyes," Acha says.

"I am sorry."

He bends down and gives Acha a kiss on his forehead. The smell of his skin is not of death but of an object that has not been touched or used for years, so different from the perfumed skin he last kissed, with its smell of strength, vitality and freshness. What connects the man who was his father and the one sitting in this chair?

The air in the room is still. The curtains are drawn and what little light there is has stolen in through the gaps. Each piece of furniture is as he remembers it, sitting where it belongs. He looks around the room for a sign of change but sees none. He feels reassured that the objects around him serve as true and steadfast markers of the past.

Aini is no longer with them; she has slipped out of the room unnoticed.

"Sit down. I want to ask you why you took so long to come home, why you didn't call as soon as you got the news about me, why you left so suddenly three years ago, why the deep silence between the letters you wrote once a year. And a hundred other questions." Acha pauses, for effect Anil thinks, before saying, "But I will not. It would be too sudden and too easy."

Acha continues talking but Anil loses himself in the pleasure he gets from the sound of his voice and no longer hears what he says. Acha's words form a veil around him. In the dark the initial shock of seeing his father so changed melts away, as he shifts his attention from his father's body and face to his voice. It is still strong and does not betray him. The voice fills the room. He longs to be swept away by its strength, back to his childhood.

"I cried a lot when you left," Normah says.

A smile spreads across her face and it creases the skin around her eyes, forming a net of fine lines. She has aged, this childhood friend of his, but age suits her well. The shop her father left her when he moved to Kelantan must be a burden.

Anil and Normah used to play in the *rambutan* and *durian* orchard behind her house when they were children, careful to avoid Osman the orchard keeper. She would pretend to feed him the leaves and grass she cooked in a rusty tin can filled with water, saying, "Eat, eat, and you will be stronger than all of them." She was like an older sister to him, the one who nurtured and cared for him with simple words and gestures.

"I had to go away," Anil says.

"It has been so long. Three years, more? I received one letter from you in all that time, two years after you left."

"You shouldn't complain. I wrote to my father just three times, once every Deepavali."

"What happened to Santhia? In the letter, you said you were in love with her."

"She is carrying my child."

Anil steals through the passageways on tiptoe with bare feet, moving towards the tall Chinese vases standing like elegant guards outside Acha's study. He looked for Aini earlier in all the usual places but he couldn't find her. As he walks past the vases he lifts the heels of his feet higher to avoid making a sound. The muscles in his calves stretch and scream.

South Indian calves and ankles have never been the foundation they should be. The typical leg starts promisingly at the well-formed hips, swelling gently into strong thighs, but below the knees the tragedy begins. Spindly calves, betraying the body, taper down towards fragile ankles, rescued only by graceful feet. He stands outside the room, cursing the bottom fourth of his body.

He almost forgets where he is, but a groan, animal and alive, brings him back. The door to the study is open. He pokes his head out enough so he can see right into the bedroom. Acha is bent over in his chair, his lips brushing Aini's hair. She kneels before him, head in his lap, her thick hair spread over his thighs like a blanket to keep his legs warm. He begins to sob. His hollow chest heaves in and out. Aini remains where she is, her body moving in rhythm with his.

"Move," Normah commands.

"I'm glad to find out that you're not a virgin. Who was the

culprit?" Anil says.

"The milkman. Are you going to spend the whole night questioning me?"

"Please, just tell me this one thing."

"No, move."

Later Anil sits with his back up against the headboard. Normah is fast asleep, her head on his stomach. A lock of her hair sticks fast to her cheek, glued by her sweat, or his. He runs his hand over her back. The skin on her body is smooth but her hands are calloused. They almost scratched him when she gripped his shoulders; the hands of a worker. Her mouth remains slightly open, as if she wants to reveal something.

The white Mercedes roars to life, spewing clouds of rich, black smoke into the humid air. He backs out slowly, careful to avoid crashing into the gauntlet of flowerpots lining the driveway. "Don't hit the flowerpots," Acha warns. Anil slows down almost to a halt. "Don't worry, I had a good teacher. She is a crazy driver but you need to be one to get anywhere in the city." He has never driven Acha's car; Santhia had taught him to drive a few months after they met.

Leaving the neighbourhood behind he turns left onto the road to town. They have made this trip many times before, but never just the two of them; Abdul-the-driver was always there. Abdul-the-driver, never just Abdul, or driver, but always a marriage between the man and his occupation.

Abdul-the-driver has disappeared along with all the other servants, except Aini, who said that Acha is shedding all the luxuries he had acquired during his years of success and is now preparing to meet death bare and alone. "Take care of him," she whispered to Anil as they left for town. "This is the first time he has left the house in over a month. He keeps on saying that he is tired of going out into the world, of seeing it any longer. He wants the world to come to him."

He feels Acha so very near and large; the physical presence of the man dominates the large interior of the car. His father has suddenly grown from a small, shrivelled shell to a giant shield protecting him from the sky and the elements. This shield has always blocked out rain and chaos and chance, leaving him dry and safe and barren.

The monsoon rain crashes against the glass and obscures the view of the town, but the outlines and the blurred facades are enough for him to identify the buildings and know where he is. He remembers the town well enough and little has changed.

"Do you want to stop somewhere before going to the office?" he asks Acha.

"Let's go straight there."

A streak of lightning flows across the sky like a great river with many tributaries. It approaches the horizon with its delta of light. Its companion arrives six seconds later, rattling the windows of the car. The thirteen-storey UMNO (United Malay National Organization) complex is suddenly illuminated. A symbol of the dominance of the Malay party over the ruling coalition and the country's political life. It stands next to the hundred-year old, cream-washed, colonial town hall, looking down on it as if to say, "Look how far we've come since the Yes, *Tuan*-You are right, *Tuan*-days. Now you're in my shadow." Not when it rains. The black and blue monsoon clouds hanging low above the land make all shadows disappear, except during brief flashes of lightning. Then they dot the landscape like an army of black phantoms, appearing and disappearing in an instant.

The builders and architects were careless setting the UMNO building on reclaimed land by the river without a stable foundation, and it has acquired a premature stoop. It is a tired building. Most of its hotel rooms and convention halls are vacant, now that the north-south traffic that used to pour through the town across the bridge has been diverted to the North-South highway twenty seven kilometres inland.

Karim greets anyone who wishes to pass through the doors of the building without a word but with a gesture of penance; he stands on one leg and holds both hands high above his head. Karim has taken a vow of silence. The story goes that he is a political activist who adopted this stance when the foundation stone for the building was laid. He is reported to have said, "This is a symbol of evil and greed. Only when the river eats it up will I speak again." That only explained part of the mystery — the silence, and not his stork-like pose — but it was enough to turn the story into a tablet of truth passed around among the coffee-shop dissidents, carried from conversation to conversation as evidence that there was true opposition to the stranglehold on Malaysian politics exerted by UMNO, MCA (Malaysian Chinese Association) and MIC (Malaysian Indian Congress), the unholy triumvirate divided along racial lines. In the beginning the security guards would chase Karim away every morning after they unlocked the doors. He would hobble away on one leg, coming back as soon as they went in. They quickly tired of this game and allowed him to remain as long as he liked. No one seemed to mind; he was accepted as one of the town idiots who inspired laughter and sympathy. They fed him tea and cakes and brought him new clothes when the ones he had on became threadbare.

Anil parks the car in the UMNO lot. He helps Acha out. They cross the street and walk towards Pillai & Associates. He turns back to have a look at Karim, who has dropped his arms to his sides and his leg to the ground, resting his back against the wall in a moment of weakness. It appears to him that Karim is holding up the building he wants buried in the river. His face is contorted with the strain of shouldering the burden. A bearded, dishevelled Atlas.

It is an unlikely place for the offices of a law practice. Placed in the middle of a row of shop-houses, Pillai & Associates is flanked on the right by four *chettiar* shops, money-lending and pawnshop businesses run by the scantily clad Nattukottai chettiars who belong to the caste of cut-throat Tamil Vaisya businessmen, and on the left by a banana-leaf restaurant and a newspaper and magazine vendor specialising in Indian publications. An Indian street it is. The chettiars circle the five-foot way, waiting to descend on the next victim who is desperate enough to approach them for loans at usurious rates.

Anil sees a thin woman in a sari seated on a wicker mat inside one of the shops. Her head is bowed and she is crying. She has her arms held out in supplication and her hands cup a gold bracelet. On a raised platform sits a chettiar with his legs folded, nodding his head gravely. He is the high priest of this ritual and he holds the woman's fate in his hands. Specks of *basmam*, the holy powder drawn across his forehead and chest, float onto his lap as his body moves and quivers. He will wait a while without saying a word, long enough for the woman to realise the depth of her troubles. Then he will suddenly reveal the terms of the transaction, as if in a trance, as if he were an oracle channelling the words of a deity. The woman, lost and forlorn, will play her part and accept with words of thanksgiving. A transaction born out of need and greed is elevated to the spiritual realm.

As Acha walks by the chettiars they nod their heads in unison and say, "How are you, Saar?" A chorus of vultures. Barely acknowledging them Acha straightens his back and quickens his step. He plans a grand entrance but he stumbles over the two-inch door ledge into the foyer of his offices. Only the quick hands of his son save him from hitting the floor. He steadies himself and moves out of Anil's grasp, barking at the receptionist, "See that we are not disturbed. I don't want to see or hear anyone." His voice sounds shrill and unsure. He curses his decision to leave the door ledge and the façade of the shop-house standing, to keep it blended in with the rest of the row, when he had the offices modernised.

The troop of lawyers and secretaries stand up at attention as he crosses the space towards the spiral staircase that leads up to his secluded perch on the second floor. A few of the associates are about to greet him and lie about how well he looks but he raises his arms as if to shield himself, and the words die on their lips. They stay frozen on their feet as he labours up the staircase one step at a time using the banister for support, a far cry from his two-step days. Fifteen heavy thuds later he is out of view and they fall back into their seats drained, as though he has sucked all the energy out of the room. Anil slips by unnoticed, like a shadow, and runs up the staircase.

"Close the door behind you," Acha says.

Shelves of law books bound in black leather line one wall from floor to ceiling. There are a few exceptions slipped in between the legal volumes at random, or perhaps with some hidden pattern: *Sejarah Melayu*, the great quasi-fictional history of the Malay people, two parts fact and three parts fiction, a large tome on the tribes and indigenous peoples of South East Asia and a thick paperback on Indian mythology. All the furniture is Burmese, intricately carved, sturdy pieces in teak and mahogany.

On a desk by the shutters is a black and white photograph of Amma in a simple silver frame. Her unsmiling head is tilted ever so slightly to the left and her large eyes look past beyond the viewer towards infinity. She appears to be carrying the weight of the world on her slender, rounded shoulders. It is always the same with every photograph of her. No matter what she was doing at the moment the picture was taken, the camera glossed over all the other facets of her face, body and personality, and captured only the tilt, the distant gaze, the burden. To Anil they are more like spirit drawings than photographs, forever tracing out the themes of her life.

Paintings cover the other walls to form a multicoloured jigsaw. They are mounted to swallow up all available space and they clash for attention. Small paintings in watercolour and gouache mounted among six-by-four oils. Anil had searched for these paintings the day after he returned but he could not find them anywhere in the house or in Amma's studio. Now he knows they have been moved here. Acha had never understood his wife's desire to paint, what was behind it, what it meant to her, and he had always kept it at a safe distance. He seems to have capitulated after her death, allowing the paintings to be displayed, though in an office he now rarely uses, as if the answers to his questions, or the questions themselves, do not matter any longer.

The painting above Acha's head is Anil's favourite. He was there when it was made, sitting in Amma's studio staring out the window watching red ants build a nest with mango leaves. It is a copy of a Klee with a twist. Amma earnestly matched stroke for stroke but seemed to lose her will to complete the copy when it came time to add the Z that carried all its symbolic meaning. She looked at Anil and said, "Come here for a while. I want you to do something for me." He walked over to her and saw the blank face staring out of the canvas at him. "Look here. There is a Z that I can't seem to paint. Do it for me." She handed him the brush. He was about to add the missing letter but she interrupted him, saying, "Better still, paint any letter you want. It doesn't have to be a Z." Without hesitating he painted a thick, black Y, adding two dots as eyes and a thin horizontal D for a mouth. "That's right, it's not the end yet, is it?" she asked. "You are the last but one."

Tucked away in a corner is a painting he has never seen before. A woman dressed in a sari is standing, holding on firmly to the back of a chair, as if to steady herself. From her distant gaze, pointing towards infinity, he recognises the figure as a self-portrait of Amma, although the woman in the painting looks nothing like her. Standing beside her is Acha, dressed in a suit. He too is staring out into the distance, looking longingly out the window at an event unfolding far away. It is impossible to make out what the event is, but it is painted with quick strokes in shades of yellow and red that suggest motion and violence. Everything appears in subdued colours but for the scene outside the window. On the chair is a naked child. It is fat and androgynous like the cherubs or baby Jesuses in European religious paintings. The calm and static surface of the scene in the room is ruptured by the child's actions. From afar it looks as if the child is feeding from its mother's breast but moving closer Anil sees that it is eating her entrails.

The story the painting tells disturbs him. An almost studio-like portrait, calm and normal in every way at a distance, turns violent and gruesome up close. *Is that how she saw us as she painted this? When did she paint it?* All his strict and stern artistic judgements and views of Amma's paintings crumble under the weight and strength of this one work. So she could paint in a different way after all, with a measure of freedom and abandonment. Are there more paintings like this one hidden away or destroyed?

"Come here," Acha calls out.

He sits beside Acha and sees a labyrinth of names, numbers and notes stare out at him from the pages of a few notebooks. "Who am I?" Acha asks. Anil waits to see if this is a trick or rhetorical question. Acha says nothing, so he replies with a frown, "You are my father."

"What else?"

"You worked your way up from a boy growing up in a family on a rubber estate to a successful lawyer and businessman. And you were Amma's husband."

"You are not wrong. But I am more."

Pointing to the UMNO building Acha says, "That is where my story begins." The leaning tower looks even wearier from here, hardly capable of holding itself up, let alone being the starting point of a story, of a life.

"That is where my secret starts," Acha says. "That's not entirely true because it started much earlier, at the time of independence. But for me, the point of entry into my story was the building over there. Your grandparents gave up your birthright and mine on independence day. Your grandparents, all the other non-Malays, the British. The Malays were trying to take everything they could to make up for the shame of the colonial period and the others let them."

Acha closes his eyes and continues, "I once had a dream in which I was Tunku Abdul Rahman. I was standing in the newly built Stadium Merdeka on independence day, proud to be our country's first prime minister. I shouted, 'Merdeka! Merdeka! Merdeka! Merdeka, Merdeka, Merdeka, Merdeka!' and with those seven cries we were a free country. The crowd in the stadium echoed each cry of independence. We were no longer part of the Empire and I could feel the joys and anxieties of everyone around me. Somehow I found a way of holding all of us together, of keeping us from imploding or exploding, if only for an instant.

"I dreamt I had four masks. The British mask I put aside forever. I am a Malay prince, a leader of my people who are farmers and fishermen, so I wear our mask most of the time. I like the Indians in a distant, paternalistic way and wear their fragile mask when I am with them. I can see them as traders in the early centuries, and then as workers in the rubber estates and civil servants under the British. The Japanese marched thousands of them off to build the Death Railway in Burma during the war. I can see they are struggling to find their voice again. I hold the Chinese mask a few inches from my face when I have to. They trouble me. Their story here does not go back as far as the Indians' and they have not really shared their culture and ways. In my dream they appear like giants stretched across the South China Sea, with one leg in Malaya and the other in China. And yet they have made the most of themselves here, these tin miners and businessmen.

"I can't deny that most of the images and words in this dream were taken from books I had read and footage of films I had watched over the years. But I could swear I was in Tunku Abdul Rahman's head and heart and body in that dream. I was thinking his thoughts and seeing with his eyes, or so I felt when I woke up. That dream has stayed with me ever since."

Anil looks at Acha intently, wondering where he is going with all this. He sounds like a history book coming alive in an intimate, first-person narrative. If only his teachers at school had been as entertaining.

Acha loses himself further in his story.

"The Malay had his political power and Islam, and the Chinese his wealth and industry. But I often asked, 'What did we, the Indians, have?' At best, only our ability to talk, to get ahead with a few words. Not that this gift saved my father when the Japanese dragged him off to Burma.

"I was a young lawyer in KL (Kuala Lumpur) when the 13 May incident happened. I saw the Chinese and Malays kill each other over a five-year economic plan and I saw the Indians stand aside and watch. On the fence as usual, waiting for the right side to jump to. To be fair, they couldn't do anything else, being a small minority. Some say high-ranking members of UMNO and MCA were involved in the slaughter. I realised that the Malays and Chinese would hate each other as long as the Malays remained privileged under the constitution as *bumiputeras*, princes of the soil, and the Chinese remained in control of the money. It was obvious that they would hate each other as long as they could not find a way to share the land as equals.

"The Indians had something in common with the Chinese; they were both non-bumiputeras. But the Indian had given much of his culture to the Malay over centuries. He first brought Hinduism to the region, then Islam. He is a neutral link between the two, trusted and mistrusted in equal measure by both, yet powerless, impotent. I knew that I would have to wait for the time when I could turn this into an advantage, into a form of power.

"I said to myself, 'I will fight the Malay and Chinese by using them both and stealing some power for my own kind.' The fight would not be out in the open in broad daylight but behind the scenes in the shadows. It was not to be open confrontation but guerrilla warfare. I had to wait many years to set my ideas in motion. I moved to this town and made a name for myself with my law practice. I married your mother. I used a favour owed to me by a Chinese businessman whom I kept out of prison to get into property development."

Acha has rehearsed this performance over and over again in his mind, but like an inexperienced actor on stage speaking his part for the first time to a live audience, he becomes overexcited and speaks too quickly, gesticulates too wildly. His eyes are open wide. The words are a weight he must cast off, the story told as he wants to tell it.

He stops to catch his breath.

"Then the day came. It was not long after the UMNO building was built, some fifteen years ago. I had been involved with the MIC party in the town since I had moved to Muar. But it was nothing more than cutting a few ribbons and drawing curtains at opening ceremonies and witnessing the party faithful break chairs over each other's heads at the annual meetings in the town hall. A call came from Dr. Razak Mohammad, the president of the Johor UMNO party. He wanted to meet me to discuss some business opportunities, he said. I went up to his office on the thirteenth floor and we talked for a long time about the town and its history. We went as far back as Parameswara, the founder of the Melakan empire. Then he started on a different track altogether, saying that he had heard I was a dedicated member of the National Front. I protested and said that I was involved every now and then with the MIC but that I wouldn't describe myself as such. 'You're too modest,' he said, 'I've heard very good things about you.'

"What he went on to propose was almost too good to be true. He would give me the contract to build over ten thousand units of low-cost housing in the district. All I had to do was set up a company with a few Malay directors on the board and put in the bid under that company. He was even kind enough to suggest the names of potential directors. One of them was his brother. With a nice Malay company name and a few Malay directors I would be assured of winning the contract no matter what the bid was because they were no other bumiputera companies involved. So it was settled.

"My chance had finally come. This would be my entry into the world of politics and power. I could use my contacts with Chinese businessmen and builders to carry the project through and my new connections with Malay political might to win further contracts. I was lucky to have aligned myself with Dr. Razak. He was, and is, an ambitious man. Together we built one of the biggest business groups in the country. Property, highways, shipping, communication, we do it all. Dr. Razak has become one of the top men in UMNO and I have spread my influence to the national level. I declined all offers of a political post because I always knew it would be best for me to set the stage for those who would play the real game. I would like to think of myself as the Joseph Kennedy of Malaysia, building secretly and waiting for the right moment for one of his own kind to burst into the limelight."

Acha is exhausted after the long speech and leans back to rest his head. He places the notebooks on Anil's lap.

"This is my legacy to you. The important names and numbers and transactions of the past fifteen years. There is much more but you can find that out easily enough. Also, a list of people you can depend on, the companies I own, where all the money is. All this will soon be yours. I have made arrangements to have everything transferred to you after I die. Apart from some money for Aini, everything is yours. You can do with it as you please. You can give it all away if you want. But remember what I said to you. I have set the stage and you must decide if you want to act. Not in a small way as you have done till now, drawing cartoons and taking your little stabs at those in power. There is nothing you can't do with the money and influence I have left you. Don't stay locked away in a room somewhere pretending that you are changing the world with your art. In a way you will have to choose between the gifts I have now given you and those your mother fed you with as you were growing up."

Illuminations

Anil's first lesson in painting was a form of punishment. He had been running around in circles shouting at the top of his voice, a boy of seven seeking attention from his mother who was seated at the far end of the shed buried in her work, her back turned towards him. At first Amma continued painting, ignoring him, but the climbing pitch and volume of his cries broke her concentration. She turned and said softly, "Stop that now." Her quiet words surprised him; he stopped yelling. "For that you are not to speak or to make a sound for an hour. You can still talk to me if you like but not with your mouth. Anything you want to say to me you will have to draw or paint."

She handed him a sheet of paper, a piece of charcoal, a palette, a brush, three tubes of watercolour paint, and a jar of water. "Remember, no written words. This will teach you how weak words and sounds are," she said. As he reached out to gather his new tools of communication he was about to thank Amma but he stopped himself just in time.

How do I say thank you without speaking the words or writing them? This was the first task he set himself. He tried thinking up a symbol but nothing came to mind. He closed his eyes and imagined the scene of a little boy thanking his mother as he accepts a gift, but he quickly came to the conclusion that without writing the words, the end result could easily be mistaken for a picture of a little boy receiving a gift from his mother without gratitude appearing anywhere at all. He knew he did not have the ability to convey the message by getting the facial expressions right. And even if he could, that was not exactly what he wanted, because he could easily imagine himself saying thank you without a single ripple of expression spreading across his face.

He felt trapped, he felt cheated by Amma. The objects she had given him were poor substitutes for words, and yet she had said that they would teach him how weak words and sounds were. He pushed on. Grabbing a sheet of paper he started drawing, hesitantly at first, but as his anger grew, the movement of his hand across the surface became wilder and bolder. When he emerged from the spell he was under, a mass of lines, wild and formless, greeted him. What had he done? He was not quite sure what to make of it. The effort looked unfinished, incomplete in some way. He poured blobs of colour straight from the tubes in patches at the centre of the drawing. Blue, red, yellow. He added a few drops of water with the brush. The paint smeared across the surface of the paper and where they touched he saw green, purple, orange, black and many other colours he could not name.

After an hour of getting stuck, thinking as hard as his mind would allow, expressing his exasperation, evaluating his first effort, experimenting with colour, he had travelled far from his original desire. He had travelled so far that what he had wanted to say was almost invisible, a tiny dot from which he began his journey. He ran towards Amma and thrust his 'first work', as he would call it later, at her. "Alright, let's see what we have here. I'll tell you what I see first and then you can explain to me what you were trying to do," she said.

He was anxious. What if Amma does not see anything? What if she sees something that is not there? She pointed to the centre of the paper and said, "I see thin and tentative lines here. This is where you started the drawing. The lines become thicker and deeper as you go out slightly. You have pressed hard into the paper, probably because you were angry. You were trying to say something and couldn't. As you grew calmer, the lines became playful, as if you had completely forgotten what you wanted to say and were happy just to draw." She could see that he was confused but she carried on. "It is easy to see that the colour was added last because the lines are buried underneath. You have reinvented the wheel. The colour wheel I mean. That's one lesson I won't have to teach you. If you look at this closely you will see how the colours I gave you mix to form other colours. And they all come together to create black, darkness."

Amma talked for a long time and said many things he did not understand. He was amazed that she could see so much in one painting, his painting. When she finished, he started his explanation. He was bursting to tell her what she had missed, what was missing from the painting altogether: the origin, the first thought. All of it came out in a hurry, in fits and starts, and he felt embarrassed. He borrowed words and phrases from Amma. He realised he was not speaking clearly. His words were getting mixed up with hers and with the painting itself. Lines, words, colours, sentences, meaning were boiling away in a pot, and the smell was unfamiliar. He couldn't say for sure if his first attempt was a success or failure. Amma's wide smile gave him some comfort.

Over time it becomes a game between them. Anil speaks with a painting, she guesses what he is trying to say, describes what she sees and replies in kind. Then he tries his hand at interpretation. He finds himself developing a strange vocabulary, quite distinct from Amma's, to explain what he thinks is hidden beneath the layers of paint and lines. He says, "Those lines are dancing and crying drops of paint at the same time. You are sad." Or, "I see fire. Everything is hot, everything is on fire. The face, the flowers." Amma laughs when he speaks like this. She is not a woman who laughs often, but when she does, laughter takes hold of her in a tight grip. She doubles over as if in pain. Her eyes grow bigger, she bares her teeth, her eyebrows arch to touch her forehead. Short, sharp sounds, like muted barks, escape her mouth. Anil loves her laughter. It tugs her back from a distant land and places her squarely before him, contorting flesh and sound. In laughter she becomes solid, her pleasure deep and crystalline. He knows that if he reaches out to touch her then, he will feel all of her.

Anil remembers watching her paint. Amma would always sit for a long time, brush in hand, staring at the canvas, past the canvas. There was something at the end of the world tugging her towards it. An invisible rope pulling her in towards infinity. Without warning, as if her muse had switched her on when she was least expecting it, she would come to life in an instant. The muscles in her arm would tense up, and the brush would touch the canvas in slow, measured movements. She couldn't paint any other way. No wild gestures, no quick strokes, every action was painfully deliberate. She would work steadily for hours on end, building the painting as if she were rolling a boulder uphill, fighting against its weight, struggling against gravity. It never came easily for her. Perhaps it was a matter of talent or something in her nature that wouldn't allow her the spontaneity he longed to see as she worked. At the end of a session she would calmly put the brush and paints away and look around the room. She would fix her gaze upon him, as if saying "I am back now," and he would run to her, knowing she was safe to touch and talk to once again. The shed remained unchanged but for some more paint on a canvas. What was the meaning of this, what was the use of hours of work if nothing changed and no one saw the fruit of her labour? Anil could not understand all that dedication, day after day, all that seriousness, all that weight. Maybe that is why when she died he abandoned everything he had learnt from her, years of practice and discussion, for cartoons. They seemed lighter, more capricious and free from her spell. She would have hated him if she had known.

Leela is playing in front of the house. Long, thin blades of *lalang* prick and poke at her small, bare feet and she performs a St. Vitus' dance, each jerky movement wilder than the one before. She hears a motorcycle approaching. The roar of its engine becomes louder and higher pitched. She stops suddenly, gesture frozen in mid-air, fists clenched and arms held slightly away from her sides, eyes squinting against the glare of the morning sun, lips pouted. This is how Acha sees her for the first time. He slows down to a halt, turns off the engine and stares at the lovely young girl with the funny expression. She looks back at him, unafraid of the stranger.

He would say to her after they were married that he was in love with her most at that moment. He feels that if a sudden wind picks up on this bright and clear day, she will topple over and break into pieces, so slight and fragile she seems, and that the funny expression will live forever on her face. He rides away and she comes back to life, allowing herself a smile.

Acha visits her parents the next day. He introduces himself and talks about his parents, who are dead, his past and present, and the town. Leela runs into the room and out again to steal a glimpse of him; she instantly recognises the stranger on the motorcycle. Acha ignores her and looks straight at her parents, talking hurriedly to keep his concentration. She hears him say when he gets up to leave, "I want you to promise that you will allow me to marry your daughter when she is old enough." Her father coughs. "Mr. Pillai, she is only fourteen. You will have to wait at least four years for that. Maybe that is too long for you."

"I will be back here in four years," Acha says as he walks to his motorcycle.

A week before the four years are up, Acha sends a note to her parents saying that he will visit the following Saturday. Leela spends all that Saturday morning and early afternoon preparing for his visit. She washes her body and her hair, and then sits in front of the mirror looking at her face and breasts. She thinks her features are now set and she will probably look the same, but for the effects of time, for the rest of her life. Her breasts have grown heavier and fuller in the past year. She parts her legs and touches her pubic hair and thighs. What will he think of her now, four years later?

Her mother is outside the door. "Leela, he's here. He's here. Hurry up and come out." This is one of my better days, she thinks. With her sari tied carefully, revealing just enough of her midriff, and her hair pulled back in a bun, he will now see a woman, not a child. Her mother smiles when she opens the door. She leads her by the hand to the kitchen. A large tray has been laid out with two cups of tea and savoury and sweet cakes. She reaches out for some candy, but her mother slaps her hand gently and tells her to take the tray out to her father and Mr. Pillai.

Throwing the sash of her sari over her left shoulder, she steadies her nerves and body and carries the tray into the living room, all the while looking slightly downwards to avoid catching his eyes. She leans forward as she approaches him. Just as he is about to reach for a cup of tea, she takes a step forward and catches the hem of her sari underfoot. The tray with all its contents flies out of her grasp and lands on his lap. His suit is drenched with tea but he sits there calmly, smiling at her. She bursts out laughing and doubles over as if in pain. Her eyes grow bigger, she bares her teeth, and her eyebrows arch to touch her forehead. Short, sharp sounds, like muted barks, escape her mouth. Her mother and father apologise profusely for her behaviour and ask her what she thinks she is doing. She kneels in front of Acha and picks the cakes from his lap and puts them back on the tray, all the while looking at him with an expression that says, "This is what you are getting."

*

All around Leela are colour and sound and smell. Her sari glitters silver and gold in a sea of bright silk, cotton and polyester. Reds, browns, greens, yellows and blues bob up and down, heaving violently like a many-coloured monster enfolding her. The cream pillars of the temple and the pale green leaves of the coconut trees along the high walls of the compound offer the only respite from the visual onslaught. The white jasmine flowers in her garland are fresh. Their scent, which mixes with the fragrant smoke from the incense burning in front of her and the unpleasant smell of the priest's sweat trickling down his forehead and naked upper body, overpowers her and makes her feel disoriented and nauseous. A thick cloud of sound hangs over the scene. A fat, squat man, whose cheeks and chin swell up like a toad's every time he blows hard on his instrument, makes piercing and reedy cries with the *nagaswaram*. His son caresses the tabla with his long beautiful fingers, producing a pulsating rhythm. Sombre and monotonous prayers in Sanskrit trickle towards the concrete floor, children's cries and laughter fill the background.

She is seated in the middle of the temple with her back facing the altar. There are people around her as far as she can see, but the gods and goddesses are behind her in the inner sanctum and above her on the five levels of the *gopuram*. With her eyes closed she can see the three serene faces, all placed on one neck, of Sri Mariamman in the centre of the first tier, flanked by two strong attendants with tilted heads. She imagines herself taking the place of the goddess, radiating her healing powers to all who walk through the gates of the temple. She can see the blue shepherd boy Krishna, her favourite god, close to Sri Mariamman, and the gigantic yellow statue of Vishnu.

The wedding garlands have been exchanged and the priest leads the couple three times around the sacred fire. Showers of yellow rice fall on her head and body. She looks straight ahead and sees herself outside the temple gates, playing hopscotch with her childhood friends. All of them are happy, so brightly happy.

A week later, after a short honeymoon in Singapore, she is in her new home. The official wedding picture sits in an ornate frame on Leela's dressing table. If she looks at it long enough, her stomach knots up and the fear refuses to leave for hours afterwards. She remembers being in the studio immediately after the ceremony in the temple, ushered by the photographer from one pose to the next. The picture was shot against a background of lakes and trees. She is still in her wedding sari. The flowers in her garland have wilted in the heat. Her husband looks ahead with a firm and steady expression, but the lit cigarette in his right hand betrays his nerves. He takes a quick puff every time there is a break in the action. She can summon her state of mind during the studio session with ease. All through the drive to the studio, and for hours after the pictures were taken, she could not get rid of the images of her playing hopscotch with her friends. The last frames of the movie playing before her eyes are ones where she freezes up and cannot bring herself to make the simplest of jumps to pick up the stone and win the game for her team. Her friends are urging her on. They grow tired of her cowardice and start shouting at her and calling her names. She finally tries to jump but she falls outside the square and scratches her knee. Her friends run away and leave her alone with her wound seeping bright blood onto the white chalk.

*

The small sign next to the front door of the shophouse gives nothing away. Tom Artosy, it says. No one is in the large front room. A ceiling fan knocks loudly as its blades spin and wobble. Countless canvases and frames are stacked against the walls. There is no furniture in the room and it appears to be more of a warehouse or a storage area than an artist's studio. She calls out a few times but nobody replies or comes out. She walks across the room to the far wall and tilts a canvas towards her. The painting is a portrait of a young brown-skinned girl wearing a thin blouse, her small breasts visible through the cloth. Her skin is an unnatural shade of brown and the sky and coconut trees in the background look artificial and dead. The second painting she looks at is almost identical but for the eyes, which are alive and stare out at her.

"This is how I make a living. I know you're thinking that these portraits are unremarkable and anyone can paint them, but they sell well because lots of restaurant and coffee-shop owners like hanging them up for some reason. They all call me and ask for the same thing. Sometimes when I am sitting alone and drinking tea, I curse the painter who first made such a portrait and sold it to a shop owner. Maybe the painter didn't sell it, and someone else did, a son or a daughter, but all the same it is the reason why I spend most of my waking hours painting the same strokes over and over again."

Leela turns around and sees a young man, about thirty years old she guesses, standing next to her. He is dressed in a pair of jeans and a white T-shirt covered in blobs of paint. His long, black hair falls across his face and hides his gentle features.

"I don't think they are exactly the same. You painted the eyes differently on this one. I can't say what it is exactly but they look more alive to me," Leela says.

"No matter how hard one tries to be a machine, the human element always comes into the picture. So I have a critic in my studio! It's not often that I have one here."

"I'm not a critic, Mr. Artosy, just a customer. What kind of name is Tom Artosy anyway?"

"I know who you are, Mrs. Pillai. Your husband called yesterday and told me what he wanted and I suggested that you come in at two, and here you are. My real name is Thomas Fernandes, a nice and common enough Portuguese name, especially if you're from Melaka, but it's not the sort of name you would keep as a painter, would you? Artosy is completely unimaginative I know, but I'm not good at words and names, otherwise I would have become a writer. And what is your real name? I can't be expected to paint your portrait unless I know something about you. Of course, if you want something like one of those..."

She laughs and says, "My husband would not be too happy to have a portrait hanging in our house of his wife with her breasts exposed. Something more conventional please, shoulders up would be best. My name is Leela."

He leads her through a small green door into another room the size of the first. There is hardly any natural light in the room and a few seconds pass before she sees an easel with a canvas of another portrait on it, a palette smeared with thick paint, opened tubes of colour scattered on the floor, and a young girl seated on a wooden chair. The girl has a towel wrapped around her, as if she has just emerged from a bath, and she plays with the ends of her long hair while looking at the ground, oblivious to the presence of other people in the room. "She is deaf mute," Tom says as he walks up to her and makes a few signs with his hands. The girl stands up and leaves the room, holding the towel up with one hand.

"She must be the model for all your portraits. I recognise her face."

"She is my model, my cook, my cleaner, my lover. I need someone like her, otherwise life would be too solitary."

An hour each afternoon she sits on the wooden chair vacated by the girl. He does not want or need any more of her time. She is surprised that he gives her no instructions and hardly looks her at all. He talks ceaselessly, about anything that is in his head. His hands often fail to obey his eyes and mind, and he stays frozen for minutes at a time not knowing how to continue, but he is never at a loss for things to say.

On the fourth day he leaves abruptly in the middle of a session without a word of explanation. It is the first time he has left her alone in the room. She jumps out of the chair and runs over to steal a glimpse of the portrait he has been painting for days now. What appears before her is strange and moving. She expects to see a likeness of her face, her neck and shoulders, but most of the canvas is filled with disconnected features, as if someone had mutilated a face and left the nose, eyes, ears and mouth on a large, rectangular plate for all to see. The disconcerting effect is heightened by the placement of the parts; the eyes are painted diagonally opposite each other, the nose occupies the centre below the mouth, the ears placed side by side like twin doors leading into a black hole. She thinks she recognises her mouth and eyes, but she is not certain. The nose and ears belong to someone else, but then again they could be her nose and ears, only slightly distorted.

At the bottom left-hand corner of the canvas she sees a small, nude figure on a bed. The woman is lying on her back with her legs slightly parted. Her head is raised and she is looking at something or someone beyond the borders of the painting. Leela immediately recognises herself in this painting-within-a-painting, this window. The woman's face is small and blurred but she feels that anyone looking at it would know that it was her face. The body is proportioned like hers, and the breasts, thighs and stomach look like they could belong to her body in the distant future, when her skin and flesh start to sag. Only the thick and curly pubic hair seems alien to her. She does not understand how he has stripped her clothing off in his mind while she sat in front of him fully clothed, but she is attracted by his art and wants to know how he would respond to the reality of her naked body.

She unwraps her sari, removes her blouse, *pavada* and underwear and lies on the bed behind the chair. She parts her legs slightly and waits for him. As he enters the room a few minutes later she raises her head like the woman in the painting and says, "Let us see how you deal with the real thing. I don't want you to touch me or make love to me, but I want you to put away that painting and start again with me posing for you like this. And I want you to paint a proper portrait of me too, both in three days." For once he can't think of anything to say. He puts the canvas away, sets up another easel and starts to work.

Leela allows herself to enjoy the sensation of a man looking at her body from just a few feet away. She works hard to abandon all feelings of shame and guilt, and she learns to behave naturally in this state, moving when she wants, walking around the room, standing next to him to watch over his progress. No one has ever looked at her like this and she has never before done something forbidden. She compares his gaze to that of her husband's, contorted with lust, when he is undressing her or is on top of her, and she finds Tom's strangely more caring and tender. She knows she has not gone hopelessly beyond the border of what is acceptable, but all the same she has crossed it and will be punished if found out.

Her last minutes in the studio come quickly, too quickly. Leela regrets setting the limit of only three days for him to finish his work but any more time spent posing for him would lead to questions and she wants to keep her little adventure here away from guarded answers and lies. She puts on her clothes slowly. Tom stands close to her, looking lost in his own studio. He too does not want these afternoons to end, fearing the drone of the identical days ahead, with nothing to distinguish one from another.

She gets dressed, combs her hair and ties it back in her habitual bun, and reapplies the red *potta* signifying her status as a married woman. He shows her the two paintings. She studies her portrait first. Although painted well, her features carefully recreated and enhanced to make her face more beautiful and immediate, it contains almost nothing of her. She knows it will hang on a wall like countless other portraits, eliciting polite remarks from family, friends and strangers, fading quickly in the background and casting no more than a pale shadow in the room it inhabits.

She takes a deep breath when she sees the second painting. The woman, she herself, has stepped out of the window in the corner of the canvas she saw three days earlier, has grown and blossomed and filled not only a larger surface but also every inch of space around her. She looks wise, earthy, sated, and glows through the thick paint covering her body. "That's me, that's me.

I want to paint like that. Can I paint like that?" she says in a childlike voice.

"It's not hard really. I'm sure you can if you put your mind to it. There is nothing in it I can claim to be my own. Every idea is copied, borrowed or stolen," Tom says.

She is deflated by his words. She sees something unique and magical in this painting, something that contains within it a large slice of her body and what she has experienced here, and a part of her spirit too, so surely he can't mean what he has just said?

"Don't misunderstand what I am trying to say. This is a beautiful painting I think. It has stretched me to the limits of my ability. It is the best I can do. There is so much of you in it, what you were before you first met me, what you've become by taking off your clothes and posing for me, what I saw that perhaps was not there. And that's why it is beautiful. But there is nothing new here apart from that. Every stroke is governed by a trick or two I have learnt from books. I will lend you these books and teach you what I know and maybe you will break free from all this and come up with something of your own. I know I never will.

"When I started to paint years ago, when I was about your age, I thought I would be able to stare at the plates in art books, study the technical innovations of the masters, and then experiment, develop and become great myself. The first great Malaysian painter, imagine that. It never happened. Maybe modern painting is a Western thing and there is little for us Asians to add, maybe there are no great innovations left and art is dead. Maybe I needed a master to teach me instead of learning everything on my own, maybe I have little or no talent at all. I don't know. But it never happened."

She looks at him for a long time before saying, "All the same Mr. Artosy, Tom, it is beautiful to me. I can't take it home but I will come by every now and then to gaze at it when I am tired of seeing my reflection in the mirror and I long for a different image. And I'll come to show you what I've painted and, who knows, one day you will see something different and new. You may think I am too young to give you any advice but if you're tired of painting, try writing for a change. You surely have a way with words."

This is the story of how Amma started painting.

"I don't understand it. You go to have your portrait painted and you come back an artist. Why is this so important to you?" Acha says.

Leela is angry that she has to explain what she thinks is a small request.

"This is not so much to ask, is it? Think of it as a hobby. It's not important why I want do it or if you or I understand it. All I want you to do is to give me a place where I can paint. There is no room in the house that I can use. I've explained to you that oil paints smell and give off fumes, so you need to build me a little shed at the back of the house. I'll sit there and not bother anybody. You're away at work all day and you probably won't notice anyway. The books and the paints I want are not very expensive and well within the budget of a lawyer I would think."

"Don't talk about money, Leela. It's not about the money. I just can't understand it. And what will you do when we have a child? Leave him to a servant while you stay locked away in a shed?"

"He will watch me paint and learn something from his mother."

The shed was put up within the week and Leela had her 'outhouse' to work in. All her energy and fantasy remained within the walls of the shed, nothing spilled out of it across the lawn into the house. It was as if the thick wooden planks absorbed every emotion, feeling, word and dream that flowed from her. She liked it this way. It was her wooden fortress and only she was allowed in or out. She never talked about what she did here to anyone — she only showed a painting or two every month to Tom and asked for his advice — and the hours spent in isolation were wrapped up in the same cloth that covered her days in Tom's studio.

The old man urges the girl forward but she stands rooted next to him. He places his wizened hand on the small of her back and walks towards the house, gently pushing her along. "She's never like this. I don't know why she's acting this way." He scolds her. "She's a good worker, she is. She can work all day without getting tired. You can see she is strong, good bones and skin. Some people think she's pretty," he says, pressing her arms and shoulders, as if to demonstrate that she is indeed hard and will not break easily.

The girl is very pretty, Leela thinks. She will grow into a beautiful woman. *Her limbs are long and her skin is smooth and from here she looks at least three inches taller than me.* Her thick, black hair falls to her shoulders and she is constantly brushing it back behind her ears with her fingers. *I should stop looking at her as if I were examining an animal.*

Leela takes the girl by the hand and asks, "How old are you?" Before she can reply her father says, "I've told your husband already that she is seventeen." Leela says, "I would like to hear it from her, and in English. We don't speak Malay in this house. Tell me your name too." The girl looks at her father and when he nods, she turns to Leela and says, "My name Aini. I seventeen years old."

The father smiles proudly at his daughter.

"I told Mr. Pillai that she speaks English. Me, I can only say a word or two in English, but these young people are so clever. They read and write and can fill out all these long forms. Aini is a clever girl. My wife would have been proud of her, but she died when Aini was five and didn't see her grow up. Look at her, she's here in a big town away from the paddy fields and vegetable patches, working for a big man. You will take her, right?"

She leads Aini to the house and says, "Of course we will. You needn't worry about her. We'll make sure that she becomes cleverer than she is now. She will have a good home here." The old man leaves her suitcase at the doorstep and waves goodbye to his daughter, walking away without looking back. Aini watches him until he turns the corner and is out of sight. She enters her new home with Leela, leaving the hot afternoon outside.

In time Aini learns the rhythms of the house and understands the balance of power between the couple. How Sir makes the decisions about money and big things, how the day-to-day running of the home lies completely in the hands of Madam. The little boy stands between the two, but he is growing and seems to have a mind of his own already. He knows that she is a neutral force and treats her as a confidante and a partner in crime. She doesn't know if Madam likes her. She is kind and shows her how to cook Indian dishes and spends a lot of time teaching her English, but every now and then she catches Madam looking at her in a funny way. She wants to treat her as a sister but Madam holds her a step or two away and never lets her come too close. Sir is different. He comes up to her every morning, touches her hair and her hands, asks her how she is doing and always tells her how beautiful she looks. He often says how lucky they are to have her working in the house, how she has become more than a maid to them, how Anil has become attached to her. He talks to her about his work and many other things she doesn't understand but she enjoys the attention of this big man, as her father calls him.

Pickled Snakes

"The experiment with the mad", as she would name the experience later, all began with a story Tom told her on one of her visits. Leela had read all the books he had in his collection, mastered and memorised a vast library of information, and was beginning to feel that her teacher had almost nothing left to teach her. Her skill and strokes had matured and she was beginning to show signs of being capable of breaking free, as he had never been able to do.

The paintings she considered different and special were kept hidden; even Anil was not allowed near the corner of the shed where they were stored in large boxes. Some of them were painted over when she grew out of a style she had been playing with and she was certain she had moved a step further. She realised that they were not yet complete in some way, far from being new and exciting, and she wanted to protect her 'children' from the evil eye of others. She continued to show Tom still lives and copies of paintings she had made from studying colour plates in his books. She had a great ability for reproducing paintings, he thought, and she had come far and was as good as he was, if not slightly better, but he was not convinced that she would go much further.

He lectured her repeatedly about chaos and inspiration and the unknown in art, because he was afraid she did not understand these things and thought that one could become a painter by application alone. She had grown weary of these conversations, of going around in endless circles, so one day when he was in the middle of yet another variation of the same theme, she asked him to tell her something different, something she hadn't heard countless times before.

"What do you mean? I'm doing this for your benefit, you know. I can stop talking whenever you want me to."

"Don't get angry, Tom. I know you are trying to teach me things you don't think I understand. But I am not that stupid, and I want to hear a new story. Tell me something you've been thinking about recently, something you've read that you were interested in."

"Well, do you know anything about Hans Prinzhorn?"

She shook her head.

"No, I didn't think so. He was a German art historian and psychiatrist who collected paintings, drawings, objects and collages made by patients in European psychiatric institutions from 1928 to 1931. Five thousand pieces in all. He wanted to study the art of mad people as creative works by this forgotten and forsaken slice of society and he wanted to use these works as a way of studying their mental illness. Many later artists, including Klee, were attracted to these paintings but in the 1930s the Nazis declared them to be degenerate, along with many other paintings, and the collection disappeared. Only many years later was it restored and found a permanent home in the psychiatric department of the University of Heidelberg."

"Why are you so interested in this collection?"

"I haven't seen the collection of course, but the article I read included plates of five or six pieces from it and I was shocked to see what these loonies could produce. Great works of art. Imagine these people, their minds destroyed in some way, creating objects far more beautiful and fascinating than you or I could. Works that can stand up to those of the masters. That got me thinking that perhaps I don't have that mad spark in me to make me great. Not enough chaos and inspiration, in other words."

"Don't start going in that direction again. I'm sure quite a few people out there think you're mad and would be willing to have you committed."

"Maybe, but I am not mad or mad enough. I tried a little experiment. You know Karim, the man who stands in front of the UMNO building, with one leg up and both arms held up high above his head? I gave him a piece of paper and a pencil and asked him to draw something. He took the paper and pencil, turned around with one leg still up, pressed the paper against the wall of the building and started drawing. He took all of two minutes to finish. The building had fallen into the river in his drawing, there were fish swimming all around it, and there was a matchstick man smiling on the banks of the river. It was pure garbage. Utterly devoid of anything interesting. Everyone knows that Karim wants to see the building collapse, but what else was there in the drawing? Nothing. I gave him one *ringgit* and walked away very disappointed that my experiment had failed."

The car weaves through the labyrinth of small streets in the hospital complex. Abdul-the-driver stops in front of the black, cast-iron gate at the entrance of the psychiatric institution. Not too long ago the sign would have said, "Danger! Home for the Mad!" but times have changed and, even in a small town like this, potentially offensive phrases have given way to gentler ones.

The building is no different from many others they have seen in the hospital grounds. Whitewashed, monstrously large and imposing, with a red, tiled roof. Far removed from the rest of the complex, surrounded by a high, barbed wire fence, it stands alone and desolate, a white ship steaming out to a vast, empty ocean. Leela thinks of turning back. She has gone to great lengths to get here to conduct her experiment with the mad and it is too late to give up now. Phone calls to the head of the hospital, whom her husband knew, were made time and time again before he allowed her to speak to the head of the psychiatric division. She too was sceptical about the project but she listened with curiosity and finally agreed to a trial session. Two hours with a small group of the more manageable patients, she said.

"You don't have to wait here, Abdul. It's not the nicest place to wait and I don't want you staring at a wire fence. Come back in two hours," Leela says.

The guard unbolts the gate and lets her in. His polite manner seems out place here. What a strange sight she must be, a sari-clad woman carrying a box stuffed with paints, charcoal and brushes, and a pad of watercolour paper. The head had warned her not to bring anything sharp, so she left the pencils behind.

A diagonal crack runs along the front wall of the building. She half expects to see water gushing out of it and to hear people screaming as they are drowning. But all is quiet. The reception area is tidy and bright. A few pot plants decorate the otherwise spartan room. The nurse on duty leads her to Dr. Srinivasan's office, where she waits and tries to plan the two hours ahead. Apart from spreading her wares and asking the patients to paint, she does not have a clear idea of how to fill the allotted time. Perhaps she should first show them how to use charcoal and watercolour? A short demonstration, nothing more. She is afraid that she will have nothing intelligent to say if questioned by the psychiatrist. What is she doing here? What does she want from the unfortunate creatures? What does she hope to achieve from all this? If she were honest, she would say, "I heard a story just the other day and it attracted me. I want to act it out for myself and see where it leads."

The doctor walks in. From her position at the hospital Leela knows that she must be at least forty, but she looks much younger with her short hair and fresh skin. Her eyes are big and bright, taking in the picture of the younger woman on a curious mission. She is dressed in cream trousers and a matching jacket, without a white coat on, and she seems more like an energetic businesswoman than a doctor. She notices the question in Leela's eyes and says, "I try not to wear a doctor's coat if possible. It's less threatening for the patients." Leela thanks her for allowing the experiment with the mad. She doesn't put it that way even though the phrase is at the tip of her tongue, instead she says "trial session with the patients." The doctor waves her gratitude away.

"I am not agreeing to much. We'll see how this goes and if it interests the group I have assembled. After all, it's not what you and I think about this experiment that counts, but how the patients react to it. I'll sit at the back of the room for a while to observe and if things are going well, I'll leave you with them. Of course, there will be an attendant in the room at all times."

Five patients and an attendant are waiting in the room the doctor leads her into. It is not far away from the reception area and the corridor that leads to it is like any other fluorescent-lit corridor she has seen. What was she expecting, cells on either side with madmen screaming and wailing, thrusting their hands out to touch and grab her as she walked by? If there are any cells left, they are probably hidden in the farthest reaches of the building, away from the eyes of strangers. Already her image of the experiment, built from pictures she has seen in her mind thinking about Prinzhorn wandering through what must have been prisons at that time, barbaric and cruel places housing the mad, is slowly dissolving.

She is in a classroom with desks and chairs arranged in neat rows. *Now I get to play teacher.* Prints of gentle landscapes of faraway places mounted in light, wooden frames line the walls. Places where the sun is colder and more forgiving and the grass is a lighter shade of green. The setting is calm and idyllic, but the illusion breaks into a thousand pieces when she looks out the windows and sees the wire fence standing tall and firm, reminding her of the nature of the place she is in. The patients must be used to the sight of the fence. Two of them sit looking outside, undisturbed by it. They appear sane to her from where she stands, two women and three men, all young and fit in body. She does not know the nature of their madness — she has not asked the doctor — and the word "manageable" means nothing more than non-violent to her. What is it they suffer from, why have they been locked away? She must be sure to ask the doctor when she gets the chance. A short history and description of the chosen five would help her think about what she is doing here. The attendant is the most sinister looking person in the room. He stands guard in a corner far from the rest, arms folded. He is a short, squat man, thickly muscled, with a face half hidden by his big moustache, a dark villain from a Tamil movie.

She introduces herself to the class and asks them their names one by one. They respond without fear or embarrassment. She feels a sense of relief and proceeds by explaining that she would like them to enjoy the time that follows and learn a thing or two about drawing and painting. The patient sitting closest to her, a Chinese girl named Man Mei, shouts without warning, "I can draw. I can paint." Leela smiles and says, "In that case you can help me teach the rest." The girl appears satisfied with the answer and starts humming softly. The lesson proper begins with her displaying a drawing of a boy's face. The drawing is simple and the heavy lines are easy to reproduce. She had thought of showing them how to copy the drawing but instead she just lays out paper and charcoal on the five desks and asks them to draw a face using the one she has just held up as an example. They obediently pick up the charcoal and start working.

The doctor's presence unsettles her. All along she has felt her watching and listening, a coiled snake in the corner of the room waiting to strike at her first mistake. "Would you like to draw too?" she asks. Dr. Srinivasan stands up and says, "No, not this time. I'll leave you to your lesson and will come back towards the end of it."

The rest of the two hours go by without incident. She can almost say at the end of it that she has enjoyed herself. The work the patients have produced exceeds her expectations. The matchstick figures drawn by Man Mei, the student who claimed she knew how to draw and paint, are the most childish by far, but she thinks she can see interesting lines and ideas in her drawings too. Is she reading too much into these sketches, hoping that the experiment would not be a failure from the very first day? She doesn't think so. After all, even if Man Mei's drawings are bad, surely no one can deny the power and strange beauty of the ones Ahmad has produced.

He is the most puzzling of her students. He has remained silent for the whole two hours. Not a sound has passed his lips, which have been contorted in a constant grimace or smirk. As soon as he received the paper and charcoal, he took one quick look at the example Leela had held up and began drawing without hesitation. He only stopped when he had filled every inch of the white sheet. She left a full block on his desk so he wouldn't have to ask for more paper.

She is mesmerised by the detail and ambition of the two drawings. The first is a whole world in itself. The boy's face is faithfully reproduced at the centre of the drawing but around it are humans, animals, angels and devils, and creatures from the underworld, all engaged in a ferocious battle. The boy seems to be untouched by the war that surrounds him, yet he is obviously connected to it in some way. This suggestion comes through so forcefully that she is led to think that the war is being waged over his life or soul. The other drawing is of the aftermath of the conflict. There are many dead bodies strewn all over the battlefield, and there are now two faces of the same boy, one calm and untroubled as before, the other twisted in pain.

"Impressive, isn't it?" the doctor says. The students and attendant have left the room. She has returned to talk to Leela. "You don't know what Ahmad suffers from but perhaps you can hazard a guess from what he has drawn." Leela hesitates to put a name to what she thinks she sees but she says, "Schizophrenia?"

"You are close. It is a common error to confuse schizophrenia and multiple personality disorder. Ahmad suffers from the latter. In the past three months since he has been here we have only been able to observe two separate personalities, but that doesn't mean there aren't more. He knows who we are talking about when we refer to his minor personality and he is quite aware of the two people living in his body. Maybe he is trying to tell us that there are only two. It would be quite rash to assume this right away but this is certainly interesting."

"But it wouldn't be rash to assume that you'll let me come back?"

"No, it wouldn't."

Within a month the experiment is deemed a success by all concerned and her class grows to ten. The students — she no longer refers to them as patients — develop with each lesson and now use charcoal, watercolours and oil paints with ease and little direction. Man Mei's matchstick figures grow fatter and fuller and Ahmad's vision widens beyond wars over his divided self. Even the attendant has let his guard down and begins to doodle every now and then in his corner. She knows them by name, temperament, condition and talent. She knows how to draw each of them out of his or her private cell, coaxing and cajoling the difficult ones into action, encouraging Ahmad and the two other students she believes are gifted to wander away from safe territory, to experiment. She knows she can teach. She enjoys her time here and is learning about mental illnesses by listening to Dr. Srinivasan every week.

She knows all this, yet she feels she has failed to recreate Prinzhorn's experience. The walk into something unknown, the descent below the outer surface of the mind, eludes her. Tom tells her not to ask for too much. He is impressed by what she has achieved in such a short time. "Two out of three ain't bad," he says to reassure her. "And you'll learn something about painting from this. You don't feel it now but you will, passively, through your pores." Having come this far, she wants more.

But it all ends as suddenly as it began. The students have been agitated all lesson long. Leela doesn't know the cause of their anxiety or what they are feeling. The rain pounds against the walls and roof, creating a loud, pulsating sound like steady gunshots all around them. They are restless and find it impossible to work. She walks up to Ahmad, hoping to settle him. If he begins to paint, the rest of the class will be sure to follow. Without vying for the position, he has become the unofficial leader here, the one the other students look to when all is not well. She approaches him. He looks away from her, pretending to be absorbed in a painting of his she has framed and mounted on the front wall of the classroom. She speaks to him softly, asking him to try and fill in the empty corner of the painting he is working on. He doesn't look at her. The rest of the class is watching how the scene develops, waiting for cues on how to act, and she is determined not to lose this contest that has materialised out of nowhere. She raises her voice a little and says, "Ahmad, you have to finish the painting by the end of the hour. You won't be allowed to attend next week's class if you don't."

By the way he turns to her and the look of cold anger on his face, Leela realises the threat is a mistake. He reaches with one hand to grab her neck. Before she can get out of his grasp he gets up and starts choking her with both hands. She tries to break free by wriggling and kicking him wherever she can but he is too strong for her. His hands are rough on her skin and she is repulsed by the strong smell of his skin and hair. She hears the attendant screaming, demanding that Ahmad let go of her. *Where is he?* All she sees is a gecko inching along the ceiling towards a fly. It seems to be taking forever to travel a foot, she thinks. Just as her vision starts to blur she feels his grip loosen. Out of the corner of her eye she sees the attendant wrestling Ahmad to the ground and putting him in a headlock. She wants to ask him to stop but she can't make a sound. She hits the floor and loses consciousness.

Several hours later she wakes up to find herself in a hospital bed, Anil and her husband by her side. Her husband makes a joke about her suffering for her art and she smiles feebly. Her head is wrapped in a bandage and she feels light headed. She closes her eyes and drifts off to sleep. When she opens them again a doctor is at hand, examining her and shining a bright light in her eyes. "Not to worry, it looks like nothing more than a mild concussion. You should be on your feet and ready to go home tomorrow."

The picture of Ahmad being restrained keeps playing in her head. She can see him looking lost and frightened. She feels nauseous and asks for a pan to vomit in. "Not to worry," the doctor repeats, "this is normal." She is not concerned for herself — she knows she will recover soon enough — but what about her students and the experiment? She is sure that the sessions will be stopped and that she will never see her students again. Ahmad and the others will not draw or paint as long as they remain inside the asylum. I have failed, she thinks, as she rests her head on the pillow. She pictures them lying on their beds, just like her, drifting off to sleep knowing that the narrow tunnel connecting them to the world outside is now forever sealed off.

Anil asks Amma when and why she began to paint. She thinks for a moment before saying, "Your father gave me a gift a year after we were married, an anniversary present, except the gift was not what he meant it to be. He sent me to Tom to have my portrait painted and I came back a painter. No, not a painter, but a person who wanted to paint with all her might. The reason for the change was another portrait. It's different in every way from the one you see hanging in the hallway. It's hidden away from everyone but me and Tom. So it's your father's fault, though he knows nothing about it. His present was transformed into one that affected me so deeply that it has stayed with me here, in my gut, ever since.

"In a way, it has created a wall between us. He doesn't understand what I do in this shed all day, or rather he doesn't know why I do it, and he has never tried to find out. Maybe that's unfair, because I don't have any simple explanations. I once told him that he had to spend time here with me, watching and waiting, to understand something about my painting. The way you do. I am not interested in his work either. He sometimes talks to me about what has happened during the day and I listen to him like a dutiful wife. What does it concern me if he has built another ten thousand houses or owns another company? A selfish attitude I know, because what he does could put ten thousand roofs over our heads and feed us for ten thousand lifetimes, but I can't bring myself to care about it."

She holds him by his shoulders and looks straight into his eyes. "Listen to me carefully. I am not saying that your father is a bad husband. I think I am mostly responsible for what separates us. I am saying that he is locked away in his world and I in mine."

Normah and Anil sit side by side on wooden chairs in an area of the shed Leela has cleared out moments before. Normah is facing her, posing with a book in her hands, pretending to read. Anil is seated close to Normah, touching her hair, his face in profile. They are naked. They have posed for her many times before, but this is the first time she has asked them to remove their clothes.

The nude figures she has painted have all been born out of her imagination: girls reclining in beds and fields, male and female dancers hand-in-hand in a circular configuration, women caring for their children. All these have been creatures of her mind. The flesh and body parts of the two grown people she has seen naked, her husband and herself, have been until now the only archetypes she has worked with. She has stretched, distorted and shaped them into a hundred variations. There are only so many ways you can reinvent reality, so she is pleased to have live flesh just a few feet away from her. The beauty of her son and his friend mesmerizes her and she stares at them without painting. Lean and unblemished, natural in each other's presence and hers, they are perfect. Was this how Tom felt when he saw her lying on the bed in his studio all those years ago? She is uncertain that she could have been as beautiful then as Anil and Normah appear to her now.

Later that week Leela sees Normah's father walk up to the house. She thinks nothing of it — he does odd jobs for her husband and comes by at least once a month to talk to him — and goes back to tidying the bedroom. Set on finishing the painting of Normah and Anil that day, she is eager to get to work earlier than usual. She makes the bed and puts her nightclothes away in a hurry. As she is about to leave the room she hears heavy footsteps running towards her. Aini turns the corner and says breathlessly, "Madam, Sir wants you in the living room now." She instructs Aini to prepare her breakfast and goes to meet her husband calmly; it still does not occur to her that something may be wrong.

As she walks into the room she sees the stern faces greeting her. Instantly she knows Normah's father is here about the painting.

"Mr. Rahman tells me that you asked Normah and Anil to pose without their clothes on for you. Is this true?"

She looks down at her feet, unable to face this inquisition. Her first experience painting nude models has quickly led to this intrusion into her work. What a heavy price to pay, she thinks. She remains silent. Her husband gets to his feet and grabs her by her shoulders.

"Leela, answer me. Did you ask Normah and Anil to take off their clothes?"

She looks at him coldly, angry that he has chosen to make a scene out of this in front of an outsider.

"Is it a crime? I used them as models for a painting. It was innocent."

He lets go of her and raises his hand to strike her. It happens too suddenly for her to avert the slap, and she feels the full force of the blow on her face. Her ear starts ringing and she loses her balance, stumbling backwards. She grabs hold of the back of a chair to break her fall and steadies herself slowly. She can feel her face and neck burning and turning red, from the slap and the shame and anger of being humiliated in her own home. Her eyes fill up with tears and they start to trickle down her cheeks. She wipes her face with the sash of her sari and looks at her husband defiantly. He is about to hit her again but Normah's father jumps up from his chair and holds him back.

"That's enough, Mr. Pillai. I did not want you to hurt your wife. Telling her not to ask Normah to do that again would have been enough," he says.

"Leela, have you gone mad? How could you have thought that asking two fourteen-year olds to pose for you naked was innocent? Go, get that painting and bring it here."

On the way to the shed she wonders how Normah's father found out. Normah did not seem the type of girl who would run and tell her parents about such a thing. She wouldn't have asked her to pose if she had thought the girl was a telltale. She is probably not to blame; it may have come out in the open by mistake. Or she may have talked to some other kids in the neighbourhood and the story may have been carried from house to house until it reached her father's ears. How would she face her neighbours if the latter were true?

She studies the painting for the last time. She knows she will be able to recreate what she has done so far and finish the painting in secret. Once again she will have to use all her skill and guile to work from stored images, memorised and locked away in some part of her brain. At least she will have two more real bodies as starting points.

Her husband is already prepared for the slaughter when she returns to the living room. Knife in hand, he commands her to give him the canvas. He thrusts the knife through the centre of the painting into pure space, as if carefully avoiding the seated figures, and slices it into thin strips. The scene of this ritual sacrifice has turned comical and she has to suppress a smile.

"Mr. Rahman, I think this is a satisfactory resolution, don't you? The painting is destroyed and you have my word that my wife will not use Normah as a model from now on. Leela, if anything like this happens again, I swear I will burn that shed down together with everything in it. And you can be certain you will never be allowed to draw or paint anymore if we have to go through another scene like this one."

Normah's father apologises to her as he leaves the house.

From her desk Leela can see the solitary coconut tree towering above the secondary forest beyond the fence. No one climbs the tree to pluck its fruit; there are no notches cut along its trunk for footholds. The crown of leaves moves in the breeze, a mop of hair gently tousled by the wind. Each day, at three in the afternoon, a monitor lizard begins its eight-metre climb up the tree. As if governed by an ancient rhythm no other creature can feel or hear, it inches its way up to the top, stops a while to survey the kingdom below, a dense undergrowth of smaller trees and shrubs that have replaced the pristine rainforest which once grew here, and then returns to where it came from.

An inner clock ticks inside her too; each day, after lunch, she retires to her desk in the spare room in their rented house. Her husband is away at work, Aini is busy cleaning and preparing dinner. Anil leaves the house as soon as he puts the last morsel of lunch into his mouth and doesn't return until eight. Leela is worried about her son. Ever since they moved here she has hardly seen him. Where does he go off to between lunch and dinner? Why doesn't he stay with her in the afternoons like he used to? She doesn't have the energy to find out and she finds herself avoiding him. She has retreated further into herself.

The builders demolished her home three months earlier to start building her husband's palace on stilts. Every day she returned to her studio, until they could not longer work around it and had to tear it down too. Watching from a distance she saw the bulldozer raze the shed in one go and when it turned around there were only planks of wood and a zinc roof in tatters flattened to the ground, covered in a swirl of dust. She had planned to throw a small party for its anniversary, inviting the few people who knew she painted and cared for her work, but there it lies dead three months short of its twentieth birthday.

Painting at the desk in the rented house has become a struggle for her. She tries hard to concentrate, but nothing comes easily and she finds herself thrown off by everything around her. The changing light through the small window, the distant sounds of children playing, the lizard's clockwork journey each afternoon, all these daily events distract her from her work. In the months she has been here she has not finished a single painting. It is as if the bulldozer had severed the connection between her mind and her hand. The watercolours she paints with — her husband has forbidden oil paints here — do not obey her will and they smear and streak across the paper of their own volition, creating patterns and formations she doesn't understand. She hopes that when the monstrosity is built, she will have her own space, and her painting will flow again. But she fears that this may be the end of her twenty-year journey; her painting is in some way intertwined with the shed and the space within. Her strength is ebbing away but she forces herself to return to the desk day after day without fail, waiting for the moment when life will slip back into her empty and weakened body.

According to legend all the steps of *kampung* houses in Melaka are made of stone because Sultan Mansur Shah's favourite son slipped and fell from a wooden one five hundred years ago, dying at the age of fifteen. The sultan decreed that never again would a house be built with wooden steps in his kingdom. This story is not to be found in any book of the period but teachers of history lessons and old men in the state recount it tirelessly as if it were the truth.

I turned the corner and saw you lying at the bottom of the steps. I ran towards you shouting, hoping that you would wake up, get to your feet and start talking to me. Who has not heard the story of the stone steps in Melaka? There you were lying, silent, dead to my calls, your blood trickling from your mouth onto the wet stone. Red on green stone, red diluted by rainwater. Not the colours you would have chosen to paint your death. I bent down to touch you. Your face was still warm, twisted away from your body like a broken doll. Your eyes and mouth were open. I forced them closed, fearing that someone else would see you with that grotesque expression. No matter how hard I tried, I couldn't erase the look of shock on your face. As if you were asking, "Is this it? Is this all there is?" I started screaming, calling for attention. Aini arrived moments later. She broke down and started sobbing hysterically. I tried to get her to call Acha and an ambulance but she would not move, so I had to do it myself. You were cold by the time they arrived. The monstrosity, Acha's palace on stilts, was the death of you, as you had prophesied.

The teak coffin lies in the middle of the room, surrounded by rings of family and friends. The order is obvious: the ones closest to her by blood form the inner circle, while the rest jostle for position outside the stronghold. Amma is laid out in a plain white sari, with a red *potta* on her forehead. Garlands and loose flowers fill the coffin. Her small face pokes out from behind the floral screen. The white and red flowers are the only form of decoration allowed in the house. All things festive and gay and colourful have been put away or covered with white cloth. She looks calm and peaceful. The undertakers must have worked hard to remove the expression that was frozen on her face when Anil found her. The scent of jasmine and roses and rosewater rise from around her body and mix with the sandalwood incense the priest is burning.

When he was alone with her the night before, speaking out loud and stroking her hair, he could smell the fumes of chemicals rising from beneath her skin. What do they use to preserve bodies, formaldehyde? Touching her hands and face reminded him of playing with pickled snakes; they were cold and clammy and ancient.

He has been instructed by someone — he can't quite remember who asked him to do this — to greet every mantra the priest utters with "Siva, Siva, Siva." Why he has to repeat this response endlessly he doesn't know, but he blindly obeys and finds himself drifting away from the room. Anil floats above the house and sees it put together like a giant quilt, each piece sewn along its borders to the next one. The cursed Melakan wing will forever stand out for him. He will say, "This is where my mother died. She fell down these stone steps and broke her neck." He sees the street wind through the neighbourhood to the main road. The hearse will travel slowly along this street while the neighbours witness the spectacle. He floats higher and the whole town appears far beneath him. Through the clouds he sees the river flowing into the Straits of Melaka. That is where he will scatter her ashes.

He returns to the room to find four thickset men standing around the coffin. They lift it above their shoulders and walk towards the door. He is pulled to his feet by several pairs of hands. He is told to walk behind the coffin, touching it at all times. Acha appears next to him and Uncle Ravi, Amma's brother, is close behind. He sees Tom propped against a wall, crying silently, and his three young cousins running wildly, playing a game. They follow the coffin to the hearse, where it is laid down gently. The hearse begins to move. Behind and to both sides of it is a throng of men with palms placed flat on any part of the vehicle they can touch, chanting loudly. Only men will be involved in the ceremony from now on; the women are left behind to grieve and prepare the evening meal. No cooking is allowed when the body is in the house. Anil holds on to his *munda* with one hand. He has tied it around his waist carelessly and he feels it slipping down as he leans forward to touch the hearse. The skin of his arms and chest presses against the cool metal. For now the journey ends at the main road. They let go and return to the house, watched by the neighbours who have spilled out onto the street to witness the procession.

They will go from here to the cremation ground at the edge of town, ten kilometres away. Son, husband, brother, cousins, priest, self-appointed elders of the Malayalee community: only fifteen of the many who have played a part in the funeral accompany the body to the place of ritual burning. A band of half-naked men, dressed in white mundas and streaked with holy powder, guiding the dead body to the place where it will be consigned to the flames.

Acha sits next to Anil in the backseat, turning to him every now and then as if he is about to say something, but he doesn't speak. Abdul-the-driver drives looking straight ahead, his lips sealed too. The day outside is bright and hot. The windows are rolled down and Anil can smell melting tar as they travel on a freshly laid road on the far side of town. Will burning flesh and bone smell the same? He has not seen his father cry. Maybe he has done so in private, but he wants to see him shed at least a tear before this day ends. Acha lights a cigarette and leans out the window to blow the smoke.

They arrive at the cremation ground. It is nothing more than an acre of land surrounded by a six-foot high, solid wooden fence. There are pits the size of human bodies dug out of the thick layer of sand laid along the perimeter; they remind Anil of barbecue pits along the beach. The caretaker leads them along the path to where Amma lies in her coffin. Along the way he sees the dying embers of a fire. Who was cremated yesterday? Tomorrow or the day after, someone else will walk down this path and ask the same question.

The coffin lies open on the funeral pyre, resting on neatly stacked logs of wood. Kindling and small pieces of charcoal are stuffed between the logs to help the fire take. There is a strong smell of kerosene splashed on the wood and coffin. He doesn't know what is expected of him. Nothing has been explained or laid out. They are moving and acting according to the priest's instructions. The prayers start again. As soon as they end the priest leads him by the arm to the pyre. The others remain behind. He sees Amma's face surrounded by flowers. He is given rosewater to sprinkle on her face and body and is asked to repeat a few mantras.

Out of nowhere the caretaker appears with a burning torch in his hand. He passes the torch to Anil, who now realises what he has to do. His body goes weak and he struggles to hold on to the torch. The priest holds on to him tightly and says, "You must be strong. This is your duty as the eldest son, the only son." He is surprised by how strong the small priest's grip is. The man does not come up to his shoulders, yet he is able to hold him up and keep him from falling. Once he has steadied Anil the priest pushes him forward. Anil closes his eyes and says, "Get up and run, Amma. Don't make me do this." He counts to ten and opens his eyes, but she is still there. He lunges with the torch and the wood bursts into flame. This is not enough. He wants to walk away, throw cold water on his face and head and try to erase this brutal ritual before it sets deep in his mind, but he is led around the pyre to set it alight at another five points. Finally, the priest says to him, "We can go now. You have done your duty."

He walks, then breaks into a run, to get away from the sight of flames rising, engulfing the coffin. He can already smell the flowers burning. Before long he knows he will be able to smell burning cloth, hair and flesh. He sprints to the car, gets in, rolls up the windows and shouts at Abdul-the-driver to start the engine. *Why are they taking so long?* He sees Acha and Uncle Ravi strolling behind the priest towards the entrance of the cremation ground, while a few others are still standing before the pyre, palms touching in prayer. The caretaker is tending the fire, making sure it does not go out.

Sweat trickles down Anil's chest. He is burning. Burning, shaking, crying. Abdul-the-driver says, "You can rest, son. It's all over now."

But it is not all over. The next day he is awoken at dawn. He can't remember when he fell asleep the night before. Upon returning to the house after the cremation he rushed to his room and has stayed there since. Aini brought him some food before dark, but the plate remains untouched. He did not drink the water she left either; his mouth is dry and his throat parched. He forces himself to think about his mother, travelling across her hair and face and body to memorise what she looked like when she was alive. Memory will play its usual tricks and these pictures will yellow and fray at the edges in less time than he imagines. For the moment he wants to believe that he can cheat time and memory by freezing her image.

He thought about her life and her stories and found himself resorting to cheap words and sentences to describe the years of her existence. This exercise tired him quickly and he drifted off to sleep. He dreamt all night long but he didn't dream of her. Not once did she appear in scenes of long walks in the forests, swimming in the river, fights with children in the neighbourhood. Even when he dreamt about painting in the shed she was curiously absent.

He drinks a glass of water in the kitchen but refuses to eat breakfast. After the commotion and noise of yesterday the house feels oddly silent. He is bundled into the car again and this time he ends up at the temple. The same kindly, short priest leads them to a room beside the main altar. On the floor is an earthen tray, filled with her ashes and bones that refused to burn. The charred remains have been arranged to recreate the geometry of her body; there are bones placed to suggest her arms, legs, head, torso and hips, and flowers fill the gaps. The whole arrangement sits on a bed of ashes.

Later, when he is in the city, he will buy a picture book on anatomy and study all two hundred and six bones in the human body. He learns that babies have more bones, two hundred and seventy soft ones, and some fuse before the age of twenty-five. Tibia, femur clavicle, ilium; these are some of the bones he remembers from his biology classes at school. Leafing through the book at night he reads out loud the names he has never heard before. He likes the sound of distal phalanx and manubrium. Which ones did he see in the tray? Most probably parts of the larger, stronger bones which were not completely burnt to ashes in a fire that lasted the better part of a day. The tibia connects to the patella, which connects to the femur, which connects to the ilium, which connects to the vertebrae, which connect to the skull. This way he travels up and down her skeleton, his, all the skeletons that have ever existed, of people dead or alive.

He touches the flowers, ashes and bones lightly during the prayers, as if caressing her body for the last time. No one forbids him from doing so and he doesn't care if he is doing something wrong. The contents of the tray are poured into a large urn after the prayers end and they travel with it to the mouth of the river.

There is a narrow strip of artificial beach where he can perform the final rites. It is a perfect day. The sun warms his body and the coconut trees sway in the sea breeze. In the distance he can see the outline of the island, Pulau Besar, which sits on the horizon in the Straits of Melaka. He steps into the water with the urn on his head. He walks with careful steps until the water is chest-high, then he drops to his knees and tips the urn forward. Underwater he sees the flowers and ashes float to the surface and the bones sink to the bottom of the riverbed. He remains in this position until he is sure that he has emptied the urn. He has stayed under for more than a minute and he quickly gets to his feet, breaking the surface, gasping for air. The urn is still in his hand. He throws it as hard as he can away from him. But the tide is coming in and the urn slowly drifts back towards him. He turns and runs back to shore. The undertow will drag the bones to deeper water, the ashes will float away to the straits and perhaps journey to the seas and ocean, but the urn does not want to leave.

For six days and nights Anil wanders through the maze. He moves from wing to wing, up and down the interconnecting passageways and steps, an explorer in his own home. Furniture, the texture of wood which makes up each part of the puzzle, ornaments and vases; he studies all these things. He wants to pick up Amma's presence, her trail, before it goes cold. A tracker carefully retracing her steps and the imprints she may have left behind.

What has she bequeathed? A batik sarong bought in a market in Kota Bahru draped over an armchair, a simple Chinese vase on her bedside table, a splash of red paint on the wall. And the expression on her face when he found her, her death mask, which never leaves him. Apart from these trinkets, and her painting (but that was always there staring him squarely in the face — he wants more), he finds no other trace of her. It is as if she were caged in the Melakan wing that she had turned into her studio and surrendered the rest of the house to Acha. He lifts the cloth over her portrait in the hallway to see her face again but it no longer resembles her. Her body has vanished, and with it her spirit.

The numbers dwindled quickly. There were over a hundred people coming and going the day of the funeral, twenty remained the next day, and only a handful of the closest friends and family were to be found after that. Now there are three. Acha has returned to his life and work away from home and Aini is busy restoring order and cleanliness. Anil is tired of being alone and goes looking for his father. Wandering through the house endlessly the days before, he has learned to walk like a ghost, creating no sound and leaving no tracks. He heads toward Acha's study. He has not seen Aini this morning; she was not in the kitchen as she usually is at this time.

The seven days of mourning are over. The white cloth covering the paintings and decorations has been removed and colour has been brought back into the house. Life is supposed to return to normal after just one hundred and sixty eight hours. Outside the study the tall vases are bare and beautiful. The door is slightly ajar and he pushes it open further without knocking first. It moves without creaking. In the bedroom beyond the study he sees his father in bed with Aini. The muscles in his back and buttocks tense as he thrusts into her. They move silently. Her eyes are closed. He finds himself stuck to where he is, watching his father fucking the maid. The days of mourning are truly over.

He closes the door and walks back to his room. He feels like running but he knows that the floors will heave and scream if he does. Without thinking he packs his clothes neatly into a suitcase and looks for his identity card and bank book. When he was eight he ran away from home after receiving a spanking from his mother who found out he had been stealing money from a boy at school. He became hungry after a few hours and the orchard began to look menacing. He tried hard to stay away forever to punish Amma but he could not and came home before dark. It was a trial run for the real thing.

He returns to the study when Acha leaves the house later that day. He opens the drawer where he knows Acha keeps bundles of notes and counts out two thousand *ringgit*. Together with the money he has in his bank account, he will have enough to keep him going for a few months wherever he chooses to go. He writes a note and leaves it on the desk.

I have to leave. I don't know where I am going but I will let you know that I am safe. Please don't have anyone look for me. I don't have to remind you that I am of legal age and can choose to go where I like. You may notice that some money is missing. You don't owe me anything, but I need it.

"*Pakcik*, can you tell me when the northern train leaves?" Anil asks.

"It's delayed but not for long. It should be here in half an h⸢ Just wait here. Where are you going?" the platform conducto⸢

"To the city, I think."

"You think? Either you're going to the city or you're not. All the young people want to leave for the city sooner or later."

"I meant that I'm going there now but I don't know if I'll stay for long."

"A wanderer I see. Don't worry, the city is a big place with many worlds in it and I'm sure you'll find one where you fit. My son did and he is happy there."

On the train Anil realises that he has not seen his father cry for Amma. This gives him the final push he needs to break away from the town where he has lived all his life. He feels the train speeding ahead through the landscape.

The City

Dusk arrives and with it comes the noise of hawkers setting up their stalls along the street outside his window. Ah Nam, who fries Anil's *Hokkien mee* three nights a week, waves at him from below. The shutters are wide open and will remain so until he goes to bed past midnight. Anil likes it this way, allowing the bustle and life of the evening and night to drift in to puncture his solitary existence. And the smells and words. Leaning out of the window as far as he can, he sees the crescent moon hanging low in the sky.

The walk from the train station to Puduraya took him an hour. Anil lost his way and had to stop twice to ask for directions. Dragging his suitcase along the ground and looking up at buildings slowed him down even further. Once he gets to know the city the same route takes him less than half the time. His first task was to find a cheap hotel. The taxi drivers outside the station were good sources of information; they suggested looking in the backstreets behind the main bus station. "Don't be stupid and choose a ho' on the main street. Only white backpackers do that. You pay r for nothing," one of them volunteered.

He had seen KL before, but not like this, not on foot. Walking the streets on a mission with his eyes wide open taught him more in an hour than he had learned travelling for days through the city with his parents in the backseat of a car. He noticed immediately that people were more energetic here, as if everyone he encountered was moving towards a goal he could not see. *Doesn't anyone here know how to stroll like they do back home, walking aimlessly?* After a while he found himself changing his pace to fall into step with the crowd.

He walked past the first four hotels he found. He could not say why; they all looked much the same from the outside. A white signboard above the door, peeling paint on the front walls, windows with grilles and wooden shutters. He entered the fifth for no other reason than the name: Super City Hotel. Now that's the way to start my life here, he thought. The toothless Chinese man at the front desk led him up the stairs after they had settled on the price. He was to take the room for a week at a discounted rate, full payment upfront. He was careful not to lean on the broken banister while walking up the steps.

The room was small but clean enough. He could not spot any stains on the striped sheets, at least not from where he stood. The floral wallpaper and the soft light coming in through the large windows gave the room an almost pleasant feel. "You like?" the old man asked. "Sink here, toilet and bathroom outside," he continued, pointing a finger at the corner of the room where the sink and mirror stood and then waving his hands in some general direction down the corridor. Anil nodded and took the key from the man. He dropped his suitcase near the desk, locked the door and drifted off to sleep. For the first time in his life he was exiled from the comfort that he had been accustomed to since the day he was born.

"Aini, can you speak up? I can't hear you."

"Anil? Where are you?"

"I'm in KL. Can you hear the noise outside this phone booth? It's deafening."

"Anil, please come home. Your father is angry. Do you want to speak to him?"

"No, I'm just calling to say that I am here and safe. I won't be coming home Aini. Tell him that for me. I won't be coming home."

The days of wandering continued, but he now had a whole city before him instead of the palace on stilts and its compound. Anil would wake up early in the morning, before dawn, wash quickly before the other hotel guests stirred, and leave just as the old man began his morning exercises in the courtyard. A cup of tea and *roti canai* at the corner coffee shop and he would be ready to start the day. The itinerary for the next twelve hours was roughly laid out the night before with a marker in hand and a map spread out on the desk. He avoided public transport as much as possible and would walk for hours at a time breathing in the city and its fumes. When he tired he would stop for drink and food for half an hour, no more, and then continue on his way.

In this manner he swallowed the city within two weeks. The main sights were devoured systematically, in the way a German tourist produces a list of things to see when he first arrives in a new place and proceeds to check them off as he goes along. He had time to revisit places and buildings he liked and to get to know them intimately. He would always stop for a moment as he passed the Sultan Abdul Samad building, to marvel at its singular and childlike Moorish architecture, or to gaze up into the sky at the scaly sea monsters that were the twin towers. If he was not exhausted after dinner he would sit in Merdeka square and watch the children play under the glare of the spotlights and couples walk hand-in-hand along the promenades. All this he did in silence. Apart from words that were necessary for transactions — ordering his food, buying tickets for the bus or light rail on rare occasions, and explaining his plans to the hotel proprietor — he did not speak to anyone. To make up for the lack of conversation he would talk himself to sleep while lying in bed at night, speaking with people from his past and present, and with imaginary interlocutors.

He thought he recognised at least one person each day, but he would snap back into the present by telling himself that the chances of such a person, a classmate or the owner of the shop in Muar where he used to buy his monthly football magazine, being in KL at this time of year were too small for him to seriously consider these encounters as real. These imaginings, as he knew them to be, were mostly of people who were on the fringes of the life he had left at home, of bit players. But on two occasions, which happened a day apart, he thought he saw Amma and Acha separately.

The woman he saw walking near the Klang bus station bore a striking resemblance, from a distance, to his mother. Her long hair, speckled white, framed her beautiful and severe face. She wore a simple and elegant sari, exposing only a hint of her midriff. Her head was tilted ever so slightly to the left, the weight of the world pushing down squarely on her slender, rounded shoulders. After she disappeared in the crowd of people walking northwards from the station, he had to hold on to a lamppost to steady himself.

The man he thought was Acha walked out of the Dayabumi complex just as he passed the entrance. The man bumped into him and knocked him to the ground. He turned around and apologised, helping Anil to his feet. He asked, "Do I know you?" Anil shook his head, and the man lit a cigarette and walked away, whistling one the Malay pop tunes that played daily on the radio at that time. He did not see the man's face clearly but he noticed that his thick hair was combed back neatly and he wore a small Hitler moustache and a cream linen suit. Anil followed the man at a safe distance for fifteen minutes until he too vanished in the crowd. He rushed back to his hotel room to clear his head and rest.

Was he going mad? Apart from these phantoms, who materialised and evaporated suddenly each day, he could not put his finger on anything abnormal. He talked to himself at night, but surely it was out of loneliness more than anything else? He washed and ate regularly, slept for eight hours each night and was getting enough exercise walking the city by day. He studied his face in the mirror and was relieved to find that the only thing that had changed in the past weeks was the stubble on his chin. There was no history of mental illness in his family — at least no cases were ever mentioned openly — but he was afraid that this difficult period was taking its toll and marked the beginning of a complete breakdown. He decided to escape to the cool air of the hills and left for Genting Highlands the next morning. He paid the old man a week's rent in advance and left his suitcase in the room, carrying only a small sports bag with him.

He was at one thousand six hundred metres above sea level. The sky was clear and he could see the hills and valleys populated with trees for miles around from where he stood near the waterfall. The forests at this height were less dense and a lighter shade of green than those further down. He dipped his hands into the stream and splashed the icy water over his face and hair. Only five days here and already he felt refreshed; the ghosts were in hiding. With the fog over his mind clearing he spent his mornings and afternoons walking along the paths snaking up the highlands, moving away from the hotels, resorts and theme parks below. The highlands had become a popular getaway for the city people ever since the first hotel was built almost thirty years earlier. Construction continued at a frantic pace and the devastation wrought on several hills by the building work dominated the view. Trees had been chopped down for yet another luxury hotel and casino and bulldozers were levelling the ground. The piling would begin after this was done and the cranes and workers would swing into action. He chose trails that led him over the hills, away from the ugliness and destruction.

After dinner he would walk into the very same buildings that he found ugly by daylight. His favourite was the Hotel Merdeka, where he would sit in the lobby café undisturbed, nursing a small beer for an hour and watching the guests come and go. Most of them were from the city (he could tell right away), comfortable and relaxed in these surroundings, but there were a few who seemed out of place in the ostentatiously decorated ground floor of the hotel. To his surprise the bouncers, standing at attention in their red uniforms with gold tassels, allowed him to enter the casino dressed as he was in a pair of jeans, a white T-shirt and a cheap cotton sweater he had bought when he arrived. He played several rounds of blackjack at the minimum-betting tables and then roamed the different rooms. There were professional gamblers playing for high stakes, Chinese women laughing and cursing loudly at the mahjong tables and desperate souls gambling with furious intensity as if their lives depended on a roll of the dice or a card, along with those who were there to kill time with some harmless betting at the slot machines. He saw a few Malays around the tables, despite the large sign at the entrance of the hotel prohibiting Muslims from drinking and gambling. The hours passed quickly. When there was nothing interesting left to observe, he would step out into the cold night, invigorated and entertained and ready to return to his room in a modest hotel a mile away, to rest untroubled by dreams.

One evening, the whole gambling room erupted in a shout. The shout trailed off into a long groan and then murmurs all around. The cause of the commotion was a man at the roulette table who had lost another ten thousand ringgit. This was the fourth large bet he had placed and lost, but he laughed out loud, thumped the table a few times and squeezed the waists of the two beautiful girls next to him. Cognac, Hennessy XO, was passed around freely to his retinue of fellow-businessmen and a chorus of young girls, heavily made up and dressed in almost identical low-cut evening gowns. He stroked his balding head and wiped off the sweat from his face.

He glowed in the light of the elaborate chandeliers hanging low from the ceiling. Looking around the room he asked, "Again?" to which the crowd gathered around the table answered with a resounding "Yes!" And again he gambled away a stack of chips.

Anil had been observing the man since he appeared in the casino, his followers behind him. It became clear to him after two bets that the man's goal was to show his friends and the women, and whoever else cared to witness the spectacle, that he could throw an obscene amount of money away without a care. Anil approached the table and stood by one of the girls, smelling the perfume and excitement on her skin. He asked her who the man was. She looked him up and down, surprised that a casually dressed young man was allowed into the casino, before replying, "You don't know Mr. Lim? He is one of the richest men in Malaysia. Look, fifty thousand ringgit is nothing to him." He stared at her marble-white neck and face and wanted to ask her what she was doing with him but instead he said, "What is he doing here in Genting? Just gambling away his money?" She shook her head and said, "No, he is trying to make more. Tomorrow, he has a meeting with another rich man, Mr. Pillai. I don't quite understand it, but it has something to do with a shipping company or something like that."

Upon hearing his father's name, he lost all interest in the girl and everything around him. Even here, high above the sea, he was not safe. "What's wrong?" she asked. "Are you OK?" He touched her hand lightly and felt the warmth of her skin. She did not pull her hand away. He felt her pulse, her strong and steady heartbeat coursing through the veins that were visible beneath her delicate flesh. He realised than this was the first time in weeks he had touched another person. Blood flowed back to his head.

"Do you know when Mr. Pillai arrives? Or is he here already?" Anil asked.

"I know he is not here yet. Maybe later tonight or tomorrow morning," the girl said.

"I have to leave. I'll tell you something before I go. You may repeat it to the next person you meet but it doesn't matter if you do. Mr. Pillai is my father. I ran away from home a few weeks ago after my mother died. I saw him fucking the maid. Fucking Aini a week after my mother was cremated. I don't want to see him or to have him see me here. You're the first person I have told this to," he confessed.

She held his hand tightly, as if refusing to let him go. A false intimacy born of his confession. He pulled away from her grip, kissed her on the cheek and ran out of the casino. He threw his things into his small bag, checked out of the hotel and caught the next bus back to KL.

He ran his hand along the wallpaper by his bed. The blue flower, repeated every three inches and joined to its neighbour by a thick stem that had three, now four, serrated leaves along it, is one that he does not recognise. A flower that grows where the pattern was originally designed, England? Instead of sheep he counted flowers and leaves to lull himself to sleep.

It was good to be back in the familiar hotel room, good to see the old man again. "Oh, you back. Think no come back. Win money in Genting?" he had said with his toothless grin when he saw Anil walk in earlier that night. "No, I didn't win, but I didn't lose either." He counted the notes he had tied with a red rubber band, the notes he had stolen from his father. The trip to the highlands had cost more than he had expected and he was worried that he would have to dip into his savings before long. It's time to move out of this hotel and to find a cheaper place to live, he thought. A modest flat in a busy part of town where he could end his existence as a hermit and be part of the life he saw all around him. After he settled in he would have to find a job to keep going.

The advertisement in the newspaper said, "Large flat, cheap, central location, Jalan Tunku Watistis, near Chow Kit." Near the red light district. The agent led him up the narrow staircase by the side of the shophouse. She opened the door after a brief struggle with the rusty key; stale air rushed out of the room. "No one use for a long time. After one day, flat smell OK." He was not convinced and wanted to walk away. She opened the four floor-to-ceiling shutters and a cool breeze carried the smell of food in. He walked to the window and leaned out, his legs pressed against the waist-high railing. He saw the commotion and movement and light outside, along the street. "I'll take it. I want to move in tomorrow."

He walks up and down the street, stopping to talk to the hawkers and planning what to have for dinner. They have nursed him back to life, these peddlers and the regulars who frequent their stalls. Some of them come and go in cycles fixed and varied, others stay rooted to their chosen spots along the street.

Ah Nam was the first to admit him into the fold. He was wary at first, as they all were of strangers in their midst, but he lowered his guard once he learnt that Anil lived in the flat above his stall and was there to stay. Their burgeoning friendship was a passport for Anil to get to know the other hawkers along the street. Prabu, who sells steamed peanuts and is known as Michael York because he believes himself to be a spitting image of the actor, though, skin colour aside, this cannot be further from the truth. Guna, whose condensed-milk tea with spices and ginger keeps him awake when the conversations drift long into the night. The freshly baptised soup man John, whose name before his conversion was the rhythmic Dong Bong Gong and who now goes by the shorter, though equally unfortunate, name of John Dong.

And the quartet of Rahim, Tiok Lam, Kuppusamy and Aris. They are a motley group, glued together by the love of talking away the evenings. A university student, a trainee engineer, an insurance salesman and a magazine writer, all with their tales of hardship and escape, just like the Bremen town musicians. They bray, bark, mew and crow, and entertain Anil with their music. There was no room in the Brothers Grimm tale for a fifth player, but they took him in after he got to know Ah Nam. Within a week he was ordained a "regular", which Aris pronounced "reg", and after the briefest pause, "*ular*", snake in Malay, to a round of laughter at the silly play on words.

English is the lingua franca, as is common here when a group consists of different races. They pepper their sentences with Malay, Indian and Chinese words, speaking a street language of sorts. The conversation is light, unless politics or religion enters into it. Then Kuppusamy, or Sammy Coop as they call him, will say, "You bloody Malays, you idiot *bumiputeras*. You're all the same. With all the privileges and still you complain and act like lazy cows, chewing grass all day." Or Rahim, "Hey, *cina babi* and *keling biawak,* if you don't like it here, go home to Canton or Tamil Nadu lah." All the tensions rise to the surface and are driven underground in a matter of minutes. After running down the list of standard insults and derogatory names for each race, they fall back into light-hearted banter. It is the Malaysian version of racial harmony at the end of the twentieth century.

Anil joins the fray if he thinks he has something to add but for the most part he prefers to listen. He does not yet possess the gift of speaking at their pace and moving from one subject to another effortlessly, as if skipping on water. He knows he appears too earnest to them, weighing and choosing his words carefully before he speaks. It will take a while before he sheds his perfect sentences for the market language they use.

Ah Nam fires up the pressure lamp, pushing the piston in and out until the spark takes and the gas begins to glow. He sets the lamp on a table next to the stove and wok. Shadows are created within a five-foot circle around the stall. They are sharp where the light is strongest, fading away along the edges of the circle where they blend into the darkness of the night. Anil shields his face from the blinding light. Tiok Lam is his sole companion; the others have not arrived and Ah Nam is busy preparing for the night ahead.

"Anil, how come you never tell us where you are from?" asks Tiok Lam.

"I think I have told all of you before that I am from Muar, haven't I?"

"Yes, yes, lah, we know that, but how come a young man like you is away from home and not at university? You seem cleverer than us, speak perfect English, but you don't study."

"You not the police, why you ask so many questions? He speak when he wants," Ah Nam protests.

"Ah Nam, I am not a policeman, I know. But we are friends here, and friends tell stories. I have not heard one story from Anil."

He has not told them who he is, who his father is. Nothing from his past matters here and he wants to hide the outline and details of his old life from them. They have told him much about their lives and he is ashamed that he can only offer morsels. But it has to be so if he wants to break the spell of the life that is no longer his and to start a new one here in the city.

Later, when they are all gathered at Guna's stall, he tells them that he has left his home in Muar. He says, "My mother died not too long ago. She fell down the stairs and broke her neck. I had to cremate her, light the wood underneath her coffin, because I was the only son. She taught me how to paint." He says, "I want to be a new person here and to forget my father, my town and myself if I can." The regulars nod gravely and remain silent, sipping their tea and looking up at the moon.

On the table in the corner of the room by the shutters sit a radio and TV. Anil turns them on for an hour each day, often at the same time, afraid that he will lose his connection with the world outside the shell he has created if they always remain silent. He does not care what he watches or listens to; the ever-changing images flickering onscreen and the words and music from the box fill the room, and form invisible roads to places and events near and far. He remembers facts and figures from the news and melodies and lyrics to the songs on the radio. He finds himself humming tunes when he is distracted.

There is a trick he must perform to get the TV to work. The TV refused to display a picture when he brought it home from the junk store a few streets away and turned it on. After playing with it for days he learned that he had to turn the plug and power switches on almost simultaneously, leaving a gap of less than a second or two for the miracle to happen. He stands in his martial arts stance, arms fully stretched to reach both switches, before he can watch TV each day.

A worn-out sofa, two plastic chairs, a small wooden dining table, a chopping knife, two spoons, two forks, two plates, two glasses, a small refrigerator, a stove, and a large bed with a thin mattress. This completes the catalogue of the objects in his flat, apart from the clothes he has.

Aris points to a billboard in the distance and says, "Look, there he is." From where they stand waiting to cross the street, the figure of the man standing on a ladder appears like a large insect frozen on the face of the actor. As they come closer Anil sees the blue lettering running above the actors' heads. First the Chinese characters, then *Half a Loaf of Kungfu*. The principal character is ready to face the threat posed by the villain, who brandishes a sword, with his bare hands, while a beautiful woman, her hair pulled up high above her head and skin a pale shade of pink, looks on calmly. The hero and heroine are dressed in white, the villain in black, and they are set against an orange and red background.

"Goh Poh, come down," Aris shouts to the man on the ladder. Looking up, Anil sees the delicate balancing act the man performs to stay upright, as he leans across to put the finishing touches on the actor's face, his brush in one hand and a tray of paint in the other. "Wait, let me finish this, then I'll come down."

The man wipes his palms on his shorts and shakes Anil's hand before Aris can introduce them. "Anil, this is Goh Poh," Aris says.

"Who else? You told me yesterday that you would bring your friend Anil here. You must have told him that you were coming to see me, Chin's father. Why introduce us?" says Goh Poh.

Aris shakes his head and says, "You have to learn some good manners."

"Manners are not important to me. If they were, I would make you call me uncle, not Goh Poh. I am a billboard painter, not a gentleman."

He speaks perfect Malay, strange for a Chinese man of his age, with the musical lilt of the Kelantanese. Anil asks him if he grew up there.

"I was born in Kota Bahru and lived there until I was twenty, then I moved here. It is impossible for me to get rid of the singsong in my voice."

"I don't think you need to. Kelantanese always sounds pleasant to my ears," Anil says.

"That's the problem. Look at me. With my mouth closed, I look like a tough guy. Most people get scared when they see me and cross the street. But when I speak, I sound like a queer."

Goh Poh's features are sharp and his hair coarse and thick. His body is lean and muscular and his skin is burnt brown. He is dressed in a pair of shorts and a sleeveless, white undershirt, both smeared with paint and dirt. They laugh because there is some truth in what he has just said.

"So, you want to work for me. There are not many jobs left in this line of work, but enough to keep my business going. I'm the best around, at least in this city. Almost all the cinemas now use printed posters. But there are still a few who want hand-painted ones, mostly the cinemas showing Chinese, Indian and local films. I'm getting too old to do all the jobs myself and I wouldn't mind having an assistant. My sons are not interested in the business. They want modern jobs, nothing old-fashioned like billboard painting for them, even though they both helped me when they were young and certainly know enough to take over. Chin works on the same magazine as Aris, that gossip and fashion magazine for men. My other son is an accountant for a bank. I would like to help my son's friend's friend, but can you paint?"

"Hold the ladder and I'll show you," Anil says.

He mixes some paint in the tray and climbs up the ladder with tentative steps. Both Aris and Goh Poh brace the ladder with their arms and bodies. "Be careful," Aris shouts, "I don't want to lose your friendship just yet." With a few careful strokes, working only on the eyes and mouth, he changes the hero's expression from anger to disdain. He climbs down and hands the tray back to Goh Poh. "This guy is good," Aris says, "better than you are, Goh Poh." Anil moves towards Goh Poh and asks, "Do I have the job?"

"If you're not bothered about the poor salary I am going to pay you, the answer is yes, you have the job."

"I'd rather be doing this than working in a factory or office. Tell me where your shop is and what time you want me to start tomorrow, and I'll be there."

At this early hour before dawn, a crowd has already formed at the bus stop. There is no discernible queue as everyone jostles for position, so Anil attaches himself to the edge of the growing mass. Minibus 105 appears after a few minutes. It comes to a stop in the middle of the street, fifteen metres beyond the yellow markings of the bus stop. The crowd curses and swarms ahead. The bus is painted khaki brown with two olive green stripes running along its sides, giving it the appearance of a military vehicle. The name of the company, *"Syarikat Bas Berjaya"*, is painted in clumsy black letters almost within the confines of the olive stripes; the dots above the "i" and the "j" spill across the border.

As he boards the bus an old man pokes him in the back with an umbrella. The metal tip of the *chettiar* umbrella digs into his skin. He turns around and pushes it away from him, cursing aloud. "Don't you know how to board a bus?" the little man says calmly. "Push, otherwise you'll leave us all behind." Anil pushes as hard as he can and somehow gets to the middle of the bus. The man moves in his wake and ends up close behind him.

Anil is pressed against a young girl. He cannot see her face but her shiny black hair tickles his nose. Freshly washed and combed, her hair smells of the shampoo she uses. Her buttocks rub against his thighs as she moves to steady herself. She appears unconcerned by this but he feels an erection coming on. He turns ninety degrees to face the side windows, his cock poking the side of the plastic covered seats and not the lower curve of her back. "Don't be embarrassed," the man whispers in his ear, "it happens to the best of us. If you take away all these little pleasures, life would not be worth living." Anil looks sideways to see the man grinning. "These city girls don't mind, they're used to it. In fact, I think they secretly enjoy getting poked in such a manner. It's safe and they don't get pregnant." Anil can't suppress a smile. He looks around to see if anyone has overheard the man's remarks but the people around him are floating in their own worlds, dreaming about times and days past or preparing themselves for the hours ahead. He sees a couple with their coarse hands interlocked, both staring ahead with fixed gazes, a middle-aged Malay woman in *purdah* delicately pursing her lips to blot the bright pink lipstick she had applied moments before, and the girl with the scented hair still fidgeting in the aisle.

"Don't worry, nobody is listening. In no time you'll learn the art of shutting out the world and you'll begin to look like one of them, inmates of an invisible and all-encompassing institution on the way to work. Lost or locked in their little cells for the length of their journeys. You must be new in town, your eyes are still alert," the man says.

"I've been here for over a month but this is my first trip to work."

"Congratulations on joining the ranks of the living dead. Or are you going to do something interesting?"

"I'm helping someone paint movie posters. I don't know if you consider that interesting or not."

"At least it's something different. I, on the other hand, am like them. I came to the city years ago to escape the tedium of life in a village. I got a job in an office and I have been at the same place ever since, copying and typing letters for lawyers. I've seen the owner die at his desk, his son take his place, lawyers come and go, the walls painted over god knows how many times. The history of the space and its inhabitants, you might say, is all stored up here in my head. All these changes and movement have not affected me in the least bit. I go to work, get on with the day, register what is happening around me and then take the bus home to my little flat, but I remain untouched by what happens between the hours of nine and five. Many times I think that I have exchanged the tedium of a village for the tedium of the city.

"The only thing that keeps me alive is my reading. After dinner, I sit in my brown leather chair, the only item of luxury I own, and read without interruption, many times until well after midnight. My life during the day disappears and I live in a different place and time created by the book I am reading for hours on end. I read anything good I can lay my hands on. I don't make much money and I can allow myself to buy only one or two books a month. The rest have to come from the various libraries and collections in the city. You should test me some time. I have read the English poets, the French existentialists, the great Russian novelists, even some Malaysian writers along the way. My reading is desultory and has no goal whatsoever except as a great escape, but I have a good memory and remember large chunks of what I have read. Over time, I have become somewhat knowledgeable and learned, if I say so myself."

"Do you write?" Anil asks, eager to find out if this man does anything else but talk and read.

"I tried my hand at it but I came to the conclusion long ago that I am not blessed with a creative spark. Everything I wrote looked plain and tiresome to me, at least compared to the books I was reading, and I gave up after several attempts. I was not too crushed when I finally realised this because I have found my little place where my small joys and pleasures come readily. There are too many writers in the world already. I often worry that by the end of my life I will not get to read more than a tiny fraction of all the great books that have been written."

Anil continues listening to the man while looking out the window. As daylight breaks the streetlights are turned off and the dirt and grime and bustle of the streets are revealed. Traffic and people fill the roads and sidewalks. The melody of the man's well-rounded sentences and pleasant voice plays above the background of the roar of engines, the blaring horns, voices raised in the bus and on the streets below, and the indecipherable white noise of the city. The conductor performs a delicate balancing act as he makes his way through the bus, selling tickets and providing a running commentary on the landmarks outside and the stops ahead. When there is time to spare he cracks a joke or informs the passengers about current events or sports news. All this, and the excitement of the first working day of his life, keeps the thought of turning into one of them, the living dead, away from Anil's mind. A frozen, vegetative state seems a lifetime away. He catches his faint reflection in the dirty window and is content with what he sees.

As he prepares to push his way forward to get off, an hour after he boarded the bus, the man says, "Be sure to catch the bus at the same time tomorrow if you want the pleasure of my company." Anil doesn't reply but waves goodbye.

Goh Poh's shop is in a cul-de-sac at the end of an alleyway, twenty metres from the main road. Narrow drains run along both sides of the path leading to it. Pieces of newspaper, juice cartons, plastic straws and bottles lie half submerged in the murky brown water fighting to flow around the obstacles. Bamboo poles laden with bright clothes put out to dry hang from windows on both sides of the path, like flags and banners held by invisible schoolboys to greet him as he walks by.

Two gnarled jasmine trees lean and touch at the entrance to the shop, forming an archway of twisted branches, glossy green leaves and white flowers. Anil picks up a flower, crushes the soft petals to release its fragrance and rubs it over his hands. The delicate smell stays with him until he walks in, when it is overpowered by paint fumes. *I'm back in Amma's world.*

Goh Poh waves to him as he walks in. "You decided to accept my lousy offer."

"I told you I would be here bright and early. I don't really know what your offer is, you only told me that my salary would be poor. You wouldn't cheat Aris's friend, would you?"

"I would cheat Aris, but not his friends. I'll be fair, don't worry," Goh Poh assures him.

Goh Poh appears to be wearing yesterday's clothes but as Anil walks up to him, he notices that the blue shorts and white singlet are spotless and not stained with paint and dirt. Later Goh Poh will tell him that he owns seven pairs of identical Pagoda blue shorts and white underwear, and seven white Crocodile singlets. He replaces his collection every six months. These are the only clothes he has, except for a pair of tailored trousers and a short sleeve shirt he wears on special occasions.

A large wooden table sits in the middle of the shop. On it lies a poster Goh Poh is working on for another martial arts movie and a few cans of paint. Along the walls are metal filing cabinets, mounted shelves for paint, brushes, paper and canvases, a small television and VCR. Rolled posters of different sizes are stacked upright in plastic containers in the far corner of the room. Each is labelled with the name of a movie, cinema and customer. Anil is surprised to see how neatly ordered everything is, in contrast to Goh Poh's careless appearance. "I like to keep my shop nice and tidy and I won't tolerate a mess," Goh Poh explains. "You can use whatever you see in this room for work except things that are labelled for a specific job. If you can't find something you need, just shout and I'll find it for you in the shed outside. There is nothing you can possibly need that I don't have here or in storage. If there is something I don't have, it must be a want, not a need, and you'll have to make do without it or buy it out of your own pocket. The staircase leads to the second floor, where I live. You're not to go there unless invited. That should cover all the basic rules."

"That's clear enough."

"Before I put you to work, let me show you my garden, my second obsession."

Anil has already caught glimpses of it through the wide-open shutters all round the room. Goh Poh leads him out the back door, down a few steps and into the garden. What he sees is unexpected and he stands rooted to the ground, looking around him in wonder.

There is a large pond in the centre of the garden filled with floating lilies and golden carp. A bamboo bridge spans the pond. Water trickles down over rocks and pebbles arranged intricately at the far end of the garden. Marble benches and chairs rise out of the ground beneath willow trees. Potted bonsai plants line the narrow pathways laid out in simple, geometric patterns. Goh Poh points to a delicate structure made of light wood and paper, and says, "That is my shed. Don't let the material it is made of fool you. It's sturdier than I am."

He is pleased to see Anil's reaction to his garden.

"Everyone needs a lifeline, something to keep him sane. I saw a garden like this years ago at the Japanese Centre in Petaling Jaya and I knew I had to have one. It took me quite a while to get it right but I succeeded, I believe. It looks simple but you have to think and experiment a lot before the elements blend together. Now I can't remember a time when I didn't have the garden and I can't imagine what my life would be like without it. The willows protect me from the ugly flats and houses and if you sit in the garden long enough, the sounds from the street and the world outside disappear and you can only hear the trickling water and the birds. This is far more beautiful than my living quarters so I spend a lot of time here. You're welcome to sit in the garden whenever you need a rest," Goh Poh says.

In the same way, Jim Thompson's house could have been Acha's lifeline, Anil thinks, an obsession to preserve his sanity. But the rope that kept him tied to shore was Amma's noose.

They walk back into the shop. Anil is ushered to one of the smaller tables and given his first commission, a three by four poster of a new Bollywood film. The title is meaningless to him and he has never seen or heard of the movie. There is little to work from except a few printed images Goh Poh has placed on the table. He mixes some paint and dips his brush, ready to begin. But he does not know where to start and puts his brush down.

"Don't worry, it happens to me too," Goh Poh says when he sees Anil freeze. "The trick is to rearrange all the pictures in your head and make up a strong, lively scene. If that doesn't work, try watching the movie. That's what the TV and VCR are there for. Sometimes all it takes is a few minutes of viewing, fast forwarding through the boring parts, and you're ready to paint. A small poster like that should take you three hours, at most four. Otherwise I'll lose money on the job. Once you're done with that we can start working on the main poster for the film. We'll think about what to put on it, draw the words and the scene, perhaps start painting a little. We'll finish the poster at the cinema tomorrow, on the ladder. OK?"

Anil nods. Months have passed since he last finished a painting and he feels at a loss. He longs to have his confidence back and his brush moving freely again. But he is disturbed to find his memories of painting with his mother recreated in this way. *I've run away from home only to find myself in Amma's studio again.* This is not the same, he tells himself. Then it was an act of learning, of sharing time and space with his mother; now it is a job under the tutelage of a stranger. And surely movie posters are not on the same plane as the paintings he once made? He tries to convince himself that in the grand scheme of experiences, this moment lies far below his days and years in his mother's studio. To protect the many images he has stored in his mind, to keep them clean and safe, he is forced to create an artificial scale where actions, thoughts, feelings are weighed and compared, assigned a number and locked away. He shakes off these thoughts and looks at the pictures of the actors fighting and dancing, hoping that he will find his touch before long.

It feels strange being here in the city at Deepavali, away from home. Yesterday I dreamt of the cakes and dishes Amma would start preparing a day or two before and how I would sit in the kitchen watching her and Aini work. I wasn't alone today. One of my friends invited me to his home for lunch. His name is Kuppusamy but we call him Sammy Coop. The food was good but different from Amma's. Sammy explained it away by saying it is the difference between Tamil and Malayalee things in general. "Two faces of the same god," he said.

Why am I writing all of this to you? What is most important is that I am alive and well and happy. Happy although I am separated from the things and places and people I know best. My life is modest. The money I took from you kept me going for a while and I managed to get a flat in the Chow Kit area with it. It wasn't going to last forever so I had to find a job. You will be amused to know that I help this man, Goh Poh, paint movie posters. The money he pays me is enough for me to get by without worrying too much. I am no worse off than most. And I am putting the skills I learned from Amma to good use. Goh Poh is the father of a friend of a friend, one of the friends I have made while eating at the stalls on the street below my flat. They are uncomplicated people. They sit and while away the evenings talking about everything and nothing. I sit and listen, not talking much. Sometimes I feel that they think I am an impostor, not one of them. But day by day, what I left behind is fading away and I am moving closer to their way of life.

There is this dream that comes to me often. The house in Muar crumbles suddenly, shattering into a million pieces. You and I fall into deep water underneath the house, a lake or a very large pond. You are drowning and call for me to save you. I swim quickly to where you are and drag you to shore. Amma calls out to us from high above. We look up and see her in a tree, painting the destruction of the house and the scene of your salvation. She is smiling, as if all that has happened has been staged for her painting.

I think of Amma a lot. She is a ghost who haunts me at night and sometimes by day. I wish I could put her to rest. I think of you too, in a different way, though I have no wish to see you. Try to understand that I am trying to create a new life for myself and seeing any bit of my past would drag me back.

Thank you for your offer of sending me money to make my life more comfortable, as you put it. Most people would consider me foolish for not accepting your gift, but I have enough for my needs and my wants are basic and cheap enough.

Give my love to Aini and to Uncle Ravi and family. I hope that all of you are well.

Cartoons

It is mid-afternoon on a Saturday and Anil is lying propped up in bed doodling. Why is the light so feeble? He can hardly see his reflection in the mirror across the room. A year has passed in the city and still he does not have paints, brushes and canvas in his apartment. He has resigned himself to never making another 'work' again. The need is gone and he cannot convince himself to do something out of habit or just because he did it in the past.

Working for Goh Poh is as close as he comes to painting. He knows it is different, he has convinced himself that it is different. Painting posters on commission, as creative as it can be, is not the same as facing a blank canvas with no rules and guidance, no goal in sight. He will not perish if he does not paint in this room, while the food on his plate and his shelter will soon disappear if he stops working on movie posters. The smell of the acrylic paints he uses now does not remind him of oils and watercolours. Should he feel guilty for abandoning what his mother has taught him, for replacing it with a coarser art form? He is uneasy, still uncomfortable in his new skin, but this feeling does not in any way resemble guilt. He is shedding his past slowly and painfully. Born in the Chinese year of the snake, he will, like a serpent, have to cast off his outer covering again and again as he grows.

The pencil marks on his sketchpad do not amount to much. He has done this before, an hour or two spent drawing aimless lines and words that tumble together randomly. Unconscious art, some may call it, but he doesn't attach any value to these undisciplined pages. Anyone could do it. Looking through the sketchpad, he is at a loss to discern any meaning, he fails to see into his mind when the pages are filled. He needs Amma and her imaginative readings. He does not find beauty or ugliness in these doodles; they are dull, lifeless, unable to leap off the paper at him.

Let me get back to basic drawing, he tells himself, to a skill I know I have. He looks around for an object to portray. The far end of the room is hidden in shadow and the things near him are uninspiring. Pillows, a brown blanket, a side table. Looking down his body he sees his legs extended, suspended between light and darkness. They are disembodied and float in space in the play of light. He quickly draws one, then the other. The legs appear just as he saw them moments before, an exact representation of the image of his legs drifting away from him. Though the lines are strong and the drawing precise, he is not satisfied. Too easy, he thinks.

Looking at his body on the bed and the drawing he has just made, he starts again. This time he allows himself to invent. With quick, broad lines, he draws himself waist up. He stretches and distorts his limbs and features and adds a smile to his face. He separates his legs, dressed in shorts, from the rest of his body by an inch, so that they seem cut off from his upper half. He adds the bed he is lying on, with details of the pillow, sheets, blanket, and sketches in the side table. The hairs on his legs are put in as a final touch, coarse and exaggeratedly separated from one another.

What he ends up with is a cartoon, amusing and grotesque. Light and fickle, it is different from all the drawings and paintings he has ever made. It is as if he has been under a spell until now, a spell which has suddenly broken, leaving him free to play and experiment. For the first time he has created something he likes.

"That's me," Ah Nam says.

"It's obvious that's you, Ah Nam. The wok and the stall are dead giveaways," Aris points out.

"I don't quite understand why my head is stuck on a butterfly trapped in a birdcage," Sammy Coop says, puzzled.

"Cheap associations, nothing else. Kuppusamy, *kupu-kupu* is butterfly in Malay. Surely you were teased by that name when you were a child? Sammy Coop is what everyone here calls you. Coop, cage, birdcage," Anil explains.

"You're one sick bastard, you know that?" says Aris.

After displaying the cartoons of each person in the group, Anil shows them the one entitled *The Bremen Five*.

"Explain this one, Anil. I don't understand this at all," Tiok Lam pleads.

"It's from a Brothers Grimm tale called *The Bremen Town Musicians*. A horse, dog, cat and cock escape from the farm where they were ill treated and set up house elsewhere."

"I remember the story from my English textbook in primary five or six. So we're the Bremen five?" Rahim says, glad that he can finally add something meaningful about the cartoons.

"Yes, I've added myself as the fifth, a cow which doesn't appear in the original story. And you can see Ah Nam serving up a feast in the background."

They laugh and call each other by their newfound names.

"Aris, you Casanova, being a cock suits you well," Sammy Coop shouts.

"I am a cocksman, not a cock."

"Couldn't you have made me a horse or a cat? I'm a Muslim, and dogs are dirty animals in Islam."

"Have a shower once in a while, Rahim, and Anil will transform you into a cleaner animal," Tiok Lam jokes.

"This cartoon is not far from the truth. In a way, all of us have run away from home and we've set up a new one around Ah Nam's stall," Aris says wistfully.

"Enough with the cheap associations, you roadside philosopher. No wonder everyone calls you Aristotle. Now that's an idea for a cartoon. Aris as the grand Greek thinker fucking a young boy," adds Sammy Coop.

"Stop the bullshit, gang. Let Anil show us the rest," Tiok Lam says.

The other cartoons are of city scenes and characters: a wizened fortune teller reading a young girl's palm, a cobbler mending a shoe in the garden outside the twin towers, heads of passengers stuck out of the windows of a packed bus, boys playing football with a tin can in an alleyway.

"The girl has a nice arse. You could become the artist who glorifies women's bottoms. Joking aside, this is not bad at all. You should let me show them to my editor. Maybe there's room for a cartoon page in the magazine. It's a men's magazine, so you would have to concentrate on funny or sexy scenes, but it might work."

"Show it to him if you want, Aris, but I'm not working to orders or instructions. I'll be in your debt a second time if you pull this one off," Anil says.

Aris raises his beer bottle and toasts Anil. "To the principled artist! I warn you, though, that you may have to sell your arse to the devil to get ahead. You can pay me ten percent of what you make if you feel bad about depending on me too much. It's the standard rate for politicians these days."

Anil talks about the day he drew his first cartoons, how he has spent many hours scouring the streets of the city in search of interesting scenes and characters, his struggle with forming a style. He avoided studying other cartoonists until the previous weekend for fear of being influenced, contaminated.

"I think I'm there now. I spent all of last weekend looking at the cartoon collection in the National Library. Nothing that I saw reminded me of mine. So I decided to bring them out into the open and show them to you. Have I passed the test?"

"Don't forget us when you're famous," Aris says.

This is where he ought to run, get out of line. But he does not. One more man, no more than ten minutes to go from what he has seen and it will be his turn. It shouldn't be like this, at least not for the first time. Not that he holds his virginity sacred or cherishes it in any way. Anil knows he has to perform the act, to fuck, to become a man. Without a girlfriend he has little choice. There is an active pickup scene in bars he has heard of and there are girls who look at him at the stalls on the street below but he does not have the courage to play the game, to make the approach, not yet. He imagines they will be able to smell his lack of experience, his virginity, up close. A prostitute seems to be the only way out.

The squalor of the surroundings unsettles him. This underground world lies out in the open in a dead-end street in Chow Kit, a short walk from where he lives. He stumbled upon it soon after moving into his flat on one his many jaunts exploring the neighbourhood. Shacks of wooden planks and zinc sheets stand on both sides of the street, a shantytown for the unloved and unsexed. Narrow passageways lead to the entrances of the dens. Pictures of the girls inside are stuck with tape on the doors so the men can see what is on offer.

The girl he has chosen looks slim and pretty. The photograph does not reveal much else. She is forcing a smile, dressed in white shorts and a pink sleeveless top, posing on a beach, a calm sea and clear sky behind her. A school trip perhaps, a picture taken many years ago? Or a weekend escape from the city with a friend or boyfriend to see the horizon, to smell the salty air of the straits.

By day the street brothel looks out of place in the centre of the city. A piece of the urban sprawl transported from the poor outskirts to the heart of town, makeshift dwellings surrounded by shophouses and skyscrapers. By day it is quiet, almost dead. The rubbish steadily accumulating during the night has disappeared. No one walks down the dead-end street even though the neighbourhood around it is filled with people and life.

The street first stirs at five when the girls arrive, alone or in small groups, and set up shop. The lights come on an hour later, and, with dusk setting in, it begins to look like a night market with no goods on view. The men, mostly construction workers, begin to

pour in after a drink or two at coffee shops nearby. Office workers
stop by too, looking for relief on their way home to families and
wives, or from long evenings alone. How this indiscreet and illegal
activity takes place in full view, Anil does not know. The police
and authorities must have their eyes and ears stuffed with money
to allow business to continue in this way.

There is no turning back now; he is at the head of the queue.
He can see the man in the room pulling up his trousers. The
man left the door slightly ajar as he walked in and Anil has seen
his performance. Quick and forceful, he has completed the
transaction in what seemed like an instant. He grins at Anil as he
walks out, nodding, as if to say, "It's your turn."

Anil walks into the room and shuts the door firmly behind
him. The girl doesn't bother to get up from the bed. She wipes
herself slowly and carefully with a wet, perfumed cloth, ridding
herself of the previous customer's sweat and smell. She is the girl
in the photograph but she is a little older, heavier and less pretty.
Time and experience have taken their toll on her, he thinks. The
idyllic background of sea and sky has been replaced by an old bed,
dark brown sheets and a plastic bucket filled with condoms and
tissues. Hardly the surroundings to bring out the best in anyone.

"First time?" she asks. *Is it so obvious?* He remains silent. "First
time here?" she asks again. He nods. "No shy, act like man," she
says, as she gestures for him to take his clothes off. "First money."
Taking his wallet out of his trouser pocket, he looks at her and
asks, "How much?" She replies, "For normal, twenty ringgit."
What counts as normal in this room is beyond him.

He undresses and sits next to her. She tugs on his cock to make
him more erect. She rips the condom packet with her teeth and

slips the red rubber on with ease. After sucking his cock for a while she asks, "What you like?" Practised hands and mouth. He hesitates, not knowing what to say. So she lies on her back, spreads her legs and guides him in. He moves frantically, like the man he watched minutes before. She slows him down. "Not so quickly." He realises that she knows he has never done this before but she is kind enough to instruct him. His face is nestled between her neck and shoulders, his nose pressed against the pillow. He smells her sweat and sickly sweet perfume and the used condoms and semen from the bucket next to the bed. He moves his lips across her neck, over her chin towards her lips. She turns away, so he kisses her cheek instead. This is not meant be anything other than sex, he reminds himself. He thrusts harder and comes.

He thanks her as he leaves. "Come back. You nice boy, I teach you." Walking back to his flat he feels sickened but relieved.

At home he showers and sprays himself all over with aftershave. He lies on his bed and masturbates, thinking of the prostitute's body and the warmth he felt when inside her.

His second trip to a brothel is gentler, more forgiving. It is Goh Poh's idea. "You like girls?" he asks Anil.

"Of course I like girls. What kind of question is that?"

"I don't know, there are so many queers in this city."

"I'm not one of them."

"Have you had a girl before?

"Yes, but it wasn't pleasant."

Anil describes the visit to the Chow Kit brothel, insisting that he would not repeat that experience again.

"Why did you go there? Everyone knows that is the worst place to go. The girls are ugly and who knows what you can catch there.

You should have asked for my advice."

"It's not easy to ask for advice when it comes to this."

"I know. I remember when I was fifteen, my older brother dropped me off at a whorehouse, paid the pimp and told me to come look for him at the coffee shop nearby when I was done. It was interesting and exciting but not pleasant. I felt slightly sick when it was over, and believe me, it didn't last long. I wanted to talk to my brother about it afterwards but he didn't seem interested. He sat there drinking his beer, staring at the TV. Like everything else, you learn with time. At least some people do."

"Are you suggesting we go to a whorehouse?" Anil asks warily.

"This is a much better place than the ones in Chow Kit. It's discreet, the girls are pretty and they spend time with you. It sounds like you need to get rid of the taste of the first experience. Otherwise, you'll stop liking girls and really end up a queer."

Goh Poh drives him there, through back streets he doesn't recognise, across town. "This is Taman Berjaya," Goh Poh says, "just in case you want to come back on your own." He parks his beaten up Mazda in front of a row of shophouses in a housing estate and leads Anil up the stairs to the second floor. All the shops are closed but for a karaoke bar on the opposite end from where they have parked.

They walk in without knocking. The girl sitting on the sofa watching a Chinese soap opera looks up briefly and says, "Min and Lin are free." Goh Poh leads him down the corridor. "See you in an hour," he says.

This time the girl talks to him like a lover would; she pretends to make love to him. Her acting is convincing enough that at moments he thinks the emotions she displays are real and he feels drawn towards her. She allows him to kiss her, to touch her where he wants, to play with her. After he comes she holds him as he rests his head on her breast. This is what he wants, to move from lust to tenderness. He wants to wash his mouth out and replace the acrid taste of the first whore with something sweet, a taste that he can savour and hold until the next time. He wants to touch her soft skin for an hour, believing she is his.

"Was that better?" Goh Poh asks as they are having a beer in the karaoke bar. A young man with his hair slicked back is doing a poor rendition of an Elvis tune to everyone's laughter.

"That was good. I don't feel nauseous like I did after the last time. I thought I would. Discreet and clean, it's still a brothel. But I don't feel bad, in fact I feel pleasantly calm and happy. I am sure that the girl I had must have slept with you too. Strangely, this does not disturb me in the slightest."

"We forget that it sometimes takes so little to satisfy most of our desires and needs. We forget we are animals. After my wife died, I remained celibate for many years until Chin suggested that I visit this place. I almost slapped him for talking to me, his father, about sex but I'm happy he did. It's not perfect, the girls upstairs are not yours or mine, but it will do. It will keep you contented when there is nothing else."

There are books everywhere: on shelves, piled high against the wall, thrown across the coffee table next to the brown leather armchair. Anil has never seen so many books in a personal collection, not even in his father's library. You can almost suffocate on words here.

Harish clears a corner of the room to set up a folding table and two chairs. "I don't think I've ever had a guest here," he says, "I usually have my dinner outside." They sit with their knees almost touching to a simple meal of *chapattis* and *dal* curry that Harish has bought on his way back from work.

Anil watches the little old man eat. He tears the chapattis in sudden movements, wipes the dal off the stainless steel plate and carefully lifts the food to his mouth. He chews his food for a long time before swallowing. Here at home Harish is much less talkative than on the bus to work every day. Eight hours of copying and typing letters and the long journey home have drained his energy, Anil thinks. They eat quickly, without talking.

After putting away the plates and drinking a cup of Nescafe, Harish comes alive again.

"I would give you the armchair to sit on but I'm afraid I will lose my inspiration and won't be able to read well. After all this is the highlight of the evening, not the meal you've just eaten. I am feeling nervous. You know, I've never read aloud to another person before."

"I wouldn't dream of displacing you. I'll make myself comfortable here on this folding chair, out of sight. Pretend I am not here and you are reading aloud to yourself."

"Now where is the book?"

Harish makes a show of looking for the book he had placed by the armchair the night before. "Borges," he announces as he opens the book and sits. "Have you read Borges?"

"No, I have not had the pleasure."

"You have missed much. Jorge Luis Borges was an Argentinian writer, mostly an essayist and a short story writer, though he did produce some mediocre poetry in his early days. He was a librarian for many years. He was offered a job as a poultry inspector, which he declined, and was a professor of English literature at the University of Buenos Aires for fifteen years. He was close to his mother. According to a story, his father sent him to a prostitute in the red-light district in Geneva, where his family lived for some time when he was young, but he failed to do anything, thinking that his father was her client. Women were a constant source of difficulty for him but he did get married twice, the second time happily. He suffered from eye problems throughout his life and he became totally blind during the last few decades of his life."

Harish has kept his eyes on the book during this introduction and Anil can't decide if this condensed version of Borges's life is a paraphrase of the biography in the book or a summary of all Harish has read about the author. Harish turns the pages until he finds what he is looking for and begins with the title: *"Funes, the Memorious,"* he almost shouts. He lowers his voice as he reads, *"I remember him. I have no right to use this sacred verb. Only one man on earth deserved this right, and he is dead."* Gaining confidence, he moves through the story with a theatrical cadence, pausing for effect, looking at Anil to see if he is responding to Borges's words and sentences. When he sees Anil's concentration waver he repeats the sentence he has just read, adding more feeling to his delivery. He takes on the part of Funes, identifying with the character. *"I alone have more memories than all mankind has probably had since the world has been a world."* He sighs when he comes to *"Funes remembered not only every leaf of every tree of every wood, but also every one of the times he had perceived or imagined it."* It takes him thirty minutes to get to the closing words: *"Ireneo*

Funes died in 1889, of congestion of the lungs."

Anil claps as Harish puts the book down.

"Did you like it? Did you really like it? I was afraid that you would be bored."

"It was wonderful. It's impossible to get bored with a reading like that. You're right that I have missed much by not reading Borges."

"One can read him again and again and get lost in his world. Is that not the definition of a true artist? He writes about time, memory, labyrinths, riddles, circles, all the things that should obsess every thinking and reading man. There is much I don't understand, and don't pretend to understand, but what I do seems infinitely rich."

"Will you read me another story?" asks Anil.

Harish picks up the book and begins reading *Tlön, Uqbar, Orbis Tertius*. The story takes them past midnight with all its convoluted descriptions of an imaginary world.

Anil remembers nothing of it the next morning except for the strangeness of the tale — it was much more puzzling than *Funes, the Memorious* — and the following words, which he carries through the day: *Copulation and mirrors are abominable. For one of those gnostics, the visible universe was an illusion or, more precisely, a sophism. Mirrors and fatherhood are abominable because they multiply and disseminate that universe.*

Through the glass walls of the office Anil sees people moving across the floor like ants at work, stopping every few moments before scurrying around again. The circulation of the *Daily*

Planet, an independent newspaper, is less than a tenth of the major dailies but he was excited to get a call from one of the editors to come in and discuss the publication of his cartoons. A tenth of a large number is bigger than the readership of *Men's Weekly*. He is growing tired of the magazine publisher's constant demands to spice up his cartoons, to "add content appropriate to the typical reader's needs." Or in other words, to throw in sex and flesh and comedy at every opportunity for the eighteen to thirty year olds who buy the magazine every month.

"I'm sorry I'm late," the editor says as she enters the room. "We had to reorganise the entertainment page because our idiot of a movie reviewer was late with his article. I'm Santhia." She shakes his hand vigorously and takes a seat next to him.

"I'll come straight to the point. We would like to publish your cartoons in our Sunday entertainment section but you have to end your deal with *Men's Weekly*. We demand exclusivity."

"That's not a problem. I think the magazine would be happy to see me go. Somehow it's not quite working out."

"I know Lee. He is a bastard, though a charming one. It's not hard to guess that he's demanding more lascivious cartoons and you're not willing to give in."

"What will you demand of me?" asks Anil with a cheeky smile.

"Nothing more than what you're doing at the moment. I think it is good work and you deserve a bigger stage. We can't offer you the circulation of the major newspapers but you'll reach many more people than you're doing now. Your cartoons will add something new to our entertainment section," she says, not taking the bait.

This is a girl he can easily fall in love with, he thinks, while she continues to explain the nature of the arrangement with the newspaper. Does she like him?

"Is something wrong?" Santhia asks.

"No, I was just thinking that I could easily fall in love with you."

She laughs and says, "But you're supposed to be listening to me and trying to decide if you want to sign a contract with the newspaper."

"I'll sign. You just have to pay me as much as I get at the magazine and I will sign."

He pursues Santhia with all the energy he has left after working on his posters and cartoons. He calls her every day, waits for her outside her office, sends her little gifts he picks up at the night markets. There is no subtlety in his method; he thinks this is how the game is played. In return she says, "You're too young for me. I'm close to thirty, and what are you, nineteen, twenty? It will never work. You're cute and talented but you're just a boy. And I pay your wages. It won't look right if you are with me." He tries to convince her by saying that she looks young and lovely all the same, despite her age, but she shakes her head and says, "You won't get very far with me with cheap flattery."

One night, just as he is about to give up hope and go back to his whores, she seduces him. She agrees to have dinner with him in his flat on condition that he shows her how he draws. She wants to watch him in the act.

"I'm not sure how this works," he says after clearing the table.

"Where do you draw?"

"On my bed, propped up on my pillows against the wall."

"I'll sit next to you on your bed and watch you."

He hesitates for a moment but when the first line comes he loses himself in his work and almost forgets she is there. Apart from her breathing she is still. The day has been long; eight hours at Goh Poh's and another four finishing a large poster in front of the Rex cinema for a blockbuster Bollywood movie which opens the next day. After an hour, during which no words pass between them, he drifts off to sleep.

She thinks he looks beautiful while he works and sleeps. She takes the block of paper and pencil from his hands and places them on the table by the bed. He has been drawing nothing but caricatures of her. Her favourite is the one of her holding a trinket in one hand and a sword in the other with him pleading on bended knee. She first takes off her own clothes and then undresses him. He stirs when she puts her hand on his cock, but she pushes his head back on the pillow and says, "You're tired, let me do the work."

In the middle of the night he awakes to find her standing by the window. He walks up to her and holds her. "Look at the moon," she says. A large cloud in the shape of a tiger moves swiftly across the sky, swallowing the full moon. They see the faint light of the ball behind the cloud and watch as it traces a path behind the yellow veil, as if it is moving through the entrails of a beast. The cloud spits the moon out.

Anil likes waking up before her. If he does, he gets a few minutes to study her still face, undisturbed by emotions and expressions. Her skin is smooth and dark and it almost glows in the morning light.

Her hair is short and her features delicate and precise. Sometimes she looks like a young boy to him, a mirror of himself.

They move easily with each other. The chase was difficult but life together is simple and strong. Santhia spends most nights at his flat, slowly taking over his spare time. He notices her presence even when she is not there. Her clothes in his bedroom, the way she has rearranged his things, the plants and posters she has bought to liven up the flat, are all constant reminders of her place in his life.

She too becomes a regular at the stalls below, but she sometimes upsets the balance of the Bremen Five; conversation doesn't flow the way it used to when she is around. "The gang is wary of a female element in its midst," Aris says to him when they are alone. "But an older woman is good for you. You've probably learned a trick or two in bed. She swears like a sailor so I'm assuming she is not the passive type when you fuck."

Goh Poh misses his companionship on his weekly trips to the brothel but he too has to admit that a girlfriend has changed Anil for the better. "Be careful she doesn't take over your life," he warns Anil. "Keep some time for yourself. Otherwise you'll wake up one day wondering where the days and your life have gone."

Santhia is most open about her past and present after they make love. Then she talks about her childhood, her schooldays, her ex-boyfriends. How her parents died in a car accident when she was young, her teenage days with her dour aunt and uncle. "There was no happiness there. I couldn't wait to go to school and I felt like crying every time I heard the last bell and it was time to go home. I was bright enough to land a scholarship to go to university and they were happy enough to be rid of me. That's how my life in the city began."

She asks him about past girlfriends and his sexual experience.

"Girlfriends zero, sexual experience some."

"A few ladies of the night?"

"Yes, a few," he confesses.

"There's nothing to be ashamed of, Anil. But you did wear a condom every time?"

"Yes, yes I did. I won't pass you any diseases. How about you, how many boyfriends?"

"A few. The first was this boy at university who took off my clothes behind a bush in the park behind my hostel and fucked me. I'm still not quite sure if it was rape. I did go out with him for a few months afterwards, out of shame more than anything else. He was nice enough."

These revelations shock him; he thinks she is ruthless when she describes her past. She says, "But none of them buggered me. I want you to be the first." This is how she shows him that he is special to her, different from the others.

He tells her who he is, recites his history. No one in the city knows his story, not all of it. He has kept parts hidden from every person he meets, so the puzzle could never be fitted together. Now he gives her the key. She sees him walk to the funeral pyre, paint in his mother's studio, escape to the city. "Isn't it wonderful that we have all converged here with our pain and dreams?" she says.

"No one will see."

"Santhia, not here," Anil pleads.

"Come now, are you afraid of desecrating these sacred grounds?"

They are in a limestone cave on a hill, two hundred and seventy two steps above ground. It is part of a complex of caves sacred to the Hindus in Malaysia, sixteen kilometres out of the city. Long-tailed macaques, who roam the caves freely, watch as she unzips his trousers. The little statue of Krishna playing a flute in an altar carved into the stone guards over them as they make love.

We celebrated Deepavali at my flat yesterday, Santhia and I. She is my girlfriend and my editor at the Daily Planet, where my cartoons are published. Neither of us can cook, so we catered food from one of Sammy Coop's relatives. The party was a success, there were over fifty guests. It is nice that after a year and half in the city I already know that many people, though I can't claim to know all of them well. My close friends were present and that was enough for me.

You may want to know something about Santhia. She is beautiful and I always think I am lucky to have her. She is older than I am, by ten years, and is certainly more accomplished. The newspaper she works for is successful enough. Have you read it or seen my cartoons? Pick up a copy if you haven't. There is much in it that is different from the other newspapers.

I felt guilty when I abandoned painting for cartoons. It was as if I had betrayed Amma and thrown away everything she had taught me. But I feel closer to these little drawings than any painting I have made and I believe I have found my medium. Maybe you will find them frivolous and light. They are not to everyone's taste. I spend a lot of time observing people and honing my drawing skills, and what I draw is certainly different. I still work for Goh Poh. The money I make from the newspaper is decent but not enough to live on, so I now have two jobs, a girlfriend who demands much of my attention, a little more money that I need and no time to spend it. I have discovered that I have the capacity to work long and hard without getting tired. I think I inherited this trait from both you and Amma.

Talking about Amma, I bought an anatomy book a few weeks ago, a book of bones. I had always wanted to know the names of the bones I saw in the tray the day after she was cremated. The images of those bones, her bones, are still in my mind and it didn't take me long to find them and their names. In medieval times, some people kept skulls to remind them of death, or the finiteness of human existence. I use the map of these bones to keep Amma alive.

In your last letter you wanted to know if I had plans to finish my A-levels and go to university. I don't see the point of it. I am learning a lot by working on posters and cartoons. Don't worry about other parts of my education. I have Santhia to teach me about current affairs and a man named Harish, whom I met on the bus to work, is my mentor on literature and philosophy. It's not a bad education at all. You may have noticed that my writing has improved. At least, I believe it has. Harish reads to me one night a week from his vast library. We sit around over Nescafe afterwards and discuss the passages he has read and books in general. My favourite writer is Borges. His writing is convoluted and unclear to me at the best of times, but it is beautiful. Harish thinks that he, along with other writers, will open up my mind and loosen my thinking. Maybe it is all nonsense but I don't think he is wrong. This part of my education is helping my drawing in some way, although I can't say precisely how.

So you see that I am not sliding backwards and becoming a town idiot, or a city idiot I should say. On the contrary, I am progressing by the day. This is probably not what you had in mind for my future. We *never did talk about this, but I can imagine that you expected me to study law and take over your practice, or to at least to study something practical and useful like business administration. Is that what you wanted of me? There is no need to answer because I have chosen what I want to do.*

Will you give my best to Normah? I keep meaning to write to her but I haven't got around to it. Tell her that she will get a letter from me before long but my greetings will have to do for now. Give her my address, maybe she will write me first.

My love to all, as always.

From the parking lot the structure looks like an abandoned warehouse. Bright spotlights illuminate the corrugated iron sheets that make up the outer walls. The metal glows and the rust spots on them are like burn marks on the skin of a gigantic creature throbbing in the dark.

"It doesn't look very promising, does it?" Santhia says as they make their way towards the entrance, along with crowds spilling out from their cars. "But six nights a week, hundreds of people drive from the city to this warehouse in Klang Valley to see the show."

"Santhia, it's nice to see you again. How long has it been, six months?" says the bouncer at the door, a muscular young man in a sleeveless, floral dress. There are faint traces of makeup on his pretty face: lipstick, eye-shadow and colour on his cheeks.

"Probably more. I've been busy with work and I've got myself a new man," she replies, pointing at Anil. "Man? He doesn't look much older than me. Robbing the cradle?" Santhia smiles and leads Anil by the arm into the club.

They inch their way to the bar in the middle of the large, open space. Behind the long, concrete slab that is the counter, four bartenders, also in floral dresses, serve the customers. The theatre begins here. The barmen joke, laugh and shout as they toss bottles and mixers high up and slide change across the bar. Every few minutes one of them walks around with a torch, eating fire as he tilts his head back and spitting it out above the heads of the people closest to him. The arcs the stainless steel mixers trace as they glide through the air remind him of *teh tarik*. He follows the path of a gleaming container spinning to its zenith and sees the ceiling above enveloped in darkness.

Half the warehouse is lit with electric torches. The wooden stage, raised only a foot from the ground, is painted red. Plastic tables and chairs surround it in concentric circles. A row of food stalls line the wall closest to the stage. Orders are placed with the pleasant *satay* man, the gruff teenager frying noodles or the grilled fish woman, before the audience find their seats. The system is no different than that of a hawker centre. I am at an indoor street carnival, Anil thinks.

Santhia waves to some people across the room and greets those close by as they walk up to their table. This is her world. Anil has to share her with her many acquaintances on nights like this; he melts into the background as she takes centre stage. He has learned how to be invisible. "I like to be close but I don't want to be spat at. There are really no bad seats in the house," she says.

After everyone has settled down Bala makes his entrance from out of nowhere, an angel moving into the light. He looks magnificent in his gold and blue sari, a striking man dressed as a woman. He is heavily made-up, like the singers in a Chinese opera. The crowd claps and chants his name as he makes his way to the stage. He stops at their table and gives Santhia a kiss, nods approvingly at Anil and takes a sip of his beer before he darts away and leaps onto the stage.

"Why do we exist?" Bala whispers. "We don't know," the audience replies. "Because the National Front says we do," he shouts to waves of laughter and applause. He takes the audience through fifteen minutes of stand-up comedy laced with equal measures of politics, race and sex. Then his troupe of dancers and performers join him on stage for several song and dance routines. They disappear into the darkness and return with different costumes in between numbers. Wild, tongue-in-cheek and current, a transvestite cabaret with bite.

Anil smells *ganja* on the way to the bar during intermission. He knows the smell well from Aris's habit. He turns around to see a man in a black T-shirt smoking a rolled-up cigarette intently in a corner, oblivious to everything around him. Near the man stands a group of middle-aged men in suits. They appear unconcerned by what is happening in the warehouse. "Who are they?" he asks Santhia.

"They are politicians. The one in the red tie is the deputy minister for education. You see quite of a number of MPs here all the time. Don't you think it's funny, our leaders mixing with our misguided youth?"

"How does Bala get away with all this?"

"He would have been shut down years ago if he wasn't well connected. His father is *Datuk* Velappan, Mr. Ten Percent. You know, the transportation minister who everyone thinks takes ten percent of every highway project in the country. To be fair, he probably gets just a percent or two after spreading the money around, so he should probably be called Mr. One Percent. The good old Datuk disowned Bala when he caught him in his mother's nightgown but somehow the family connection is enough to keep him safe and in business. Maybe his father looks out for him out of guilt, who knows? The place is never raided, otherwise you would never get the politicos here. Someone must keep the police at bay. I have never asked Bala about it."

"Datuk Velappan, the name sounds familiar. I wouldn't swear by it but I think he visited my father at our home in Muar years ago."

"I seem to be surrounded by well-connected young men."

After the show Bala works the crowd, moving from table to table, thanking his audience for coming to see him. Exchange the sari for a suit, remove the face paint, cut his hair short, and you would have a politician in action. Does the vocation flow through his veins?

He pulls up a chair and sits with Santhia and Anil. Intricate henna patterns cover his large hands. Up close he looks even more arresting.

"Santhia, when are you going to write my show up?" Bala asks.

"When you become legal."

"This girl is too clever for her own good. And who are you?"

"I'm Anil, the clever girl's boyfriend."

"I know who you are. You're the cartoonist that all my friends talk about. I like your work but it lacks bite. The cartoons are good but they are too safe. Have you tried political cartoons?"

"I haven't. It wouldn't be too hard to draw the scenes based on what I've heard and read but I don't know if I have the humour for it."

"You can always steal my jokes. Or the countless political jokes that people make every day on the bus, in their offices or in hawker centres. I'm sure even Santhia here can tell you one or two. All you have to do is dream up a scene around the words. What do you think, Ms. Editor?"

"Stop creating trouble, Bala. Anil knows what he is doing and he doesn't need any advice, yours or mine," Santhia says angrily.

"Think about it, Anil. I've done my job, I've sown the seed. Think of how many people you can reach with your dissenting voice if you get such cartoons printed. That is if you have a dissenting voice."

Bala gets up abruptly, tosses the sash of his silk sari over his shoulder and walks away. After taking a few steps he turns around and blows them a kiss.

On the way home Anil is silent. "Is anything wrong?" Santhia asks. He shakes his head and continues looking straight ahead as he drives.

When they arrive at the flat they go to sleep without staying awake to talk in bed or to make love as they usually do after a night out. He waits for the familiar sound of her deep, low breathing when she is fast asleep before getting up and walking to the living room. He turns on the light, grabs a sketchpad and pencil and starts working.

The first cartoon he attempts is based on Bala's joke about the new highway in the city that leads straight to the political headquarters of UMNO. After several false starts he gets an idea of how to exaggerate the situation to make it work on the page. He draws the highway branching into several exits leading directly into the offices of the key figures at UMNO. The highway looks like a large horizontal tree with branches reaching out to the sky. A character who resembles the prime minister gets out of his big car and walks to his desk saying, "Now that's what I call progress." Anil is satisfied with the caption and his first political cartoon. He continues working through the night.

He presents Santhia with ten polished cartoons when she wakes up. "What do you think, will you publish them?" he asks, turning the pages of the sketchpad. Santhia walks out of the bedroom without replying. He chases after her. "What's wrong? Don't you think they're good?"

"It doesn't matter if they're good or not. They can be the work of genius as far as I care. I can't believe that you were so easily persuaded by that transvestite. Am I supposed to waltz in today to the chief editor asking for permission to print these cartoons? He knows you're my boyfriend and he will probably chew my head off and throw me out the door. Some of these cartoons go too far."

"So you won't help me? I thought the newspaper was all about independent reporting, not toeing the party line."

"There is a difference between independent reporting and this, which can easily be seen as slanderous or subversive material. Anil, the newspaper can be shut down for printing these cartoons. It's not a game."

"Don't you think my father's name will protect me and the newspaper?"

"It's well known that your father is connected to the government in some way, though no one knows how important and deeply involved he is. He could be a thousand times more powerful than Mr. Ten Percent or just a fringe figure. I don't know that and I am sure very few people do. But what upsets me is the paradox in here somewhere. You want us to print political cartoons to attack the establishment and yet at the same time you want your father to protect you. The only way that can happen is if he *is* the establishment."

Anil feels trapped; he know what she is saying makes sense. "How has this become so important to you overnight?" Santhia asks.

"I don't know but it came to me so easily after Bala suggested it. I was looking at the cartoons this morning over breakfast and I know they're very good, better than most things I've done. I am not claiming that I've turned into an activist overnight, but maybe I have a talent for turning these jokes into cartoons, giving them a different form, a different life. Would that be a good enough reason for you to print them?"

"No, Anil, no. I will not jeopardise my job or the newspaper just because you think you have some sort of talent for these cartoons. Something may have clicked in your brain last night but I want no part of it. You'll have to find some other way of getting them into print. But I hope you won't try. You're playing with fire."

They have never argued like this before. All their fights have been over little, insignificant things, fights readily patched up with a word, a gesture. This is different. He holds and kisses her before she leaves for work. Her presence vanishes immediately as she walks out the door and he feels a great distance between them. She has refused to help him. He knows her reasons are sound but he can't help hating her for her wisdom, for her age and experience. Let me do what I want, he wants to shout, let me play with fire and get burnt.

With bare hands the hero fends off ten sinister fiends brandishing sticks. The villains are dressed in identical striped, short sleeve shirts, and all of them sport long, curved moustaches. The hero has his woman by his side, keeping her safe from harm. They move from the courtyard of her house to open fields, before appearing on a hilltop where the fight scene ends in victory for the hero. She swoons in his arms and he breaks into song. "This is great," Santhia says, "I haven't been to a Bollywood movie in ages." The next scene is a song-and-dance routine in which the hero and his girlfriend go through five costume changes and dance around bushes, trees and statues. It lasts fifteen minutes.

"I'm not sure I can sit through any more of this," Anil says.

"Have you become a snob? You used to love watching movies you had painted posters for, on opening night," Goh Poh says.

"I've seen this damn thing over and over again." Anil slinks back into his seat and steels himself for the remaining hour of the film.

When they leave the cinema Goh Poh points to the poster and asks, "So Santhia, what do you think of it now that you've seen the movie?" She dances around Anil and says in a sing-song voice, mimicking the heroine in the movie, "It's a masterpiece, I love it. It is pure genius." Anil smiles and pretends to slap her. He looks up at the poster and feels disheartened. *Why I am wasting my time? I know it's a job but I should be working on things that are more important than this.*

*

Anil hears the key turn in the lock. Santhia pushes the door open and walks in, her wet hair flattened to her head. Her dress clings to her body. It has been raining since late morning; raindrops the size of small *longans* have been pounding the streets and rooftops for hours. "It's my luck that I forgot my umbrella today," she says. "Let me change out of my wet clothes."

He turns back to his book, Llosa's *War of the End of the World*. The *Conselheiro* has captivated him and he needs to return the book to Harish by the end of the week. Harish sets strict deadlines for when he wants his books back. Failing to meet the timetable set is punished by exile for a week and the loss of borrowing rights for a month. "Reading, like many good things, is a matter of discipline and these rules are meant to help you," Harish said when he first explained them to Anil. *There are so many people who want to help me, so many people who want to tell me what to do, what not to do, how to do it.*

Santhia returns in a nightdress and sits in his lap. "Put that away for a second. I've got something to tell you," she says. She kisses his forehead and plays with his hair. "What is it?" he asks.

"I'm pregnant. I went to the doctor today and he told me that I am eight weeks pregnant."

"Why didn't you tell me before?"

"I wasn't sure. I missed my period and I felt a little nauseous but I didn't want to say anything until I was certain. Are you happy?"

Anil smiles at her but he does not answer.

"I'm not giving it up. However you feel, I am not having an abortion," Santhia insists.

"Slow down. I'm happy, very happy but I am little shocked. We didn't plan this."

"No, we didn't plan this but it happened anyway."

"Shall we get married?"

"Just because of the baby? No, I don't want it that way. Ask me again after it is born and maybe I'll say yes."

He lifts her nightdress up to her waist and puts his hand on her stomach. "He or she may be the last of the line," he says as he rubs her skin gently. "What? What do you mean?" Santhia asks.

"It's hard to explain but I once painted a Y instead of a Z as my mother asked me to. When I did this she said you are the last but one. I couldn't understand what she meant at the time but perhaps she was saying that I would have one child and our line would end with that child."

"You don't believe that, do you?"

"For some reason I believe more in cryptic sayings than simple facts these days."

He puts his head on her stomach and says, "I will ask you to marry me when the baby is born."

My collection of cartoons was published a month ago. Have you received the copy I sent you? If you had seen my work in the newspaper and compared it to some of the new cartoons in the book, you would have noticed the emergence of political ones. Santhia wouldn't print them so I looked high and low for someone who would. After talking to many publishers, I found one who was willing to take a chance. His business was going nowhere, so the thought of being closed down did not scare him. He thought we would get away with it if we mixed the old work with the new. He was right. It has been exactly thirty days since publication but neither my publisher nor I have received a visit or a phone call from the authorities. We have been waiting for something to happen, half expecting it, but for the moment we are safe. It could be because they think that the cartoons can do no harm or that the book will be read by only a handful of people. Major bookstores have refused to stock it and it is mostly selling by word of mouth. When I last called my publisher, he said that it was doing very well and it is keeping his company afloat. I have no reason not to believe him but I guess I will find out the truth when I receive my first royalty payment at the end of the year, if he is still in business then. If the money is good, I may give up working for Goh Poh. He will be upset but I don't how long I can continue painting posters for movies I don't care about.

All my friends have bought a copy of the book and I receive letters every week from readers through my publisher telling me how good it is. People are kind, at least with words. But there have been no reviews, not a single one. Santhia is not happy at all. She thinks that I did a very dangerous and stupid thing and she said that she would have never forgiven me if I had been arrested. I don't think she has looked at the copy I left on the coffee table. It sits there, collecting dust.

Are you protecting me? I have no way of knowing and I am sure you wouldn't tell me if you were. Thank you if you are. This is important to me in some way, it feels like part of my growing up.

You are to be a grandfather soon, in four months to be precise. You can understand why Santhia is so angry I published my book given that we are to be parents soon. Being an unmarried, pregnant woman is bad enough but you can imagine how difficult her life would have been if she were alone while I rotted in jail. Am I exaggerating the dangers? I think it's hard to know where the line is drawn, it is difficult to decide how far you can go in this country. I understand Santhia's anger but I had no choice. To my mind, there was only one thing I could do.

There is some distance between us now. Things are not unpleasant but we are not as close as we used to be before I told her about the book. I hope that her anger will subside before long and that it will not hurt the baby in any way. How was Amma when she was pregnant with me? I would like to think that she was happy, that the two of you were happy together at that time.

Santhia does not want to get married until the baby is born. She does not even want me to propose now, but I will as soon as the baby is born. This has nothing to do with the book. She decided on this when she told me she was pregnant. I didn't see myself being a father or getting married at this age. This was not planned and I would be lying if I said I am not afraid. But things take their course and sometimes you cannot fight it.

I am spending this Deepavali with some friends. Santhia is away in the highlands with hers. She is tired and wanted to escape the city for a few days.

We will come to visit you after the baby is born. I want you to see your grandchild.

Anil calls out to her again and this time she hears him above the rising din from the street below.

"What is it?"

"I have to go home. My father is dying."

Without betraying the slightest emotion she turns away from him and leans out of the window, saying, "There is nothing left there for you."

"I have to go Santhia. You're probably right but I don't think he is going to last long. He wouldn't have written this letter otherwise."

"Did he ask you to go home?"

"Yes. The letter just says: 'Come home, I am dying, Acha.' "

"Is that a command or a request? Are you going to leave me alone? Have you forgotten that I am going to give birth in less than three months?"

"I haven't forgotten. I don't know how long I'll be but I will be back for it, whatever happens."

He hears her crying. He doesn't feel like comforting her and leaves the flat for the evening.

They have all assembled at Ah Nam's stall on the last night to say goodbye: the Bremen Four, Goh Poh, and Harish. Everyone he cares for in the city but Santhia. "I don't want to start crying in front of all of them. You'll have more fun without me," she said. Anil pictures her peeking out the window, spying on them from above.

Ah Nam fries his special noodles for everyone. Aris has provided the beer, cases of Anchor stacked beneath the benches in front of Ah Nam's stall. After they have eaten Aris gets up with a glass in his hand and makes a speech on behalf of the four.

"Three years ago, we allowed this snob into our midst. Now he leaves for his *kampung* a reformed character, a grown man. He can speak proper street language instead of the strange tongue he first used. How can we describe him? A painter of movie posters, a successful cartoonist, an activist who hasn't been arrested and a father-to-be. He is leaving us because something sad has happened but we hope that he will be back with us soon. *Yam Seng!*"

They raise their glasses and toast him in unison, "Yam Seng!" Goh Poh slaps him on his back and says, "You better come back soon. Otherwise, I'll be out of business with no helper."

"You were OK without me when I first met you and you'll be fine without me again. I am not that important," Anil says.

Harish, bleary-eyed, staggers to his feet and says, "I want to make a speech." Aris tries to stop him. "Enough, let the man himself speak."

"He will have his turn. But first, let me say a few words. We have an artist here, a person who is destined to be different from the rest of us. 'You are an office clerk,' you say, 'what do you know about artists?' I may be just a clerk but I'm more educated than you lot. I first met this boy about the same time you did. He could barely read proper literature back then. He had never read Borges, can you believe it?" Harish says with an astonished look, as if not having read Borges was the biggest sin anyone could commit.

Sammy Coop asks, "Who the hell is Bogel?" Everyone laughs, *bogel*, naked, conjuring up images of an author of lascivious stories.

"Borges, not Bogel, you fool. I am not going to waste my time with all of you but Anil is different. He learned quickly and within a year he was almost on par with me, a person who had read the masters all his life. When he started to draw his cartoons I knew he was on to something. Now he is a published artist and I am certain he will achieve great things one day. Well done, my boy."

Harish slumps into his chair and falls asleep. The beer bottle in his hand crashes to the ground and smashes into a dozen pieces, but the loud bang doesn't wake him up. "The genius is drunk and asleep. Hurry up Anil, you better speak before he wakes up or you will lose all of us," Tiok Lam says. "And the beer is running out," Aris chimes in.

Anil clears his throat and says, "Here goes." He looks around to see if he has everyone's attention. All his friends are looking at him except Harish; even Ah Nam has stopped frying noodles to listen to what he has to say.

"I don't want to get sentimental at this late hour. The alcohol has gone to my head and I am floating, floating above you all. When I first met these guys, the Bremen Four, I thought I was watching an advertisement for racial harmony. Two Malays, a Chinese and an Indian, what better mix could you ask for? It has turned out to be much better than an ad, much better. They argue, we argue, insult and call each other names, laugh and everything stays the same, it's all OK. And to find two Malays who drink and are willing to drink in public is truly the icing on the cake. Add Ah Nam, Goh Poh and Harish, and one couldn't ask for a better group of friends, teachers and misfits."

Anil steadies himself and takes another swig from the bottle.

"Misfits, Malaysians, countrymen, lend me your ears, and your last beer. You have been kind to me but I have to ask you for another act of kindness. The woman in that flat, Santhia, my wife, not in the eyes of the law but my wife just the same, is going to give birth in less than two months. I have to leave, you all know why, and I can't take care of her at a distance. Tell me you will instead."

They all nod; even Harish appears to be moving his head up and down in his sleep. Does he want to leave Santhia in the care of his friends? Does he want to leave all this behind and return to his father's house? He has spent three years building this delicate structure and he is afraid that it will all come tumbling down if he goes now. Perhaps Santhia is right, perhaps there is nothing left for him at home. Does it matter that his father is dying? After all, he didn't feel anything when he read the letter, at least anything resembling sadness or pity or love. But he feels compelled to go home, not out of duty, but to see what is around the corner, what is in store for him.

Father and Son

He feels water on his face. The shutters are open and the strong winds drive the rain into his room. Anil lifts his head off the pillow and runs his tongue across his upper lip; the raindrops taste sweet and fresh. Jumping out of bed he runs to close the shutters. He ties a sarong around his waist and puts on an undershirt. The air is cool here when it rains, much cooler than in the city.

Aini is already in the kitchen so early in the morning. He was expecting to be alone but she is moving around noisily, rummaging through cupboards, banging pots and pans, singing to herself.

"Did I wake you up?"

"No, the rain did. My room is too far from the kitchen for me to hear the noise anyway."

She continues cooking up a feast. Until a few days ago his first meal of the day was a hurried, meagre affair. A cup of coffee, a slice of bread with *Kaya*, no more. Here it is elaborate, leisurely. He eats whatever Aini makes with relish, savouring every bite. In turn, she is happy to be cooking grand breakfasts once again, recreating the mornings from years ago.

"I've had to clean all the breakfast utensils. They've been sitting in the cupboards getting dirty and dusty since your mother died. Your father had tea and bread, and he was out the door. At least that was true when he was still working. He hardly eats or drinks anymore."

"All we need is for you to come and wake me up like you used to and life will be the same again. Remember? You would cradle me and I would wake up smelling the food on your skin."

"You're too old for that. We're both too old for that. I don't think it will be the same again whatever we do."

His days begin to acquire a new pattern. The dust kicked into the air by his arrival has now settled. After breakfast with Aini he spends his mornings walking through the orchard, in the neighbourhood, or in town. A wanderer in his old surroundings, learning to grow familiar again with what he had chosen to forget. If the rain becomes too heavy, he seeks shelter at Osman's shed in the orchard, at Normah's shop, or under five-foot ways. Anil digs out his old green raincoat, the 'spaceman suit' that served him so well in his schooldays, so that he is not completely at the mercy of the weather. But even the spaceman suit is not enough at times to withstand the force of the rain and winds during the first days of the monsoon.

His clothes are as he left them, neatly folded in drawers or hanging in the cupboard. They smell of things unused for a long time, of must and damp. He tries them on; nothing fits but for the raincoat. He realises how much he has grown when he sees the legs of his favourite pair of trousers end above his ankles. He must be as tall as Acha, or taller, now that Acha has shrunk.

Lunch and afternoons are reserved for Acha. They dine together in the kitchen with Aini moving quietly in the background. She is careful not to make much noise because it disturbs Acha. Any sudden, loud sound drives him mad. This is the only time of day when Acha looks something like his old self. He dresses up in a suit, combs his hair back and tries to sit up straight, but the show is not convincing no matter how hard he tries. The suit hangs on him like clothes on a scarecrow and he picks at his food, hardly eating. They talk like adults, like strangers, about the events in the world, about things in general. After lunch Acha returns to his room and changes into his sarong. Anil sits with him, reading and talking to him until he drifts off. He often lingers to watch Acha sleep or to read. When he tires of this he walks to Amma's studio in the Melakan wing to draw for an hour or two. He needs to keep his skills honed and he likes to draw where she worked on her paintings.

Normah is his escape in the evenings. They eat together and walk through the neighbourhood after dinner, returning to lie in her bed. He never spends the night at her house; he needs the time before he falls asleep to himself, to digest the day.

In the corner of Acha's room, just above the teak chest, is a cobweb. He wonders how it has escaped Aini's attention. She is a meticulous cleaner and not much slips by her unnoticed. He remembers how she would dust every inch of his room once a week and throw everything that was not neatly put away into the rubbish bin.

The small, diamond-backed spider sits imperiously in the

centre of its world. He reaches out and breaks one of the strands attaching the web to the wall. The web swings to and fro for a few moments before coming to a stop, the spider hanging precariously at the end of a thread. Another swipe of his hand and it will fall to the ground. A light step would be enough to end its life. But he does not do this. Instead he watches the spider spin furiously to keep itself balanced. Soon the web is reconstructed and connected once again to both walls. The spider lies in wait, perfectly still, for its next victim.

"Are you still here?"

Acha looks towards him but his eyes are unfocused; he is floating between sleep and consciousness.

"I was reading while you were asleep. Why didn't Aini remove this cobweb?"

"I told her not to. It keeps me company, this little spider. When my face is turned towards this wall, away from the window, it is the only living thing I see."

"You may not need it anymore now that I am here."

"Leave it alone. You are only here for a few hours a day."

Anil decides not to tell him what he did to the cobweb.

"What were you reading?"

"The story I was reading to you before you fell asleep, *Tlön, Uqbar, Orbis Tertius*."

"I like that line, whatever it means. What is it, mirrors and fathers are abominable?"

"Mirrors and fatherhood are abominable because they multiply and disseminate that universe."

"You didn't look at the book at all, you must have memorised that line. I hate mirrors now but I loved them before I was sick.

I hardly remember my father, certainly not enough to hate him. He was a man no one noticed, a man who made no impression on the world around him. He disappeared during the war and never came back. He certainly won't be remembered for that. He will just remain one of the nameless souls who died during the war. There will be no record of him, no trace of him."

"Will *you* be remembered? And what does it matter anyway once you're dead?"

Acha grimaces as if in pain and turns away from him. Anil reaches out to touch him but he brushes Anil's hand away.

"I don't think we have enough time left to be polite and careful with each other. If we're going to get anywhere, we have to be able to speak freely without getting angry."

Acha turns to face him.

"You're right. No more tantrums. What did you want to know, why it is important to be remembered? I never thought about it when I was young but as I grew older I became more and more concerned about my image after death. That's the only thing you leave behind that you have some control over. Your children go their own way. There is something of you in them, features, temperament, but nothing concrete. No one will say in twenty years, there goes Anil the son of Sankaran Pillai. But they may remember me for all the things I have done in business and politics. It almost doesn't matter to me now if they remember me fondly or hate me for what I have done. Maybe that's not entirely true. As long as I am remembered without distortion, I won't turn in my grave. Can I use that turn of phrase even if I know that I will be cremated?"

Anil ignores the question and asks, "Do you think I'll feel the same way when I grow older?"

"Don't fool yourself, it has already started. Why did you publish your book even though you knew it was not a safe thing to do? You are already craving attention, drawing the world towards yourself. You are on your way to moulding your image for after you've gone. That is the way it should be, at least for those who are not mediocre. It is one of the things that keeps you going if you don't believe in God or an afterlife."

Anil thinks of Amma painting day after day in isolation, never once talking about showing her art to the world. He used to wonder about the meaning of such hidden work and had questioned his mother's talent and spontaneity until he saw that painting in Acha's office.

"Do you think Amma was mediocre? She never once wanted attention for what she did best."

"She used to show some of her work to that painter, Tom. She had you as a captive audience, so I'm not sure that she didn't want any attention. You are right that she never tried to sell her work or have it displayed somewhere, at least not that I know of. I don't pretend to understand what drove your mother and I never understood her art. I don't have an eye for such things and I can't say if she was good or horrible at what she did. It simply didn't interest me, just the way that what I did was not interesting to her at all after a while. What do *you* think?"

"I had my doubts until I saw that strangely moving painting in your office, the one with the child eating its mother's entrails. Everything I saw before that was either copied from some other painting or too laboured. Where did you find it?"

"It was in her studio, on one of her easels in the corner of the room. I found it when I was choosing paintings from her studio for my office."

"When did you do that?"

"About six months after you left. I wanted to cover my office walls with her paintings. I didn't understand what they meant or what they were about, but I wanted to have some things of hers around me while I worked."

"Was there anything else like it? I walked into the studio after she died but I must have missed that painting."

"Nothing else that I could see."

"I should go look one of these days. After I saw that painting I developed this theory that she kept the best pieces of her work hidden from everyone. I should try to find out if this is true. If she had been born somewhere where her art could have flourished, maybe she would have become great and famous, I don't know. There is so much luck involved in success."

The reading sessions began on the third afternoon after his return. Acha woke up abruptly from his sleep screaming. Anil couldn't make out what Acha was saying except for a line he repeated again and again: "The cloud is swallowing me, the cloud is swallowing me." He asked Acha which cloud, what cloud, absurd questions given the state his father was in but he could not think of anything else to ask or say. Acha stopped speaking and fixed his eyes on Amma's photograph on the desk along the wall. He lapsed into complete silence for a few minutes. Suddenly he started shouting again, "She's dead. What is she doing here? She's dead." Anil walked to the desk, picked up the small photograph in a silver frame and shoved it into his trouser pocket. Acha fell back onto his bed, his face pressed against the pillow, sobbing and convulsing uncontrollably. He rubbed Acha's back, caressed his hair and head, whispered soothingly that it was all a dream and that everything was going to be alright but nothing he did helped. Then for no reason at all, at least as far as he could recall afterwards, he picked up his book and started reading aloud.

The Garden of Forking Paths is an enormous riddle, or parable, whose theme is time; this recondite cause prohibits its mention. Acha howled through the first sentence of the Borges story, moving his head from side to side and his legs restlessly. Anil continued reading: *To omit a word always, to resort to inept metaphors and obvious paraphrases, is perhaps the most emphatic way of stressing it.* By the end of the paragraph Acha was perfectly still and alert. He sat up straight at the side of the bed, his head turned towards Anil. Anil paused reading only to catch his breath, afraid that Acha would begin sobbing again if he stopped for too long. He read page after page of *The Garden of Forking Paths* until Acha drifted off to sleep. Harish's reading lessons have come in handy, Anil thought. He spoke the final words of the story to himself: *I am a mistake, a ghost.*

The next afternoon he asked Acha if he should read to him again.

"Yes. No one has read to me in a long time, not since my schooldays. I remember sitting with my classmates, listening to the teacher read out aloud, usually some tedious story or lesson from a schoolbook. I have never had anyone read to me alone. The sound of your voice calmed me down. It reminded me of mine when I was your age. It was as if I was reading out loud to myself, across time. I could only describe it to myself later as an echo from the past. The strangely beautiful words, the sound of the paper moving as you turned the pages, the smell of the book, all of this took me out of myself and after a while I could not remember why I was so upset. So yes, read to me again."

It becomes part of their afternoons together. Acha doesn't demand continuity; the meaning of the story or novel seems unimportant to him, as if the only value he finds is how the words it contains sound when grouped together, what they mean in tight bunches. Anil dips in and out of the books in his collection he is reading currently or ones he finds in the public library which he thinks might interest them both. Borges, Conrad, Le Carré and many others help them pass time and ease the pain and weight of their conversations. And they help Acha to sleep.

"Did your mother read to you?"

"Not that I can remember. I can't recall ever seeing her with a book that was not about painting or some painter. She used to read magazines, but not aloud to me. It was all painting and drawing between us."

"That's good, reading will become something between us. Something you will remember of our time together."

Normah's voice floats in from the bathroom, bounces off the walls in the hallway and turns the corner into the bedroom where he is. It is not a pleasant sound; she butchers the song with a high-pitched, weak and uneven voice. She sounds so different when she talks; her speaking voice is gentle and comforting, drawing him into her words. But he enjoys listening to her lost in the tune as she bathes vigorously. There are heavy slaps as she breaks the surface of the water in the earthenware cistern with a plastic dipper and pours the water over her head from high above. He hears her gasping for breath as the water splashes over her body onto the floor, struggling to keep on singing. He hears the sound of the towel rubbing against her skin and hair.

She appears moments later at the bedroom door, her hair still damp. She sits at the edge of the bed, confident and assured as he looks at her body. So unlike the first few times when she had her towel wrapped tightly around her, dropping it to the floor just before she jumped under the thin cotton blanket spread over the bed. He had told her again and again she was beautiful, that she needn't be embarrassed about letting him see her without her clothes on. "What is beautiful about me?" she said. "I am just a plain and skinny girl." And he would say, "Your silky hair, your small, wiry body. There is so much strength coiled in it. Your big mouth, your pretty little ears, your always bright eyes, your almost hairless pussy." He would continue saying such things until she smiled and pushed the blanket away from her.

Now the light brown skin of her shoulder and face is lost against the colourful threads of the blanket. But her eyes and hair are lit up by the reading lamp at the side of the bed. She always says before she presses her body against his, "I've washed the smell of the shop and the day off me."

Anil hopes they will pave the street one day. By the time he reaches the main road his shoes are muddied. He will have to clean them with leaves before he reaches Uncle Ravi's house.

The walk there takes him through a clearing in a secondary forest. The path is soft and damp but not as muddy as he thought it would be. The trees that line the path have protected it from the rain. He sees a monitor lizard on the coconut tree outside the house they once rented. So it is still alive, he thinks. Its movement appears much slower than it was three years ago; gravity is getting the better of the lizard in its old age.

Anil remembers Amma talking about the animal, how it reminded her of some prehistoric beast one sees in books on dinosaurs and extinct animals, how it marked time for her when they lived here. She had said, "It is strange why the Malays and Chinese call Indians *biawak*, monitor lizard, when they want to insult us. We don't look anything like these beautiful creatures, do we? They think we eat its meat but I have never known a single Indian person who has tasted it. Maybe they used to years ago, I don't know." He stops to watch it climb the tree. It stops to rest. He sees its eyes rolling from side to side, watching and waiting, perhaps looking at him. It starts climbing again, its leathery body gripping the trunk of the tree as it moves upwards.

He sees one of his cousins playing in the garden. He must go in and do his duty, visiting with Uncle Ravi and his family, making small talk and whiling the afternoon away eating and playing with his cousins. "How thin and dark you've become," Uncle Ravi says to him as he walks in. "At least you've become taller and kept your handsome face." Anil nods in agreement, refusing to be drawn into a conversation about his colour, weight and looks.

Uncle Ravi is a fat and dark man with oily skin. He looks nothing like Amma, his sister. Amma once told him that when it came time for Uncle Ravi to get married, the only thing he wanted from his parents was to find him a fair Malayalee girl. "I don't care if she is fat and ugly or if she does not have any money. Just make sure she has fair skin," he said. So they found him Aunty Shanti, her skin as white as snow. She is plump and jolly and she has given him three boys, more than Uncle Ravi could hope for.

"It's good to see you. We don't see Sankaran very much anymore since Leela passed away. I can't believe it's been three years," she says as she starts crying.

"Why did you have to bring that up? You haven't seen the boy for a long time and the first thing you do is upset him," Uncle Ravi says.

"Don't worry Aunty, you haven't upset me. It has been three years."

She feeds him cakes and tea and makes him play with his cousins. They are polite boys who are happy to see him. "You've grown so much," Anil says, "you will all be as tall as I am before long." He immediately becomes irritated with himself for not having anything to say to them except the two lines he has heard from many adults while he himself was growing up. He acts out the scene and plays with them for an hour.

Before he leaves he asks Uncle Ravi, "What was Amma like when she was young?"

"She was a nice sister to me. She was a very loving girl but she was often alone. She liked playing by herself. I'm not sure of the right word to use."

"Distant?"

"Yes, that's right. Distant. She was separated from us in some way."

"Do you remember her painting as a child?"

"No, I don't think she did. I don't remember her drawing much either, not more than any child does. But she did like making up stories."

"What kind of stories?"

"She pretended to be someone, for example a queen, and told us long stories about that person. She had much more imagination than I did. I only wanted to play with toys and build things. That's why I ended up a mechanic and she started painting."

"Are there any artists in your family, a grandfather or an uncle perhaps?"

"My parents didn't mention anything like that. They didn't tell us much about our grandparents and family."

He wants to ask more questions, to probe deeper but he can see that Uncle Ravi is becoming uncomfortable. He decides to stop for now and says, "I have to go. Thanks for the answers and the lovely cakes." Uncle Ravi says, "Don't worry about what your mother was like when she was young. Try to remember her the way she was as your mother." He kisses Aunty Shanti and his cousins goodbye.

The shout comes piercing through the window. Earthquake, it sounds like. But the old man on his bicycle is saying *tahu-chueh,* soft beancurd in sweetened soy milk. He comes by in the early afternoon every day, selling his wares. Acha sleeps through his calls. When the man has gone his voice is replaced by the words and laughter of a group of girls or young women. He finds it pleasant to hear human sounds float in as he sits reading by Acha's bedside. The silence of these afternoons often leaves him sad and anxious. He walks to the window and sees the teachers who live a few houses away walking home after school. They wave to him and he waves back. They seem to know who he is even though he has not introduced himself. Normah must have said something to them. He watches them enter their house before going back to his chair. Acha is awake.

"They have lovely voices. They sound like little birds when they talk and laugh," Acha says.

"Did they wake you up or was it the earthquake man?"

"I just couldn't sleep any longer."

Acha looks as if he wants to ask him something.

"What is it?" Anil asks.

"I'm not sure if I should ask you this."

"Didn't we agree not be careful with one another?"

"Alright, what do you think of women?"

"What do you mean?"

"Do you like women?"

"One of my friends in the city once asked me that. He thought I was queer."

"I don't think you're queer. I just want to know if you like women. Do you fuck a lot?"

Anil is embarassed and looks away.

"So there are things we should be careful about," Acha says.

"I don't quite know what a lot means. I've never heard you speak like this before."

"I've used many words like it but not in your presence. You're old enough to hear such things I think, even from your father. When I was your age I used to fuck a lot. I couldn't keep my cock in my trousers. It got me in trouble sometimes but I couldn't control my urges. I want to know if you're the same."

"I don't think so. I like women but I don't think I'm built that way."

Anil does not know if he should keep this conversation alive. Acha seems to be waiting for him to press on, so he asks, "Did that change when you met Amma?"

"It did for years. Your mother attracted me sexually and I think she found me attractive too at first. I told you that we drifted apart. We stopped sleeping with each other and I started looking elsewhere."

"Anyone I know? Aini?"

"Aini was one of my lovers. She still is but she has become more than that. She is my companion, the only human contact I have since I got sick."

"I saw you fucking her a week after Amma died."

Acha does not respond. Anil shouts, "Why do you think I ran away? You bastard, at least you could have waited." He has never before raised his voice at his parents, he has never uttered an obscenity in their presence. Anil gets up to leave the room. He had thought he could stomach a lot by now, talk to Acha about anything, but this conversation makes him sick. He thinks he will taint the memory of his mother if he continues with it.

"How long should I have waited? A month, a year, would that have been enough? I cared very deeply for Leela but we hadn't been like man and wife for a long time before she died. Surely you noticed that we stopped sleeping in the same room in the old house and occupied different parts of this house when we moved here. Don't judge me, Anil. I'm sorry you had to find out what was happening the way you did. It is not something your mother or

I could have easily talked to you about. This may happen to you someday and maybe then you will understand. Sometimes no one is to blame."

Anil thinks of his own deception with Santhia and Normah and he walks back to his chair.

"I won't judge you. But promise me that we won't speak of this again. I know we agreed we could say anything to each other but I want us to leave Amma out of it."

"What's your first memory of me?" Anil asks Normah.

"I remember you standing outside your house throwing stones at some birds. How old were we then? Five, six?"

"Did I catch you watching me? I can't seem to place the scene. My earliest concrete memory of you is the first time you cooked leaves for me. I think I can recall other images of you from before that moment, but they are all blurred around the edges. I may have made some of these up along the way. The *masak-masak* scene is the first memory I can be certain of."

"Do you always talk like this? You never did speak normally, did you?"

"It's my mother's fault. She brought up me up that way."

"I was thinking the other day of the time she asked us to pose naked for her. Do you know if my father asked her about it?"

"He told my father. I didn't witness it but Amma said that Acha slapped her and cut the painting up. She was almost laughing when she told me the story. I didn't understand why she found it funny. How did your father find out anyway?"

"If I had known what had happened, I would have explained

it all to your mother. I blurted it out to one of our friends in the neighbourhood. He told his father, who mentioned it to mine. You know how it goes in small towns. This bit of news moved so quickly that my father asked me if the story was true the next morning. I said yes. I didn't want to lie to him. He didn't get angry with me. That was the last thing I heard about it. Your mother must have hated me. She must have thought I was a stupid girl who couldn't keep her mouth shut."

"I don't think she hated you. She was not the sort to hold grudges against people, especially against a fourteen-year old girl. As for the stupid girl part, I am not sure. I would have thought you were silly for blurting it out if I had been slapped for it."

Normah takes Anil's hand and forces it against her cheek. "Take that as payment for what happened to your mother." It is not a forceful blow but he can see the red rising in her cheek and a tear forming in her eye. "Consider your debt paid."

They fall asleep next to each other. He wakes up to find her sitting up in bed, watching him.

"Did you plan to seduce me when you came back?"

"I didn't plan for anything to happen. This may insult you, but I never thought of you that way before we first made love. Not quite, even when we posed for Amma. I felt a little awkward at first but I don't remember feeling excited. I think I looked between your legs to see if you had the same hair there as the girls in the dirty magazines I had read. I don't remember getting hard."

"You didn't. I would have noticed."

"After a while, I wasn't aware any longer of being naked in front of you and Amma. It felt natural."

"It felt the same to me. I had never seen a penis before, so I did look at yours a little longer than you stared at my pubic hair but I wasn't excited either. I am a bit insulted that you never dreamt or thought of sleeping with me. Not once?"

"I confess, I did think of you once or twice while masturbating. It was innocent, I swear."

She laughs and says, "I began to think of you as a man after you left. I told you I cried a lot for a while, every time I thought of you. I realised that my feelings for you were not purely sisterly after all."

"So you seduced me?"

"I made myself available and you took the opportunity. Did I force you to do something you didn't want to do?"

"No. The same not-so-brotherly feeling must have been somewhere inside me too. Otherwise it wouldn't have happened."

Anil is describing how Santhia told him she was pregnant, the way she came back home wet from the rain, how she sat in his lap and told him he was going to be a father. "How did you feel when she told you the news?" Acha asks.

"I was stunned. I wasn't expecting it. She was on the pill and I didn't think she would get pregnant. The first thought that came to my mind was marriage. The second was a strange sentence Amma spoke once about my being the last but one. I took it to mean that the baby would be the last of our line."

"Leela used to say many strange things. I think it was more for effect than an attempt to prophesy. Don't tell me you believed what she said."

"Santhia asked me the same question."

"Clever girl, at least you have someone to keep your feet on the ground. Otherwise you would float away like your mother did."

"I told her that it was easier for me at that time to believe cryptic messages than simple facts."

"That sounds like something Leela would have said. I can tell you I was happy to hear your mother was pregnant. I can't quite remember how she told me the news but I know I was happy."

"It took me a long time to get over the shock and to be able to feel anything. I told Santhia I was happy right away but that wasn't true. I saw her smiling at breakfast the next morning and only then did I feel a pinch of happiness."

"I think it is going to be a boy. I hope I get to see my grandson before I die."

"Don't say that, I am sure you will. And it may be a grand-daughter."

"When I felt 'pregnant', it was my death sentence."

Is Acha hallucinating?

"I was tired all the time and one day I woke up to notice that my belly was slightly swollen and hard. It didn't take long for the doctors to find out I had stomach cancer."

"Couldn't they do anything?"

"I saw five specialists, I even had one flown in from the US. They all said that it was too far advanced and nothing could be done. It had spread everywhere. I was not prepared to die on an operating table or torture myself with chemotherapy just to prove them wrong. Isn't the baby due soon?"

"In a month."

"That's a strange coincidence. I found out I was sick eight months ago. I only wrote to you when I was sure there was no hope of recovering. Look how my belly has grown."

Acha pulls his undershirt up and shows Anil his stomach. He puts his hand on it just as he did on Santhia's when she told him she was pregnant.

The air turns strangely cold when the rain stops, as if the receding drops have sucked away the heat from the earth into the clouds. Acha stirs from his sleep and asks Anil to pass him the blanket at the foot of the bed. He drapes it over Acha's body and sits by his side. Goose bumps dot Acha's arms, little cones of flesh rising from the surface of his dry skin. Anil remembers that Amma would always tell him to place a light blanket across his stomach and chest to keep warm at night even when it was hot outside. To keep from catching cold, she said. Before Acha drifts off to sleep again he asks, "Did you protect me?"

"From what?"

"After you found out I had published my book of cartoons, did you do anything to protect me from the consequences? I asked you that in one of my letters and said you need not answer but I want to know now."

"If I say no, you will be upset that I didn't care for you enough to protect you. If I say yes, you will blame me for smothering you and not allowing you to live your life without interference. I lose in either case. I would call that an unfair question."

"Tell me the truth."

"I got a call after your book was published, a week or so later, from a person I know at the CID. He asked me if I knew you had published a book of cartoons. I said no. He told me about the contents of the book and said that they had to bring you in for questioning. I asked what would happen to you. He said if it were someone else, they would consider confiscating all copies of the book, shutting the publisher down and bringing a case against the author and publisher for slander and libel. I told him not to do anything until I spoke to Razak. I found out that the book was selling but not through the mainstream bookstores. I called Razak and explained the situation to him. I suggested to him that it was an opportunity for the government to appear tolerant at no cost. 'What is a book of cartoons going to do,' I said, 'cause a revolution?'"

"You really believed that my book had no power to change things at all?"

"No, I don't think so. Not against the power the government and my political partners and I have."

"Then why were you afraid of a book?"

"It is not one book that changes things. But if we allowed all such books to be published, we could be in trouble. Everyone would say that we had gone soft and that would spell the end."

"What did Dr. Razak say?"

"He agreed, saying that it was probably the best move. He knew we could always go for the harder line if necessary."

"I could ask you why you did it."

"It would be a silly question. You'll find out when you become a father. And I have grand plans for you. I didn't want to see them ruined over a book."

"How many boyfriends have you had?"

"Don't speak so loud. I don't want your friends next door to know all about my private life."

"I'll whisper. How many boyfriends have you had?"

Normah pretends not to hear the question. She walks around the shop putting everything in order, humming to herself.

"Come on, you can tell me," Anil insists.

"Why is this so important to you?"

"It's not important but I want to know just the same. It's not going to change anything."

She pulls a stool from behind the counter and sits next to him.

"One. One boyfriend."

"Anyone I know? Someone from around here?"

"Not from the neighbourhood, you don't know him. I prefer to keep these things away from here."

"Are you afraid that the officers from the *kadi's* office will get you for *khalwat*? They spend most of their time shining torchlights underneath bushes along the river, searching for the smallest signs of fornication. You're safe as long as you do it indoors. Unless of course you have enemies."

"I don't have enemies but everyone knows me around here."

"Aren't you afraid that they will catch us in the act?"

"A little, but you've been my friend since I was a child. No one will suspect anything."

"Any lovers apart from the one mysterious boyfriend? What happened to him?"

"He got a job in Singapore and left. He asked me to marry him and go with him there but I couldn't bring myself to move. He was a nice man but I wasn't ready to get married. I had one lover before the boyfriend."

"Who is he?"

She blushes and says, "No, Anil, stop this. You asked me that the first night we were together and I didn't answer. I am not going to answer now either."

"Why the secrecy?"

"It's better this way."

"I'll tell you about my love life if you care to ask."

"I don't want to know. It doesn't matter to me if you've had one or a hundred girlfriends or lovers. I don't have a hold over you anyway."

"I'll tell you this one thing. You're the first Malay girl I've slept with."

"Are we different?"

"Well, your pussy is darker than the Chinese girls but not as dark as the Indians. The rest is the same, give or take a few minor things."

"Amazing. I could have told you that without having seen a naked Chinese or Indian girl."

She pulls the stool from under him and hits him playfully in the stomach. "Get out of my shop, I need to get some work done." He waves goodbye as he walks away. "Anil, please don't bring this up again," she shouts after him.

Silent gaps start to form in their evenings together. They grow longer and more frequent with time. In the beginning there was excited and lively conversation, energetic sex, followed by more talking before he left her after dark to return to his room. Now words are rarer and the lovemaking quieter, more tender. All this is normal, expected, Anil tells himself. There are no distractions here, no outside world to witness and talk about. Words burn out where there is no fuel. Passion becomes intimacy as every part of the other's body and erotic map become familiar. This familiarity is comforting and comfortable, yet it pricks him just the same. Do people have only a finite set of stories to tell each other? He suspects this is true. They grow tired of one another and drift apart when the store is empty. They start looking for another person to tell their stories to, hence the deep and never-fulfilled craving for new friends and lovers.

He looks across the table, watching Normah eat. He feels a tenderness for her that runs deep. She was once his childhood friend, his older sister, now she is more. Rice, *rendang* and *kangkung* with *belachan*, his favourite Malay dishes. She has taken the time to cook this food for him; he knows she is trying hard to please him. So different from Santhia. Both are strong but Normah has a soft core he finds touching. She is trying to create a little nest for them, away from life outside. The effort is endearing but it feels false and stifling. "Don't you want to get away, see something new?" He tries to bury his thoughts.

"I'm simple and I'm happy here. I don't need anything new. Remember I told you that I was offered a life in Singapore not long ago but I refused. I don't feel any different now."

"Sometimes you need to get out of your cosy surroundings to see what you are about. To shake yourself up so that what is buried underneath can rise to the surface."

"Is that what happened to you in KL?"

"I found something I'm good at. And I found Santhia."

She winces at the mention of Santhia; it is the first time that her name has surfaced. He notices her expression but does nothing to soothe her.

He doesn't know what he is doing with Normah, why she has suddenly swept into his life, into his hours and days in Muar. He is not obsessed with her as he was with Santhia when he first met her. There was no chase with Normah. As she put it, she made herself available and he took the opportunity. The opportunity to do what, to sleep with her? Is there nothing else? This thing is a strange hybrid of romance, friendship and platonic love. He doesn't have a name for it. Surely he owes her nothing. Surely he doesn't have to feel any responsibility for her. He has enough responsibility with Santhia already.

Guilt overwhelms him whenever he thinks of Santhia but it slips away when he is with Normah. He is unsure what he is really guilty of. What guise does Normah wear, that of a lover, a mistress? Santhia is his wife in all but name; he can't tell what Normah means to him. At her best she is his respite from everything heavy and ponderous. He likes to think of her as a light breeze brushing his hair and skin as he dozes off in the afternoon.

She senses all this, she is aware of her tenuous, precious position. She knows that she can keep him interested, keep this going, perhaps indefinitely, if she plays along and makes everything light, if she refuses to clarify and name it. But she can't help asking, "What do I mean to you? Where do I stand?"

"Such weighty questions, such serious words. I have this theory. That the heart has four chambers and so it can love more than one person at the same time."

"You should become a Muslim, you can have four wives along with your theories."

"What would I do with four wives?" he replies, frowning in irritation. With just two short questions she has broken her spell over him. She has brought down to earth what was floating unnamed in the air around them.

It suddenly becomes clear to both of them that this won't last. Hybrids are often strong but this one is too unusual and fragile to survive. They know that it will live its short life and then die out, leaving no trace behind. She hopes they will return to their friendship when it ends. But there will be no record of the words and feelings that passed between them during this time and the pleasure they felt while making love. They will never speak about it to each other or to anyone else. She wants a memento, a real thing she can hold on to as a reminder of what happened.

"Will you paint me?"

"In the nude, you mean?"

"Yes. Will you paint me?"

"Not if you're going to blurt it out to the next person."

"I've learned my lesson. Please paint me."

"I don't paint any more, Normah. I can draw you in a classical way but I would prefer a cartoon. That is what I do best."

"A cartoon? If that is all you can offer, I have to accept it."

Hidden Legacies

The cupboard is locked; a small padlock across the latch bars his entry. Anil walks out into the garden to find something heavy to force open the lock with. There is little chance he will find the key in all this mess even if Amma hid it here. He removes a brick from underneath a flower pot. A piece chips away on his first attempt and the padlock breaks open easily when he hits it harder. He smells damp as he swings the door open. The cupboard is large and deep; it is almost a separate room attached to the studio in the Melakan wing. There are rolled up canvases and frames everywhere.

As he unfolds the first canvas, he knows he has found Amma's cache. It is a painting of him and Normah, not a recreation of the one Acha destroyed but something altogether different. The brushwork is assured and strong, much like that of the painting in Acha's office. He and Normah are in a clearing in the forest, sitting on a fallen tree trunk. All around them is lush and wild vegetation, dark and foreboding. The area around their bodies is bathed in bright light. The source of the light is a mystery; there is no lamp or fire in the clearing and the plants and trees that surround them thickly will not allow sunlight to burst through with such force. Their heads are bowed slightly. Following their line of sight Anil realises they are looking at each other's genitals. But their expressions are innocent and serene, without the slightest hint of arousal. They look perfect and beautiful. He decides that he will give this painting to Normah. She deserves to have something more enchanting and substantial than the cartoon he plans to give her.

Every one of the paintings he finds here is remarkable and striking. There is no trace of the heavy, artificial style Amma used to make copies or variations of paintings from books. He has seen enough in those very books to know that these paintings are original and of a high order. He is intoxicated by the discovery of Amma's secret. The dates below the signatures on the paintings span from a few years before he was born, when she first started painting, to the year she died. So she was painting like this all along, he thinks. She chose to keep her real work totally hidden from view. *Has anyone else ever seen these paintings, Tom maybe?* He doubts it. He says aloud, "Why did you keep these hidden? They deserve to be seen and admired." He imagines her replying, "I painted for myself, not to be seen or admired. I was not sure how they compared with the work of great or even good painters and I didn't care enough to find out."

"Didn't care? Your life would have been completely different if you had made them known."

"Do you think they are that good?"

"I think they are remarkable."

"That's the nicest thing you've said to me. Too bad I am no longer alive to hear it."

"Maybe you were too scared to find out if they were good or not."

"Scared? A little, perhaps, but I don't think fear had anything to do with it. It would not have mattered much to me. I didn't need the money to survive, to continue painting. These paintings were part of my world, a world no one else could see or touch."

"How about fame and recognition?"

"What would fame and recognition have done for me?"

"Acha said to me the other day that people who are not mediocre crave attention and draw the world towards them. They start moulding their images for after death."

"Take everything he says with a pinch of salt. Take everything I said with a pinch of salt too. Facts are changed, stories and histories rewritten, to preserve your wholeness. There are many ways of explaining your life to yourself and to others around you but all these explanations don't matter in the end, except to keep you sane. I was sane. Perhaps I was happy in my own way, although I am sure that wasn't very evident. Would my image have saved me from breaking my neck?"

"I'll make sure your work is known."

"You can do with them what you choose. I am not around to stop you. This is my legacy to you."

He spends the rest of the day studying the paintings closely. Luckily none of them have been damaged by the damp and humidity. There are more than enough to fill a gallery; he counts sixty-two finished paintings and twenty in various stages of progress. He plans to seek Tom's advice on what to make of her work, how it will stand up to display and scrutiny.

He closes the cupboard door and latches it shut. No need to

lock it, no one has come here in a long time; the dust and cobwebs are evidence of this. The unfinished paintings on the other easels in the studio are not her special ones. Was she working on the painting in Acha's office just before she died? Perhaps the paint from her last brushstrokes was still drying when she fell down the steps. She may have gone outside for some fresh air, to escape the paint fumes for a while. If this is true, the painting is her death mask, or her soul mask, an imprint of her spirit at the moment of her death. How strange that the child eating her entrails was her last word. Did she have a premonition of her death? He must go to Acha's office to study the painting again.

"Have you decided what you are going to do with your inheritance?" Acha asks.

"No. When you first mentioned it I thought I would give it all away just to avoid the responsibility, to avoid thinking of what to do with all the money. An hour later, I wasn't sure if that was the right thing to do. I am thoroughly confused now. There are a bewildering number of choices and I don't know what I will finally decide."

They are playing a game he and Amma used to play when they got stuck with each other, when they needed to get questions and answers out in the open. It helped clear the air and get them back to where they could talk and act naturally. Three questions each, fired in rapid succession. No more than five seconds allowed between the end of an answer and the beginning of the next question, otherwise one question was forfeited. Each answer had to be at least twenty words long and no answer could be avoided.

They had been lost in silence for over an hour and Anil thought the game would help them start talking again.

"My turn. Why don't you visit Uncle Ravi and Aunty Shanti any more?"

"I can't stand them. The only reason I put up with them was because of your mother. I don't think she liked them very much either. The kids are fine but I can't see them without visiting those two. They don't interest me at all."

Anil smiles and says, "They're not that bad."

"I thought we weren't supposed to comment on the answers."

"You're right. Next question."

"Can you remember your mother's face without having to remind yourself of what she looked like with a photograph?"

"It fades away at times but it becomes clearer the longer I think of her. I hadn't seen her photographs for three years until I saw the one by your bed. The picture I had in my head was different and I was surprised how distorted memories can become. But I thought afterwards that it doesn't matter."

Anil touches his right temple and says, "The image I store here is more precious." He pauses for a moment as if to recall the image, and asks, "Why did you stop at one child?"

"It was Leela's decision. I wanted to have a big family, five, six children but she didn't want to have any more. She had her tubes tied soon after she had you. She didn't tell me she was going to have the operation and I was angry with her for a long time. I don't think we spoke to each other for weeks afterwards. There are no rules about the questions we can ask, are there?"

"No rules."

"Do you love me?"

The question shocks him. It is a simple one, not against the rules of the game, but he would never have expected Acha to ask him that. Not in a game like this, not even during their most serious conversations.

"I am waiting for your answer."

"I am not sure."

When he hesitates Acha says, "Sixteen words left."

"It is a complicated feeling. I didn't quite know as I was growing up whether I did. I knew I loved Amma. My feelings for you were different in many ways so I didn't know how to describe it. Your presence was insignificant compared to hers and it was not important what I felt for you. That's not quite right. I could always feel your presence but it was in the background, almost like a shield. I can say I hated you when I left for KL. I am not sure what I feel now."

Anil can see that Acha is hurt by what he has just said. He continues the game by asking, "Do you love me?"

"Are there any rules against asking the same question?"

"No. Answer the question."

"Yes."

"Nineteen more words."

"I am a simple person emotionally, at least compared to you or your mother. A father loves his son just as a son should love his father."

"You told me not too long ago that you couldn't remember enough about your father to decide if you hated him or not. How does that fit in with your simple rule?"

"You trap all my words and spit them back at me. I should be careful what I say to you. Well, anyway, the game is over. That's enough for one day."

The final round of questions and answers has made things worse between them. We should never have played this game, Anil thinks. It always worked with Amma; they knew how to use it well. They kept the questions light and easy, yet interesting enough to open up new paths they could explore later. He wants to know as much as he can about Acha but he has to learn to be more careful with him, out of compassion for a dying man who should not be subjected to more pain than he already has to bear. And out of fear that Acha will shut down if he is too honest. All this truth, all these revelations are beginning to wear both of them down. Time is running out, but they have to learn to slow down and not rush as if this were a race with a prize waiting for them at the end. They are trying to recapture lost years with simple descriptions, questions and answers. A difficult and almost futile exercise in summarising and condensing, like the précis he had to write in school for his English exams, or attempting to explain and describe Amma's paintings and the books he has read with short synopses. He knows that summaries are necessary at times but they can never replace watching, observing and living with the person or thing you are trying to understand.

The buffalo horns of the Minangkabau roof reach up to meet the falling rain. They celebrate the victory in a battle which saved the Minangkabau people from Javanese domination. He knows the myth well; it was one of Amma's favourite stories and she loved reciting it to him as a child. He would always laugh when she explained that Minangkabau meant buffalo victory. It was funny to him that a people should be named after an animal and an ugly one at that.

The roof looks like a capsized *sampan* to him, flipped over by the force of the wind and rain. He opens the shutters and sits by the window. The monsoon has gathered strength and the rainfall is increasing day by day. The clouds are thick and still; he knows he will be trapped in the house for the rest of the day.

Amma liked this wing best. She used to say that it was the most pleasing to her eye and she thought that the Minangkabau had a lot in common with their caste, the Nairs. They were both matrilineal societies. "Until a generation ago in Kerala, the Nair women had all the wealth and power. A woman could leave her husband's sleeping mat outside the compound if she was unhappy with him. Unfortunately, modern life finally encroached on this society and the system was dismantled. You would have taken my surname and would have been a Menon and not a Pillai if it had survived," she said. She would have preferred to have her studio here in the Minangkabau wing but Acha wanted to use it as the formal dining room of the house because it was near the main kitchen.

If he were a songwriter, he would compose a song to celebrate all this rain. He would write a song for every day of the monsoon, a song cycle to celebrate the season. The texture of the raindrops, the light and cloud, the breaking of the monsoon, the changes from day to day would all be witnessed and set to music. What would the song of this day be? A loud introduction to suit the crashing rain, followed by slow and melancholy passages as he thinks about Amma.

She is present now that he has found her real paintings. He can feel her again, not only in her studio but everywhere, through the furniture and decorative pieces she picked out, and by imagining her movements and her life in the house. Her trail is warm once more.

He thinks of how her life would have been if she had become a famous painter. He dreams of a different life as the son of a famous painter. He may have followed in her footsteps and become a painter himself. Did he abandon painting for the wrong reasons, false ones? Does he still have the gift flowing through him?

"What do you think, Amma? Did I have any talent for painting?"

"I am not sure. You didn't try hard enough. But you were always good at drawing."

"I abandoned what you taught me for something light and fickle. I thought what you painted was too laboured, not good enough. Are you saying I shouldn't feel bad about this?"

"I didn't say that. You should feel bad for assuming I had no talent from what you saw."

"How was I to know that you hid your best work? I could only judge you from what I witnessed day after day."

"I suppose you're right. Why are you troubled then?"

"I want to know if I should start painting again. Is it too late?"

"I don't know if it is too late. But it's silly to assume that whatever talent I had for painting was passed on to you in some way. You have to find your own way of saying things. Haven't you found it in your cartoons?"

"I think so. But they appear frivolous and too light compared to your paintings."

"Give it time, maybe you have nothing serious and weighty to say now. Not all good art has to be heavy. You will grow into your own skin one day and only then will you be able to decide if you have found what you were looking for in your art."

He draws two sequences of cartoons: one of his life as it has turned out to be, the other an alternate world where he is a painter, carrying the torch his mother has passed to him. For the first time he gives his characters words.

The bakelite telephone sits camouflaged and hidden on the ebony table. Black against black, blocked from sight by the curved lamp. It is the only old phone in the house; the others are top-of-the-line gadgets with scores of buttons and functions. He loves its chrome dial, the braided cord, the little drawer at its base where he has his lucky one-cent coin hidden. This is where he waits for Santhia's calls. They have come up with a system. She tries him at six o'clock every weekday, just before she leaves the office. If one of them misses the appointment for some reason, he calls her at home the next morning before she goes to work. They give themselves the weekends to rest and recover from their conversations.

The telephone rings, its deep, rich sound flooding the evening silence. He allows it to ring five times before lifting the receiver.

"How are you?"

"When are you coming home?"

She asks this question almost every day and he always replies, "I don't know." She expects this answer and moves on quickly.

"I met the gang at dinner yesterday. It was the first time in weeks we were all together. All except Goh Poh, but he never appears without an invitation. Even Harish turned up at some point. We didn't plan it but it just happened that we were all there."

"How are they?"

"Everyone is fine. Prabu has left for Hollywood. He is convinced that he will make it there. John converted back to Taoism or Buddhism, whatever his religion was before he became a Christian. No one knows why. So he is Dong Bong Gong again."

Anil laughs loudly. He is glad to have these comic interludes.

"And the quartet?"

"Same old, same old, except for Aris who has just been promoted to deputy editor of the magazine. You should see his strut. Harish was worried that you would have no good books to read. I told him that you carried quite a few in your suitcase when you left and you have been borrowing books from the public library. They all asked about you. I said you're fine but I am not sure how you are."

"Ask me."

"How are you?"

"I'm OK. There is a lot to think about but I am coping. How are you, Santhia?"

"What do you want me to say? I'm getting heavier by the minute. It is getting more and more difficult for me to drag myself around. I think I will have to stop working soon."

"Why don't you come here?"

"Why should I? You promised you would come home before I gave birth. I don't know if you realise that the baby is due in a month."

"I know that but things are complicated here. Acha is very sick, I can't abandon him now. Do you have any help?"

"The guys have been wonderful. They are doing what *you*

should be doing for me. Goh Poh is the kindest of the lot. He repainted the flat and helped me buy the pram and cot and all the other baby things we will need."

"He looks like a thug but he is quite an angel."

"He is. He told me to ask him for help whenever I need it. He has a lot of time on his hands after he decided to give up his poster business."

"What? Is he retiring?"

"I don't think he can handle it now he is working alone again. Don't feel guilty for leaving him stranded. I think he would have quit a long time ago if you hadn't started working for him."

"I thought he was joking the night before I left. He said that he would go out of business without my help. What will he do?"

"He wants to tend his garden and rest."

With Goh Poh gone the painted poster world will shrink further and it will soon give way completely to printed advertisements. A dying art is one step closer to death.

"I've got some bad news."

"What is it?"

"I was told by the chief editor that we can't publish your cartoons anymore. I asked him if he was pressured into the decision but he didn't want to talk about it."

He says nothing. The room is bathed in red as the suns sets in the sky.

"Anil, are you there? Are you upset?"

"I don't care," he says.

He sees himself drawing in Amma's studio day after day, with no outlet for his work. The baby will be born and when she is old enough he will teach her how to draw cartoons. He hopes it will be a daughter; he dislikes little boys. She will grow up close to him, drinking in the air and ink of the studio, questioning the value of all the hours he spends hidden from the world drawing. She does not see the numerous blocks he fills with special cartoons and hides away in the cupboard. She will abandon the cartoons for something else, painting perhaps? That would complete the circle.

The only connection he has left to the city is Santhia. And his friends, but they will forget him quickly and accept someone else in their fold to take his place. Only Harish and Goh Poh may truly miss him. There is no work for him to return to. Goh Poh has retired and no newspaper or magazine will touch his work. Could Acha have been behind this? He is too weary to find out. *Let it all sweep me along.*

The dull thud of a bell announces his approach.

"That must be 007. Sharp two on Sunday as always," Acha says.

Anil pokes his head out of the window and sees Mr. Ramalingam struggling to keep his balance as he tries to bring the bicycle to a halt. He jumps off and allows the bicycle to fall to one side. Its front wheel comes to a rest an inch away from the front gate.

"I think he's fallen off his bicycle," Anil says.

"Don't worry about him. It's always the same. I don't know why he doesn't lower the seat or learn to ride that bicycle of his properly."

The man who serves as Acha's eyes and ears in the town is big and heavy. His protruding stomach presses hard against his white shirt and he wears his trousers well below the lower curve of his belly. His small nose and mouth look lost in such a large face and his eyes droop almost to the ground. Rocking gently on the balls of his feet, he stands helpless and abandoned next to his Raleigh bicycle.

Acha first heard about Mr. Ramalingam's gift from one of his friends. "There is nothing this man doesn't know or can't find out. He is a teacher but he seems more interested in stories and gossip than his job. The strange thing is that everyone trusts him despite this," his friend had said. Acha hired him as his spy after he got sick. "He is my secret agent, my 007," Acha said when he explained to Anil who this man was.

"Ask Aini to let him in. I'll change and join you in a few minutes."

Mr. Ramalingam walks into the living room and slumps into the chair facing the windows. "Mr. Pillai likes me sitting here, so he can see my face in the light and know whether I am telling the truth. As if I would lie to him," he says as he chuckles. Anil can understand why you would want to tell this man everything. There is something in his face, something in his oafish manner that breeds instant trust.

"You must be Master Pillai."

"I'm Anil, Mr. Pillai's son."

"I've heard a lot about you, from your father and many other people. I have seen your cartoons."

"What do you think of them?"

"They are funny and amusing but my opinion doesn't count for anything. There are many others you should pay attention to."

Before Anil can ask him what he means by this Acha walks into the room. Aini arrives behind him with tea, saying, "With lots of

sugar and condensed milk Mr. Ramalingam, just as you like it."
She leaves the room after serving everyone.

"You are looking well, Mr. Pillai."

"For a dying man, yes. What do you have to tell me this week?"

Acha looks at him with disgust, as if being in the same room
with this man makes him feel dirty. Mr. Ramalingam does not
seem to notice or pretends not to be bothered by Acha's expression.
He slurps his tea happily and smacks his lips to show his approval
of how Aini has prepared it.

"That woman is a genius with tea. It is hard to find anyone who
can make tea like this nowadays."

Acha shows no interest in discussing Aini's skill in brewing
tea, so Mr. Ramalingam continues, "The most important piece of
news I have to tell you is that Onn Rahim's trial begins soon."

"I know that. I pay you to tell me things I don't know."

"I was going to say what you probably haven't found out yet is
that the judge for the trial will be *Datuk* Ismail. It's not official but
someone I trust at the courthouse told me this yesterday."

"Are you sure? That's strange, I thought it would be someone
else."

"Everyone thought so too. This gives Onn a fighting chance.
Datuk Ismail is not the biggest government supporter and my
source thinks the outcome could go either way."

They go on to talk about many things Anil doesn't know
about. He plays along, acting as if he is interested in the bits of
information 007 presents to Acha, but all the while he is studying
their faces and gestures, collecting material for his cartoons.
Acha gets tired after an hour and says, "That's enough. Leave the
rest for next week." Mr. Ramalingam hesitates and remains in

his chair, staring at his cup.

"Mr. Pillai, I am not sure how to ask you this. You know I wouldn't ask for help unless I really needed it."

"What is it? Just tell me."

"My daughter wants to get married but I don't have the money for the dowry."

"Who is she marrying?"

"Siva, Mr. Guna's eldest son. He is a nice boy and he has a good job but his parents are monsters. I don't think it's Mr. Guna's fault really. I'm sure it is his wife, that snake of a woman. They want twenty thousand *ringgit* for the boy. Where am I to get that kind of money? He doesn't weigh more than seventy kilos so that makes it close to three hundred ringgit a kilo. He is more expensive than anything you can find in the market, except saffron, at least according to his mother."

Acha laughs at Mr. Ramalingam's comparison of his future son-in-law to something in the market. "Do you want to borrow the whole sum?"

"Yes, Mr. Pillai. I have some money saved up but I have to think of all the expenses for the wedding. Those monsters are not likely to contribute much."

"Anil, you decide."

Mr. Ramalingam shakes his head and starts to protest. Acha puts his hand up to silence him, saying, "Don't look surprised. I am handing everything over to Anil. It is time he starts making decisions where his money is concerned." Mr. Ramalingam looks at Anil and grins uncomfortably. "Is she happy? Is this what your daughter wants?" Anil asks.

"It's not a love marriage, Master Pillai, but my wife and I

did not force her into this. She was introduced to Siva through a common friend of our families. She likes him very much and wants to marry him. She cried when I told her that I didn't have enough for the dowry."

"I'll take your word for it, Mr. Ramalingam. You'll have the money as soon as I can get it for you. Is that alright, Acha?"

"I've said it's your money. Just go and talk to Lee Meng at the office and he will arrange it."

"Thank you Mr. Pillai, thank you Master Pillai. I'll go now."

The spy slinks out of the room. "How did that feel?" Acha asks.

"That wasn't difficult at all. If I'm going to be as rich as you say, twenty thousand ringgit is nothing. I did it more for his daughter than for him."

"A sentimentalist. Don't be too easy with your money. I would have asked 007 how and when he was going to pay it back. That question would have given you control over him even if the sum means nothing to you or you don't care when he clears the loan. You need to learn to always get something for your help. It is simple accounting, credits and debits. I am sure he is grateful and will be beholden to you for the rest of his life because of the way he is. But not everyone is like that. Some people will even hate you for helping them. The hate does not matter as long as you can get something important in return from them."

All he wanted to do was to decide quickly and simply if Mr. Ramalingam deserved the money, to act decisively in the game Acha asked him to play. He can see now that it was never going to be just a simple and honest gesture; nothing is ever as easy and uncomplicated as it first appears. It was a test Acha set for him, but a test with no consequences. He has failed, but he knows he will still inherit Acha's fortune. More than a test, it was a demonstration of the might his inheritance could wield. A fraction of his worth, no more than a few days, or even a few hours, interest on the money that will be his, was enough to bind a person to him for the rest of his life. Acha wanted to say, "Look at what twenty thousand ringgit can do in an instant. Think of what you could do with all that I am leaving you." It was a practical lesson about the power and control Acha had talked about and the impotence of Anil's art in contrast. He is unsure that his cartoons could ever move a person the same way.

Aini stretches to reach the clump of dust stuck between the chest of drawers and the wall. Her blouse glides up her torso and he sees the soft curve of her stomach. These three years have not touched her, Anil thinks, at least not on the surface. The skin on her face, neck, arms and stomach is smooth and she is as agile as ever. The only creases he spots are on her hands, from all the cleaning and washing she does. Anil lies on his bed and studies her features and body. He can see why Acha fell for this girl, this woman. To him Aini was always the maid, Amma's helper and the girl he could confide things in when he did not want to reveal them to Amma. He has never stopped to look at her carefully, he has never thought about her much. Now he can see that her face oscillates between prettiness and beauty, her limbs are long and slender, her black hair comes down to the middle of her back. She talks and hums while she is cleaning the room.

"I think I am getting old. I used to be able to clean the whole house without getting tired but it's getting harder all the time."

"I don't think you've aged at all."

"You have your father's gift of saying nice things."

"Tell me something about him."

"I think it is good for him to have you around. He is more alive now you are here. He used to talk about death and dying all the time before you arrived but he has stopped talking about these things. He seems more interested in living. But I'm a little jealous that you have taken away some of my time with him."

She smiles at him but she immediately realises what she has said and stops talking. Her face grows cold and she presses the rag hard against the table she is cleaning, pretending to be absorbed in her work. She turns away to hide her reddening neck and face.

"How long have you and Acha been lovers?"

"We are not lovers."

"I don't care what you call it but I have seen you fucking him. I have seen you sucking his cock."

"Don't speak like that! Please don't say such things."

She throws the rag at him and sticks a finger in each ear, trying to block out his words like a child who refuses to listen. Anil walks over to her, grabs her arms and pins them to her sides.

"Don't be a child. I saw you fucking a week after Amma died."

She wriggles to get free but his grip is too strong. She screams, asking him to let her go. He refuses, and says, "Look me in the eye while you keep on denying this." She screams again and spits in his face. Her warm saliva trickles down his cheek and brushes the side of his lips.

"Acha and I have talked about this, Aini. It's OK, I know."

"You think you know everything. You think I am a prostitute."

"No, not a prostitute. I'm not sure if I have come up with a word for you."

Anil lets her go and takes a few steps back.

"How about step-mother?"

"Are you getting married to him?"

"No, but I am pregnant with his child."

She pats her stomach and says, "This is your brother or sister in here." Anil walks away from her and sits on the bed. "Does he know?" he asks.

"I haven't told him. He is going to die soon and he doesn't need to know. It will make it much harder for him I think."

"But your stomach will grow bigger. How will you hide it?"

"It won't really show for another month or two. He doesn't notice much anymore, he won't see it until it really starts sticking out. If he survives until then and asks me, I will tell him."

Amma was at least half wrong. You are the last but one, she said. There will be two, although one will have no trace of her blood.

"What was that last line?" Acha asks. Anil repeats the sentence he has just read aloud but Acha looks away and doesn't seem to hear the words. He moves his arms and legs restlessly and pushes the blanket away from him. He gets up and circles the room a few times before he goes to the window and throws the shutters open.

"Shall I continue reading?"

"Don't let me interrupt. I am trying to listen."

"Are you in pain?"

Acha walks back to the bed and lies down again.

"It always starts as a dull ache in my stomach. Then it spreads, not evenly but randomly across my body. I feel it moving from my back to my legs, to my arms, to my head. Sometimes it feels like even my hair hurts. It's like a giant mosquito darting inside me and biting me every ten seconds. After a while I feel it all over. No part of my body is spared. It becomes a stabbing pain."

"Why don't you take your medication?"

"My drug you mean? It's too late now for little pills. The only thing that helps me is morphine."

"Take your morphine now," Anil pleads.

"I usually inject it when I can't stand the pain any longer. If I took it every time I felt discomfort or pain, I would be constantly on it and my mind and body would be dull and dead all day and night. I've learned to concentrate and think at some level with the morphine in my body but it still feels alien. I am a stranger to myself when I take it. It makes me constipated and nauseous if I use it too often."

Acha reaches over and pulls open the drawer of his bedside table. It is filled with vials and syringes, a few open and used, the others still in their covers and boxes.

"Aini cleans this drawer from time to time."

He tears the plastic covering off a syringe and snaps open a vial. He fills the syringe and stretches out his left arm. His hand shakes slightly as he brings the needle to his vein.

"Do you want me to help you?"

"No, I can manage this time. I don't think you've done this before. Aini helps me when my hands shake too much or I can't find a vein. I have to use a rubber band when that happens. What do they call it, a tourniquet? Look, here is one I can see clearly today."

Acha's whole body is tense; the muscles in his arms are flexed and the skin across his face and neck is stretched tight. Anil sees the dilated blood vessels at his temples. The liquid in the tube enters his vein as he slowly presses the head of the syringe with his thumb. His fingers are curled around the syringe as if he is holding a knife, stabbing his arm. He drops the syringe on the table and leans back. He presses a small ball of cotton against the punctured skin but not before a trickle of blood escapes from it.

The morphine acts quickly and the muscles in his face relax. His chest rises and falls as he breathes calmly and deeply. The picture of deep meditation is complete when he closes his eyes. As Anil is about to leave, Acha says, "There will come a day soon when I won't be able to take this any more. I am a strong man but I know that fighting this pain constantly will be too much for me." There is no sign of agitation on his face as he says this.

"Will you help me when that day comes?"

"How will I help you?"

"Six of these vials will put me to sleep forever. If I don't have the strength to do it myself, you would have to break open the vials, fill two syringes and inject the morphine into me. That's all. We can plan on a signal I can give you if I can't speak, to let you know I'm ready. I can move my little finger like this."

Why me? It can't be right for a son to kill his father, even if he is in great pain.

"Why does it have to be me? Why can't Aini do this for you?"

"I know her. She won't be able to do it. Who else can I ask? It seems fitting that you should help me die and take over from me."

Will he be able to steady his hands and plunge the needle into Acha's vein? He doesn't know if he can be cold enough to go through with this when the time comes. He finds it difficult to breathe as he pictures himself murdering his father.

"I don't think I can do it either. Don't ask me to do this."

The air in the room is moist, almost wet. All the shutters have been thrown open and the fan spins at its highest speed, but the humidity still clings stubbornly to everything. The sun came out brightly in the morning and lifted some of the water off the ground. It will stay this way until the rain washes the moisture away and cleans the air.

Acha lies asleep with only a sarong tied across his waist. He threw his blanket off earlier and removed his undershirt. His forehead and chest glisten with sweat. Anil dips a towel into a bowl of fresh, cool water and wipes Acha's face and upper body. Acha murmurs his approval. But he immediately becomes restless again and tugs at the knot that keeps his sarong fastened. He folds his legs towards his chest and the sarong slips off easily. Anil is embarrassed. He has never seen his father like this. He turns away when he sees his penis, shrivelled and hidden in a mass of pubic hair. He slowly turns back and looks at Acha. What does he see? Thick and dishevelled hair, rich curly locks fall across his forehead and the top of his ears. Grey hairs sprouting in his moustache and on his chest. A face that is tired but strong. His nose sits high and square above lips that are too sensuous for a man. Arms and legs once strong are now atrophied and are like sticks attached to his frame. His cock, always ready for action in his younger days as he said, sleeping across his thigh. His skin stretched tight across his protruding stomach.

This is how he plans his cartoons; he has developed the technique of sketching and thinking about every detail of his characters before distilling them into a few simple strokes. With Acha he knows that he will remember only his stomach, swollen and teeming with cancer cells multiplying day after day, choking his insides. What will remain of Acha when they cremate him? The same bones that Amma left behind or will a different map of his skeleton emerge? The man looks nothing like him. He takes all his features from Amma. What has he inherited from Acha? Perhaps some part of his blood, something of his character and the way he feels and thinks. Precisely what he does not know. He may discover this as he grows older. He may have to wait until he lies on his own deathbed, when all the lights and decorations have been stripped away and he is left alone with nothing to hide behind.

The Second Adam

A bearded man stares at him as he stands outside the entrance to the office. Anil has been observing him for a while. The man is not alive; he is merely an image left behind on the wall outside by water rising from the ground below. A damp patch that has yellowed and aged to reveal the face and body of an old man in long robes looking at the ground below. It is the lightest and most delicate of forms, like a faint watercolour done in ochre monochrome by a skilful hand. He walks in and asks Lee Meng, "Have you seen the bearded man outside?" Lee Meng looks puzzled and says, "What bearded man?"

"There is a patch on the wall outside that looks like an old man dressed in robes."

"Oh, that stain! We'll have it painted over once the monsoon season is over."

"Don't touch it. It's the most beautiful figure I have seen in quite some time."

Lee Meng does not respond. Anil tells him to let him know before any work is done.

"I am not sure why you want to worry about a patch when there are so many other things to think about. But it's up to you."

"Just let me know."

He raises his voice and says to Lee Meng, "Can I see you upstairs?" The whole office looks up when Anil says this. He walks up the steps, with Lee Meng following closely behind. As soon as he shuts the door Lee Meng blurts out angrily, "As far as I am concerned, Mr. Pillai is still in charge."

"That's true, but my father is a very sick man. All this will come to me before long. You will have to listen to me soon, so you may as well start doing that now."

Lee Meng looks away and heads for the door.

"I am not here to interfere with your work. You can stay in charge if you would like to. I don't pretend to know all of this better than you do but I would like you to humour me. And do not contradict me or speak back to me again in front of the whole office. You can say whatever you want here but not in front of the rest. Do you understand?"

Lee Meng turns to face him and says meekly, "It will not happen again."

"Please arrange for twenty thousand *ringgit* to be sent to Mr. Ramalingam. It's a loan for his daughter's dowry. Before you protest, Acha, I mean my father, has approved this."

"I'll do this right away. But the money can't be released without Mr. Pillai's signature."

"Send the papers to him at home and he will sign them. Can you please have someone send up some chicken rice and *cincau*? I would like to remain alone here. Make sure no one disturbs me after that."

He is surprised how his voice changed during his conversation with Lee Meng. When he spoke loudly or forcefully, all sweetness and fragility vanished and were replaced by the stentorian notes of Acha's voice, as if those alien sounds lay waiting in his voicebox for the right moment to surface. Sweetness and fragility were the words Santhia used to describe the way he spoke on their first date after they slept together. What words would she use if she heard him boss Lee Meng around?

The office is as he and Acha left it; he cannot spot a single object out of place. He runs a finger along the frame of Amma's photograph and looks at it carefully. Not a speck of dust. So the cleaner still comes in here. She is careful enough not to disturb anything. The distorted Klee looks at him from behind the desk. Whimsy turned this from a copy of a famous painting, devoid of charm, into one that will make him smile whenever he looks at it. A painting that brightens his face is worth the space and attention it takes up, he thinks. It also serves as a reminder of Amma's enigmatic comment that he was the last but one.

He goes to the corner to study the painting of the baby eating its mother's entrails. The delicate and detailed brushstrokes shaping the gestures, clothes and faces of the three figures suggest they are complete. Up close he sees the intestines painted with precision, its twists and undulations carefully recorded. He observes that the baby is not really eating them. Instead of sucking at his mother's breasts, he is drinking greedily from a hole in her liver. Blood replaces milk and there are red drops on the baby's chin.

Why the liver and not the heart? It was not uncommon in the distant past for people to think of the liver as the seat of the soul. The Malay expression for falling in love is *jatuh hati*, falling liver, and *hati* is used in many phrases expressing emotion. Was Amma trying to suggest that he was feeding on her spirit or draining it? Amma is sitting on a chair that is coarsely painted in a single layer and the background is patchy and unfinished. It is in every way superior to the Klee copy or any other painting Amma has made, even the ones he found hidden in the storeroom. That it is unfinished takes nothing away from it, in his judgement.

The meaning of the work eludes him and he cannot put into words why he thinks it is the most accomplished of Amma's paintings, but he instinctively knows this to be true. All the glib observations and catch phrases he learned to use when discussing paintings and drawings with Amma are of no use. It is as if he has been struck dumb by the power the painting emanates. He realises there is a strong dose of romanticism in all of this; the artist struck down as she works on her greatest painting. What does Acha think of it? The painting stood watch over him as he worked. Surely it must have triggered thoughts and emotions at least once. But there is a chance he may not have noticed it again after hanging it in the corner of the office. Anil does not know if he will ever be able to produce anything as powerful as what he sees. If he hides away for years and works on his cartoons, will his talent take him that far?

The office boy disturbs his thoughts with a knock on the door. Anil thanks him and wolfs down his food and drink. He has not eaten for hours and all the walking and thinking has made him hungry. He turns away from the paintings and looks for Acha's notebooks. He thought he saw Acha placing them in the drawer of his desk before they left the office. The drawer is not locked and he finds the ten notebooks there. They are not numbered but some entries are dated. It does not take him long to arrange the notebooks in chronological order.

At first he finds many of the names and numbers unrecognisable and meaningless, but soon a horde of them leap up at him from the ruled pages. He sees *Syarikat Bas Berjaya* on page six of the third notebook and beside it, 40%. Instantly he remembers this as the company that owned the bus he took every day when he worked for Goh Poh. When he closes his eyes he can almost see the black letters spelling out the company name within the olive stripes. There is a list of property companies in the next notebook. He is certain he has seen some of them on signboards of new developments and office buildings in the city. He cannot remember the name of the company he rented his flat from. The agent came at the end of each month to collect the rent in cash and the agreement was buried at the bottom of a drawer; he never had any use for it. Did Acha own that company too? Mr. Lim appears in another notebook. The meeting between this man and Acha drove him away from the highlands. The cinemas he and Goh Poh worked for partly belonged to a holding company Acha was involved in. And Acha was in some highway venture with Bala the comedian's father. In brackets next to his name, *Datuk* Velappan, is 'Mr. Ten Percent' with an exclamation mark. He recognises names he has seen above toll gates, along highways, on telephone booths, names painted on ships and warehouses in the dockyards in Port Klang, on light rail trains hovering above the city streets. Even the cans of paint in Goh Poh's shophouse are not safely out of reach of the web the notebooks spin.

Then he sees *Daily Planet* in the last one. The shock of seeing the name of the newspaper he worked for until a few days ago drains all his energy, and he slumps back in the leather chair.

Acha owned a majority stake in the newspaper through various subsidiary companies. The date next to this entry is three months after he had met Santhia and started publishing his cartoons there. Now he knows for certain why the newspaper no longer wants his work. Acha is trying to cut him off from his life in the city. Should he tell Santhia about this? He wonders if she would walk away from her job if she found out.

He realises his escape was an illusion maintained by his ignorance of the details of Acha's kingdom, of his inheritance recorded in these fifty-cent notebooks used by shopkeepers to write their accounts. Every moment of his existence in the city was at most a few steps removed from Acha's touch. He was under the constant gaze of all these objects and connections. They were guards watching over him, spies placed at regular intervals along his path to report his every move, beacons guiding him back to where he came from.

He feels suffocated thinking about the invisible web that surrounded him. He is still trapped in its threads. He runs to the window and throws the shutters wide open, gulping in the fresh air. *If the UMNO building had eyes, it would look down upon me with pity.* "That is where my story begins," Acha had said when they were last here, pointing to the building. The weight of the story is making the building stoop, and it is beginning to crush him.

Angklungs, hand drums and a gong lead him to the hockey field. Anil had almost forgotten about the crowd and the platform he had seen an hour earlier. He was ready to go home when he heard the music. Pushing gently he makes his way towards the dancers, stopping when he is a few feet away from the *danyang* who is leading the performance. With a whip of rope and feathers the danyang drives the other eight dancers on. They mount hobbyhorses made of cowhide, painted white and red. He has seen enough *kuda kepang* dances to know that this one is nearing the end. The music is frantic and the dancers are jumping high in the air and galloping with great speed across the stage, re-enacting the battles and struggles of the nine preachers, the Wali Songo, as they spread Islam in Java centuries ago. Their sleeveless white vests are drenched with sweat and their nostrils flare as if they are horses. All the dancers except the danyang have their eyes closed. They are in a deep trance, or they are acting very well. Some in the audience beside him are swaying to the music.

It reminds him of the atmosphere during *Thaipusam*. Aunty Shanti once carried a *kavadi* during the festival and he followed closely behind her in the procession. She was thanking the gods for Uncle Ravi's recovery from a heart attack by balancing a jar of milk on her head while walking two miles in the morning heat from one temple to another. The spears, even the little ones, pierced through the cheeks and the chariots hooked to the backs of the believers frightened her, so she chose the easiest way out. The loud, repetitive beats of the tabla drove the crowd into a mild trance. He remembers feeling lightheaded and happy as he walked. At the time he had never touched an alcoholic drink, but now he can describe his state as being slightly drunk. Aunty Shanti's plump, white body looked like it was hovering a few inches above the ground. She was not a strong woman but she danced and glided effortlessly, carried by the rhythm of the drums. Amma did not want to have anything to with the kavadi.

It was too exaggerated and forced, too unbridled for her taste. It is only for the weak of mind, she said, nothing good ever comes from such collective madness.

The *bomoh* pushes the first dancer on to the stage and sprinkles rosewater on his face. He immediately goes still. "Why is that man sleeping?" a little girl asks. Her mother says, "The bomoh has driven away the bad spirits so he can rest." Rain sweeps across the field by the time the bomoh reaches the danyang. The crowd disperses quickly but he stays to the very end, watching the last man fall to his peaceful slumber. The raindrops on their faces wake the dancers and they rise and walk away smiling, as if nothing has happened. *If only music and a little rosewater could help me rest and forget what I have learned today.*

"Are you ready?" Anil asks Abdul-the-driver.

"It feels strange being in this car again. Please give me a moment to get used to it."

"Do you mind me sitting in the backseat?"

"I prefer it that way. It will make it seem like the old days with *Tuan.*"

Anil has hired Abdul-the-driver for the day. He has not told Acha and Aini about it for fear of upsetting them. The plan is simple: Abdul-the-driver will pretend he is Acha and take him to places he drove Acha to.

"Have you been driving this car?" Abdul-the-driver asks.

"Yes. Is something wrong?"

"It's a good car. An old car but a good car. Your father has a lot of money but he did not want to buy a new one because both of us were used to it and we liked it very much. It's a faithful car, I said to him many times. But you must have the tyres changed, Tuan. They are almost bald and that's dangerous with all this rain."

"I will have them changed if you promise not to call me Tuan. I may be the little Tuan, the Tuan-to-be, but I would prefer if you called me Anil. After all, it's my name."

"I am not comfortable with that, Tuan. It is better not to change some things."

"You used to call me Anil. I am now alone in the car with you and I am paying for your work, but nothing else has changed. I have a confession to make. I have always thought of you as Abdul-the-driver. If I promise to think of you as Abdul and call you *Pakcik*, will you use Anil instead of Tuan?"

"I don't like it but we can try."

He explains his plan to Abdul. Abdul looks uncomfortable, so he says, "It will be like the old days," to soothe him. The words work their magic. Abdul smiles and repeats, "It will be like the old days."

Acha's hand is not there for him to hold as it was when he was a child. He is not listening in on conversations between Abdul and Acha. They sit in silence for a few minutes before a torrent of words start gushing out from Abdul's mouth, drowning out the steady purr of the engine. Anil is glad to hear Abdul repeating the same things he has said many times before; the words from the past put him at ease. He listens carefully to Abdul and when the opportunity presents itself, he uses a question he remembers Acha asking. A recycled question from the vaults of his memory. Abdul begins his reply with "Yes, Tuan, you are right Tuan," but Anil cuts him off before he can go any further. "I thought we had an agreement." Abdul nods and continues with his reply.

Anil notices the hair sprouting from under the collar of Abdul's white shirt. Thick, curly strands of white hair reaching out to meet the ones on the back of his head. There is nothing attractive about a man's neck. The gentle slope and the downy hairs of a woman's neck, the way it seems to trap her smell, are enough to excite him, but he can't imagine a woman giving a second thought to this part of a man's body. Is there a part, or a part of a part, that women find exciting? The cock perhaps. He should ask Normah or Santhia about this.

"Do you want me to stop at the office?" Abdul asks.

"What?"

"We're at the office. Should I stop here?"

"Sorry Pakcik, I was thinking about something silly. I was here yesterday, so take me somewhere else."

"It's getting close to lunch time. Let's go to the banana-leaf restaurant Tuan went to a few times a week."

It takes minutes of gentle and persistent persuasion to get Abdul to eat with him at the same table. In all the years Abdul worked for Acha he never once shared a meal or a drink with him. At the end of the meal Anil says, "Pakcik, I know the office and I know this restaurant. My plan is for you to show me things I don't know anything about."

"You want me to betray your father?"

Anil shakes his head and places his hand on Abdul's.

"Betrayal is not what I am looking for. I want to know Acha better. How do I explain this? Do you know the story of Adam? You Muslims share the story with the Christians. One of the important things that Adam had to do was to name all the animals

God paraded before him. He had dominion over the animals and naming was the way God allowed him to seal his authority. I am trying to do the same. I need to know and name everything that is happening to me, everything that will soon be mine, otherwise it will all spin out of control."

"I don't understand what you are saying."

"I am not sure I understand it either. But I need you to help me just the same."

"You want to be the second Adam?"

"That's it, that's it exactly. I am the second Adam."

The smell of *samsu* so early in the day makes Anil feel slightly dizzy. "What will you have?" the man asks.

"I am not sure, the bottles all look the same to me."

"A novice, I see."

"I am a novice when it comes to samsu. I don't usually drink in the afternoon."

"Can you name me one person who has died from drinking before dusk?"

"No, I don't think I can."

"Drink up then," he says as he pours out a large glass of rice wine for Anil. "Only the best for Mr. Pillai's son."

"How did you know? Do I look like my father?"

"Not at all, you look nothing like Mr. Pillai. I recognised the Mercedes parked in front of my shop and I saw Abdul get out of it. It didn't take much to guess who you were once I saw him."

"How often did my father come here?"

"He was not a regular, not one of those who come here like

clockwork at a fixed time every day. He came in only when he needed to get away from his office and his normal crowd. To clear his head, he would say."

"What did he do when he came here?"

"Drink, of course. A glass or two of the stuff you are tasting. He would strike up a conversation with me or one of the customers. He liked talking to me about politics. I may look like any middle-aged Chinese shop owner in a pair of shorts and a singlet, but I used to be a schoolteacher before I realised there was more money in this line of work than in teaching little brats."

He tries to picture Acha in his suit, seated on one of the red, plastic chairs, engaging the man he sees in front of him in conversation.

"Politics?"

"I know Mr. Pillai is an important man. But unlike many of our esteemed leaders, he seemed to enjoy listening to what people were saying on the street. Where better to hear the voice of the people than in a samsu shop? What is that saying in Latin about wine and truth?"

"In vino veritas."

"What I serve is not the vino the Romans drank but it works just as well to bring out the truth. And wisdom sometimes."

Anil gulps down the rest of the drink.

"How much do I owe you?"

"Nothing this time. I'll charge you double the next time I see you here to make up for it. Say hello to your father to me."

The next stop is along the waterfront. Abdul pulls up outside the gates of the government resthouse, once a place where colonial civil servants stayed when visiting the town but now a private club for the rich and a hotel for well-heeled guests who want a view of the river and the straits.

"Did Acha come here too?"

"When he was entertaining clients or meeting friends after work for a drink. All the rich people come here."

"What goes on inside?"

"The usual. There is also a gentleman's club that opens at midnight."

"A strip club?"

"All the drivers talk about the pretty girls who arrive at eleven for the show."

Anil grins and says, "Too bad it's too early to catch the show. We could have had a good time. Let's park the car here and walk for a while. I am sure they won't mind." Abdul ignores the joke. "Everyone knows Tuan here. We can park anywhere we like."

They walk past the resthouse and onto the promenade. There are few joggers and walkers out at this time; the crowds surface only after work and on weekends.

"When did they build this?"

"A year after you left. I am not sure where they got all the money from. This goes all the way to town. They have even given it a name, Tanjung Emas."

The large *angsanas* along the waterfront have been cleared to make way for the broad, paved walkway and a recreational park. Twenty years or more will pass before the new trees planted along the promenade reach the height of the ones that have been cut down. If the trees are the same. He does not recognise the bark and the leaves of the midgets that barely come up to his shoulders. The shade and beauty the giant trees offered are gone. So is their fruit that used to glide to the ground on wings. He would always pick up a dried one when he walked by, and pluck away at the veined, brown discs until he got to the pods. One or three he considered lucky, two a sign that the day was going to be ordinary. He would throw the pods into the river after making a wish. The dried fruit always reminded him of moths, preserved and mounted. Canvas umbrellas over the circular benches in the park have taken the place of the angsanas as protection against the sun and rain. Playgrounds, a hawker centre, and manicured green lawns fill up the rest of the space.

"Where did I throw Amma's ashes? I can't find my bearings here. When I came out of the water I had a shell in my hand. I used it to make a sign on an angsana so I would know where her ashes were scattered. I carved a little shed, her studio, on that tree. The angsanas have all gone."

"I can't remember. It was somewhere around here. What does it matter? Your mother's ashes are out at sea where they belong."

They walk back to the car. Abdul holds himself straight and moves at a steady pace but Anil doesn't want to tire him out. "Where to now?" he asks when Abdul starts the engine. Abdul looks out the window and does not answer.

"Pakcik, I need to know everything. Believe me, nothing about Acha shocks me anymore. I have found out so much since coming back that one more thing won't hurt."

"There is a girl he used to visit."

"Take me there."

Abdul follows the river until they reach the far end of the town centre. He heads past the Catholic cemetery towards St. Andrew's high school. St. Andrew's was the main threat to the supremacy

Anil's high school enjoyed and his classmates would always crack the same stale joke when talking about their rivals: "What is there to be afraid of? Those boys are as intelligent and outspoken as their neighbours six feet under."

The car turns into a road leading to a new development. Happy families stroll along clean streets on the towering signboard that says Welcome to Taman Guru.

"What's this?"

"Another new housing estate. It was built two years ago. There are more coming up every day."

"Did my father have a hand in this?"

"I think so."

Abdul stops outside a simple bungalow. The walls have been freshly painted; they are white and spotless. The houses beside it are marked with the familiar streaks of time, faint yellow and black lines starting below the rooftops and travelling down the walls. Fungi thriving on heat and damp. The little garden and driveway are filled with pot plants and flowers. Green fingers at work. A light is on in the house. Anil unlatches the gate, walks up to the front door and rings the bell. A young Chinese girl appears in a pair of yellow shorts and a pink, sleeveless top. "Can I help you?" she asks. She can't be more than a few years older than him.

"How old are you?"

"I'm sorry? I don't know who you are."

"Forgive my bad manners. I am Mr. Pillai's son, Anil. Can I come in?"

She stands by the door, unsure if she wants to let him in.

"I just want to speak to you for a while."

"Come in."

The house is tastefully furnished. Not a young girl's eye and hand at work.

"Beautiful home."

"Your father has been kind to me."

"How old are you?"

"I am twenty five."

Her English has a trace of the lilt of someone educated in a Chinese primary school. He can tell she has worked hard to smooth the rough edges of her speech. Her features are those of a doll's, fine and smooth. She is small and perfectly formed.

"Where did you meet my father?"

"A mutual acquaintance introduced us. A friend of my father's who does business with Sankaran."

He does not like hearing her use Acha's first name; it is too familiar. Why not? Does he expect her, a woman who has slept with Acha, to address him otherwise?

"How long have you been with him?"

"Five years now. I have not seen him for months but he still takes care of me."

"You know he is sick."

"He called to tell me when he first found out. I asked him to come and visit me but he didn't want to. He hasn't been here since."

"Did he visit you often?"

"Once or twice a week. He stayed for an hour, maybe two. He took me on some trips."

"What did you do when you were together?"

She laughs, covering her mouth with her hands. They are not as delicate as the rest of her; they are the hands of a person who toils with them every day. Anil is embarrassed that the question has come out so childishly.

"Apart from the obvious I mean."

"We talked. He liked playing cards, simple games like *angkat turun*. He enjoyed having someone around when he was travelling."

"Were you with him when he went to Genting Highlands three years ago? He went there to meet Mr. Lim."

"I was there."

"So was I."

She is surprised. "But I didn't see you. He didn't say you were there."

"I left a day before he arrived. Did he talk about us? My mother, me?"

"Not much. I knew of you but not more than that."

This girl, his father's mistress, is no longer important to his father, but he assumes she once was. She gave him something that he could not get from Amma, or Aini, and his other lovers. Should he pass her off as nothing more than a paid companion, a woman for an afternoon fuck and a game of cards? He should not be quick to judge and condemn. She knows many things about his father that he does not, knowledge passed through the pores and openings of the body. Flesh to flesh.

"What did you do with the rest of your time when he was not around?"

"I had my friends and plants. I have my life."

"He has chosen well. You are very pretty."

"Thank you. What do you want from me?"

"Nothing, I just wanted to see you."

"Are you sure? Do you want to stay? It is your money too that is paying for all of this."

She points to the things around her and touches her collarbone with her fingertip. A deliberate movement, rehearsed. He smells the perfume and the scent of the body when she does this. It would be easy to walk with her to the bedroom, to undress her, to fuck her while Abdul is waiting outside. The temptation to have Acha's mistress is strong. But he is here to know, to question, to name, not to possess. Or so he said to Abdul. Will he learn something about Acha by sleeping with her, will some knowledge pour out of her body into his? This has nothing to do with knowledge; the temptation is to take something that belongs to Acha, an intimate possession, and make it his.

"It is very tempting but I don't think I can do that. Thanks for letting me in."

He walks out the door, still trembling with desire. He has to walk funnily to hide his erection.

"Let's go home Pakcik. I think I have had enough for one day."

"Was it a good idea coming here?"

"I can't say."

When they reach home Abdul jumps out of the car and gets on his bicycle.

"Call me anytime you want a driver."

"I will."

"I hope you have learned something today, Anil."

He waves and cycles away, while Anil drags himself back to the house. The day's adventures have shed years off Abdul's body and face, and tied them around Anil's ankles.

*

The paint fumes carry him to Goh Poh's shop, and further back to when Amma's studio was still in use. Dead, dried paint doesn't smell the same. The air in the cupboard where Anil found Amma's hidden paintings was heavy with damp and caked paint; it didn't have the sweetness fresh oils and linseed emanate. Sweet and heady, this is how he would describe the smells here.

No one answered when he called out. The door was ajar and he walked in. Variations of the woman with her firm breasts visible through a thin blouse are everywhere. Tom is a master of breasts and nipples seen through a veil, Amma once said. He looks around for a moment before walking into the inner room through the green door. He first sees the model. Her tits are sagging, nothing like the ones in the paintings. Artistic license. If Tom can conjure up pert breasts from those he sees before him, if he has painted her face a thousand times, why does he still need to use her as a model? It would be interesting if he painted her as she is, capturing the cruel effects of time. But who would buy such paintings? Nobody wants to be reminded of old age, of decay. She makes no move to cover herself.

He sees Tom, brush and palette in hand. How much he has changed, how he has aged.

"Anil, is that you?"

"Tom, it is good to see you again."

Tom makes a few signs to the woman and she walks away. "I told her to go get dressed and to bring us a drink," he explains. "That woman has no shame in her old age. She used to turn red to her toes if someone saw her breasts, now she just sits there exposing herself to anyone who cares to look at her old body." He holds Anil by his shoulders, stares at his face and turns him around slowly. Anil smells the alcohol on his breath.

"What three years can do! You left this town a boy and now you come back a man."

"You look just the same."

"Don't lie to me. I know I look like the devil himself. I have been drinking myself to death. It won't be long before it comes. I have a secret race with your father to see who is going to get to the grave first. Or the grave for me, the crematorium for him."

He buries his head in his hands and says, "I am sorry, I shouldn't have said that."

"Why are you doing this?"

"No reason at all. Should there always be a reason for killing yourself? A more appropriate question may be, are there any reasons for living? I woke up one morning a few months after Leela died and found that I had lost the will to live. Just like that. I am too much of a coward to poison or shoot myself, or to jump off a bridge, so I decided on drink. At least I can use something I love to help me die."

"Are you sure it has nothing to do with Amma's death?"

"Why should it?"

"Did you love her?"

"Leela was intelligent, special, rare, at least in my life. How could I not have loved her? Maybe she was the last thread binding me to this shitty life."

The man he sees is a ghost, a being already living on the other side. The pores on his face are wide open, his skin is yellow. A face like a pancake being cooked. Yellow ghost, he could insult him, but Tom is Portuguese, not Chinese.

The woman returns with two tumblers of whisky. Tom says,

"Bottoms up," and drains his drink in one gulp. Anil shakes his head. "Not at ten in the morning." Tom reaches out for his drink and finishes that too in one go. His hands start shaking.

"What about her? Is she not a thread?"

"I can't explain why but she is not. It's not her fault."

"Were you and Amma lovers?"

"I kissed her once. She came here crying when she found out what was going on between your father and the servant, Aini. I stroked her hair and held her and kissed her lips. She did not respond. She was not in love with me. How could she be? A woman like her falling in love with a painter of tits? Impossible."

"But she was your friend."

Tom gets up with a start and runs out of sight. Anil hears him rummaging in the corner of the room, hidden behind a cupboard. He comes back with a painting and says, "This is the closest I came to having her." From the moment Anil sees the woman lying on a bed, her legs ever so slightly parted, he knows that this is what Amma told him about when he asked why she started painting. "Not bad for a painter of tits," he says. Not bad at all. She looks sated, real; he understands what Tom has just said about coming close to possessing her.

"I have something to show you in return."

Anil rolls out the canvas he has carried along with him and places it on a worktable.

"What do you think?"

"Is this yours?"

"No, it's Amma's. I found it in my father's office. It was mounted and framed, hanging in a corner."

Tom runs his fingers over the canvas. Anil sees he is captivated by it. He traces the outline of each figure and stops when he comes to the mouth of the baby and the drops of blood trickling down its chin.

"Are you sure it is hers? She never showed me anything like this."

"Nor anyone else. I found many others like it hidden in a locked room in her studio. Sixty-two finished paintings to be precise, and another twenty she was still working on. I studied the dates on the paintings and I discovered she was painting steadily like this from the time she started until her death, almost exactly three completed paintings a year. I think this is the one she was working on when she died."

"Why didn't she show them to me?"

"I don't know. You should come and take a look at the rest. They are remarkable, very different from the ones she showed you and me, as you can see."

Tom disappears again, this time returning with a bottle of whisky. He sits and fills his tumbler. He sips his drink slowly, working his fingers through his greasy hair.

"I could have helped her if she had showed these paintings to me."

"How? How could you have helped her?"

"Look for yourself. What you see here is just the beginning, the emergence of a talent. With my guidance, she could have taken the leap."

"She had already had taken it without you, without help from anyone."

"What do you know? This is nothing. A step in the right direction, nothing more. I have taken such steps myself but they didn't lead to anything."

"Is this not enough?"

Tom takes the canvas and throws it to the floor. "Enough for what?" he shouts. "Enough to be merely good, enough for mediocrity, just like the cartoons you draw. Enough to keep some people happy. But certainly not enough to be great. The soil in this country is not ready yet for artistic greatness. Many painters with Leela's ability will have to live and die before someone truly great emerges. I could have helped her become a bridge. Do you see?"

Anil picks up the canvas and rolls it up carefully. "I don't see and I don't care what you think, Tom. Why should I listen to a man who does nothing but paint useless pictures?" He sees Tom crying but he does not stop; he wants to punish him for what he has just said. "Why should I listen to a failed man, a dead man? I think she had gone far with her hidden paintings, far enough to be different. As for greatness, does it matter?"

He will make sure they are shown someday, great or not. More than anything else he wants Amma's spirit to escape from her studio, her prison and sanctuary, out into the open world.

Karim stands on one leg, his two hands raised high up in the air. A stork in prayer to the gods or the God he believes in. "Say something, say something to me," Anil pleads. Karim grins in reply through his tangled beard but he remains wordless. Anil reaches out and brushes the crumbs away from his thick moustache. "They say that you will stay silent until this building falls into the river. Is this true?" Karim nods, and then shakes his head from side to side. "He is really nothing more than a town idiot," Anil says to himself as he walks through the glass doors.

He takes the elevator up to the thirteenth floor. The secretary tells him to take a seat until Dr. Razak Mohammad is ready to see him. "Make yourself comfortable," she suggests, "it could take a long time. Dr. Razak is a very busy man."

Acha wanted him to see Dr. Razak. "Why should I?" he asked. "Most of your inheritance is linked with him. You have never met him before so it is only wise that you do so now," Acha explained.

He gets through most of the newspaper before the secretary speaks to him again. As far as he can tell she has not done any work during the hour he has been waiting. All he has seen her do is water a plant and stare at the computer screen in front of her. He finds it odd that the telephone did not ring even once. There is a picture in the newspaper of Dr. Razak cutting a ribbon for the opening of a business complex in Melaka. He must have just arrived in Muar. "Please go in through that door," the secretary says finally, pointing to the right.

Dr. Razak does not get up as Anil walks into the office. He leans across the desk when Anil is close enough, his hand extended. "Sit down, sit down," he says, "so you are Sankaran's son. I am surprised that we have never met." Anil shakes his plump, small hand and sits upright in the chair. If he had met Dr. Razak Mohammad for the first time on the street, the man would have left no lasting impression on him. Dressed in a pair of black trousers and a bright brown and yellow batik shirt, he cuts a slightly comical figure. Large, gold-rimmed spectacles with tinted glass hide most of his face. It is a foolish face. His nose is large and fleshy and his mouth contorts into a grin as he speaks, a grin that is not too different from Karim's. The only spark of intelligence lies in the eyes behind the glasses. Through the tinted glass he can still see that they are bright and observant. How deceptive a face can be. The man could not have risen to become one of the most powerful in the land if he were as stupid as it suggests.

Dr. Razak walks to the windows and points to the river and the bridges.

"Beautiful view, isn't it?"

"Apart from the factories and the destruction they have caused, yes."

"That is the price of progress. It would be nice if we did not have to destroy to advance but that is never possible."

He speaks in English with Anil. Anil has heard him speak Malay on TV. He uses both languages well, but with hesitation, as if he were uncomfortable with the spoken word. Dr. Razak has Arabic and Indian blood in him; it shows mostly in his skin colour and the shape of his eyes.

"Do you know that Parameswara considered founding a settlement here? I am not sure if is true but the historians have written it down, so it sticks as fact. He probably slept here on the way to Melaka, somewhere along the river. A great man lying on the soil of a village was enough to give it a name, some recognition. All he did was sleep, and urinate into the river, and we built a story around it. How times have changed. These days you have to move a mountain before they remember you."

Dr. Razak is back behind his desk, slouched in a bucket leather chair. He gently stabs the notebook on his desk with a Bic ballpoint pen as he speaks. The office is free of paper, apart from the notebook, free of files. There are no plants, there is nothing on the walls, not even a picture of the King and Queen.

"I have great affection for this town. I can say that I love it. I was born here and everything important to me has happened here, including meeting your father. I spend too much time in KL these days, I have to. But when I want to think, I come back here for a few days. I like sitting in this office and looking outside. It helps me empty my head and focus on the important things."

He feels comfortable with this man. With a few sentences Dr. Razak has transformed himself from a famous politician into a normal person sitting in front of him, speaking about his feelings and thoughts.

"How is your father?"

"Not well. I don't think he will last long."

"I must visit him."

"He doesn't receive many visitors these days."

"We go back a long way. I am sure he will want to see an old friend. And we have to discuss the Onn Rahim trial."

"What makes you think he cares about that when he is dying?"

"Don't you know it was *his* idea? Of course he cares. Onn wanted to change things. He was bowing to pressure from the West and he wanted to end corruption, he claimed. What he really wanted was power more than anything else. He wanted to climb to the top and clear the competition. He would become cleaner than white for a while to achieve that. Sankaran suggested that we charge him with corruption and sodomy. What a stroke of genius, turning the accusation against him and adding something unspeakable for added spice! Who would want to associate with him after a trial like that, even if he does not get convicted? We will make sure he gets convicted and finish him off once and for all. His Western friends will only be able to moan and groan in the background. The noises will go away after a few months, like all things do."

Dr. Razak stares at him for a long time. He looks Anil in the eye without averting his gaze. Anil squeezes his brain for a sentence, a question, but it does not come.

"Onn does not concern you. Let us drop it and talk about something else. I have already been told that your father plans to leave you everything. I am not sure if you know what this means. It will make you one of the richest men in Malaysia."

"I have not added it all up but I know it is a lot of money."

Dr. Razak laughs and says, "A lot of money? It is enough to move mountains. It took a lifetime of work and energy to build this fortune and it will now pass to you without any effort on your part. Have you decided what you are going to do with it all?"

Almost the same words Acha used a few days ago. Are they afraid of what he might do with his inheritance?

"I have not decided."

"There is not much to decide. Leave it in the hands of the people who know best."

He can hear the threat in Dr. Razak's advice. This is meant to be a command, not helpful counsel. He suspects Acha's statement that he could give all the money away if he chooses is not entirely true, or not true at all. How much of it is tied to this man and the people who know best?

"And who are they? Who are these people who know what is best for me?"

"Your father's associates, his trusted friends. The directors of his companies. There are many people waiting to help you, so you should not think you need to act alone. I know that Sankaran has great plans for you. But I can see you are not the ambitious kind. There is no cunning in your eyes. You have spent all your life away from the power he craves for you, so why should you want it now? You would have been drawn to it sooner if it had mattered to you. Instead you chose to go to the city to draw cartoons."

"That's not quite right. I didn't choose to go to the city to draw cartoons. I chose to go there but the cartoons happened by chance. I found something I was good at and liked, and I decided to work at it."

"Whatever the story is, you have never wanted to follow in your father's footsteps."

"Dr. Razak, I am grateful for your advice. There is a lot I have to think about and decide. You are not wrong in saying that my life so far has been divorced from all the things my father has done, but that does not mean it has to remain so. Who decides what they are going to do forever at my age? Did you?"

"I had already decided to be in politics at your age. It is not a good idea to use me as an example. I am not saying that you should not take an interest in what is yours. All I am saying is that you should listen to your father's friends and not go against their wishes. Do you really know what your father wants for you?"

"He said he wanted one of his kind to burst into the limelight."

"What do you think that means?"

"He wants me to use his fortune to gain power."

"That's easy. The money will automatically give you that. Sankaran has a lot of power but he wants much more for you. He wants you to become prime minister, the leader of this country. Has he not told you that? But it is impossible unless you convert. Even deputy prime minister is out of your reach. This is a Muslim country, a Malay country. It is written in the constitution. You can convert but you will forever be an Indian first, then a Muslim. I am lucky. I have Indian and Arabic blood in me like many other Malaysians but that was long in the past. I was born into a Malay family, so to everyone I am Malay and Muslim. I do not think we will see a non-Malay lead this country in my lifetime or yours. Not unless there is a revolution or a change in the constitution."

"And what if I bring about that revolution? Or at least become a bridge."

"Don't waste your time dreaming empty dreams and getting your hopes up. Just enjoy the money."

Anil feels betrayed. He thought that Acha's speech in his office was meant for him only. Now he knows that he has shared those thoughts and words with Dr. Razak. And how many others? Acha has spoken to Dr. Razak about his loftiest dream for him, and perhaps many other things he has not heard about. Prime Minister. When was Acha planning to tell him this, on his deathbed? He thanks Dr. Razak for his time and leaves the office.

He shows the batik sarong to Aini. "Is this all that is left of Amma's clothes and things?" he asks.

"Your father had all her clothing and jewellery removed after you left. All her other things too. He asked your uncle and aunty to keep whatever they wanted and had the rest burnt."

"Why did he leave this behind?"

"He wanted to keep one thing of hers. He said this was her favourite sarong. She wore it often."

"But he didn't destroy any of her paintings."

"I asked him about them. He said he had once destroyed one of her paintings and he could not bring himself to do it again. I didn't know what he was talking about."

"She painted Normah and me naked. Normah's father found out and Acha slashed the painting in front of him and Amma. What happened to her portrait?"

"He had that burnt too. He said he gave it to your mother as a present so he could do whatever he liked with it."

He takes the sarong back to his room and lays it out at the foot of the bed. Only one of her personal possessions remains, apart from her paintings and the tools of her art in the shed. This is the way it should be. He understands Acha's decision to give the rest of her things away or burn them. Who would want to leave a room frozen in time in the house he lives in, a constant reminder of the dead? The studio is already a shrine, a mausoleum without a tomb. Her paintings in the studio and office and the batik sarong are enough. And the painting in Tom's shop. He will buy that from Tom when Acha is dead and hang it in Amma's room. Her spirit and flesh are trapped in the painting Tom made of her, more so than in any other object. If Tom refuses to sell or give it to him, he will make him promise to leave it to him when he dies. When Acha is gone he will give his things away or burn them too, keeping only one possession, for symmetry if nothing else. What will be that one thing be?

The colours on the sarong have faded. There are traces of blue, streaks of red and yellow, and the floral pattern is barely visible, glimpses of what the sarong looked like when it was new and bright. It reminds Anil of the pale images of frescoes or cave paintings he has seen in Amma's books. He presses his face against the cloth. The gossamer material is the softest his skin has felt. He half expects to smell Amma but he knows this is ridiculous; the sarong has certainly been washed after she last wore it, and what smell lasts three years? The cloth is scentless. He can picture Amma in the sarong, walking around the house. It was indeed her favourite and she wore it at least twice a week. Could he have described it accurately or with more than the vaguest words if he had not seen it in Amma's room, or here at the foot of his bed? He doesn't think so. He doesn't remember how the colours faded over the five years she wore it. The only reason he knows she had it for that long is because he can place when he went to Kelantan with her.

The history and life of this object is rich and layered, but most of it is lost, at least to him. Add the histories of all the objects he has ever seen or touched and the tapestry they weave is immense, almost infinite. Thinking of all the buried stories and missing connections leaves him feeling dizzy. The sarong offers nothing else but a memento of the trip to Kelantan with Amma. It is not a sign, a symbol, a charm, a window into countless memories, a marker, it is no longer useful, it does not contain stories that can be released with a gentle touch. Will he be able to choose an object Acha owns that will be all these things? He decides he will keep the sarong Acha wears most of the time in these last days. It is a gateway into all that he has learned about him and all that he will continue to learn until Acha dies. He can lay the sarong next to Amma's; they will sit side by side like companion graves in a cemetery.

*

He removes his jeans, leaves them on the floor. First he puts on the jacket, then he pulls the trousers up, fastens the zip and the two buttons. The suit fits him well, almost perfectly. The trousers are a little long, an inch perhaps. His face borrows all its features from Amma, but his body has taken after Acha's. So he has inherited something physical from his father after all.

Acha was asleep when he started looking through his wardrobe. He wasn't sure why he was doing this, what he hoped to find. He had the sudden urge to rummage through Acha's clothes. He found the cream linen suit among the formal ones and took it back to his room.

Standing in front of the mirror he decides he cuts a dashing figure in the suit. It lends an air of maturity to his boyish face and body. The white T-shirt he has on underneath and his flip-flops cannot erase the effect it creates. He has never put on a suit before. At his most formal he would wear a pair of tailored trousers and a long sleeve shirt.

Aini walks into the room unexpectedly. He turns around to face her. She stares at him disapprovingly. He is embarrassed that she has found him in Acha's suit.

"I, I found the suit in Acha's cupboard. I wanted to try it on to see how it fits."

"He isn't dead yet."

Justice for All

The waiting room is small and badly lit. It is empty of furniture but for the eight blue plastic chairs arranged in two rows. The paint on the walls is peeling. Anil and the girl are alone in the room. He saw her seated in the front row, crying quietly, when the guard let him in earlier. He decided to sit as far away from her as possible. The guard left, saying that the warden would come for him when the inmate was ready. That's what he called him: inmate, not *Datuk* Onn.

He studies the girl, now that he is alone with her. She is Indian, around twenty he guesses. She is in a pair of stonewashed jeans and a colourful T-shirt with the words *Freedom Is Everything* written across her chest. Her face is marked by grief. Tears have smeared the makeup she wears and she looks like a circus performer with brightly painted lips and black streaks across her cheeks. He approaches her and asks, "Why are you crying?" She looks up, surprised to see that he is still in the room. "They beat up my brother. He was in hospital for a week. They almost killed him with brass knuckles. As soon as he became better they threw him in here. His trial is tomorrow. All for stealing a bicycle."

The guard returns and says, "You know that's not true. It's not the first time your brother is in jail. He is nothing but a drug addict who steals and robs to buy his drugs. The officers had to protect themselves against a known and violent criminal." She opens her mouth to protest but he cuts her off. "The warden is ready to see you," he says to Anil. They walk through a corridor to the warden's office, leaving the sobbing girl behind.

The warden is in uniform: blue trousers and a matching short sleeve jacket with silver buttons. His cap is on the table in front of him. He is a small man with a severe expression, perfectly suited to the job.

"We can only give you fifteen minutes with the prisoner. The request to see such a person was very strange in the first place. Against protocol. I would have said no if it was up to me. But I was told who you are and that was that. I had to agree. This is still my jail so I can decide how long your visit will be. I have decided that fifteen minutes is all I can give you."

Again, prisoner, not Datuk Onn. They have already stripped him of all his titles and honours, knowing what will happen. Anil nods and says, "That will be enough. Thank you for letting me see him." He had called 007 after seeing Dr. Razak and asked him to arrange a visit to see Onn Rahim. "Does Mr. Pillai know about this and approve?" 007 asked. "There is no need to bother my father." 007 called back in two hours with the time and date of the appointment. The money Anil had lent him for his daughter's dowry was beginning to pay interest.

Anil is led to the visitor's room where Onn is waiting. The warden walks away without greeting either of them. Anil goes up to Onn and extends his hand, but Onn does not take it. Anil sits down hurriedly and says, "I can understand why you will not shake my hand."

"Then there is no need for us to speak about it. Why did you want to see me?"

Anil does not know what to say. He cannot possibly explain that he has found out his father trumped up the charges brought against him, that he wants to see the man Acha is trying to destroy. He cannot say he is here to help; it would not be true. Even if he did he would not know where and how to begin. *Curiosity, Datuk Onn, curiosity is why I am here.* Maybe Onn has agreed to see him for the same reason. He replies, "I am not sure."

"I'll tell you why you are here. You are guilty by association and you want to soothe your guilt by visiting me."

"I knew nothing about your case until last week and I have nothing to do with it. Why should I feel guilty?"

"Because you are the son of one of the men who are trying to destroy me. You don't believe in the sins of the father?"

He lies and says, "No, I don't know what the sins of my father have to do with me. I don't know what his sins are."

"I am afraid you are lost if what you say is true. What do you think history is all about? Studying the sins of all our fathers, so we know how to avoid them in our own lifetimes. That's a big part of it at least. In your case, this is even more important and urgent. You will soon inherit the power and fortune your father has. It would be a pity if you do not care to know what rights and wrongs he has committed."

Onn speaks eloquently and with purpose. Anil sees the conviction in his eyes and his face. There is a bruise above Onn's right eyebrow. It is fading but he can see the discoloured patch under the bright fluorescent lights above Onn's head. In the spectral glow Onn looks like a philosopher brought back from the dead. Compared to Razak's his face radiates wisdom and intelligence.

"Tell me why you are here."

"Hasn't your father explained it to you? It's quite simple really. I wanted to clean up UMNO and the National Front. I had different ideas from the accepted ones. The big boys decided to call time on my career and to bring me down with absurd charges. Corruption and sodomy. They will be the laughing stock of the civilised world but they don't care. It won't be hard for them to come up with false evidence and witnesses. They will send me to jail for a few years and that will be enough to keep me out of politics for a decade. You know the law. I won't able to stand for office for five years after coming out."

"Are you guilty?"

Onn twists his lips into a wry smile and says, "Of what? Sodomy or corruption?"

"I assume you are not guilty of buggery. Anyway, what you do with your body is really your business, not a state affair. But why should I or anyone believe that you are not as corrupt as all the rest? A stooge of the West craving for more power."

"You could have accused me of many things in my early days as a politician. I was a Muslim firebrand and I wanted to impose my radical views on the party and country, no matter what it took. I have changed over the years. I have read more, thought more. You don't have to take my word for it. Read what I have written, speak to your friends about me. Decide for yourself if I am a power-hungry politician who panders to his white friends or if

I am something else altogether."

"Did they hit you?"

"You can see the bruise here," Onn says as he touches his eyebrow. "They boxed my ear. There was this ringing that wouldn't go away for days, but I think I am fine now. My lawyers issued a protest but they claimed I got violent while being interrogated."

"What will you do?"

"Go through with the trial. That's all I can do. I have the best defence lawyers money can buy. Except in my case I did not have to pay a cent. They are defending me for free."

"I have heard that Datuk Ismail will be the presiding judge. Surely that is good news for you?"

"You are well informed. I was quite shocked to hear it. I am still not sure how it could have happened. He is not known to be a government supporter. But I am not very hopeful. He may be able to throw out some charges but the false evidence they will compile will be too much for him to brush away. I think my fate has already been decided."

"Maybe you are destined to be a martyr and your real work will begin when you get out of jail."

"You are quite wise for a young man. Martyr or not, there are other people who can continue my work if I am found guilty. Many people. I am not indispensable."

"Who are they?"

"My wife, for one. She has formed a new party. It's called the *Truth and Justice Party*. I told her the name sounded too heavy, too earnest. She thinks that being serious and earnest under the circumstances is not the worst thing we can do. She has suffered much already so I did not insist that she change the name. They are organising a rally here on Sunday. Go, maybe you will learn something."

Anil does not answer. "You can change things if you want to," Onn persists. "You don't have to accept what is given to you without questioning the gift. Otherwise it will end up being a millstone round your neck."

The guard arrives to take Onn away. Onn raises a hand to wave to him as he leaves. In his baggy prison outfit he looks like an attendant in a hospital ward or a man preparing for sleep in rough, grey pyjamas. This is a man he can learn to trust, a man he wants to trust, more than Acha and his friends. But he should be cautious. Didn't he feel at ease with Dr. Razak until he said those threatening words? He is too trusting, too impressionable; he badly wants to believe in something or someone. He needs to temper his first impressions, his initial judgement, and wait before jumping to conclusions. Maybe there is nothing to believe in.

Anil walks through the waiting room on the way out. The girl is no longer there. He breathes deeply as leaves the prison compound. Along the street in front of the courthouse and prison the air is thick with fumes from the passing cars and damp from the rain, but it smells sweeter, much sweeter, than the trapped air inside.

"She doesn't look like much. How is that little thing going to run this party?" the man with the goatee beside Anil asks. They introduce themselves.

Anil has to agree with Sulaiman. Wan Siti, the wife of Onn Rahim, is dwarfed by the stage she is on. The microphone stand had to be lowered by a third when it was her turn to speak. She can't be more than five feet tall, perhaps a few inches shorter; it is hard to tell from this distance. The playing field was full by the time he arrived an hour after the rally started and he could not find a place closer than where he is now, past the running track. There are easily five thousand people here, maybe as many as ten. He didn't expect to find such a big crowd. He pictured a few dozen people sitting on the grass, listening lazily to endless, tiresome speeches, but this smells like a movement, an uprising.

A hundred National Front members attempted to block the entrance to the stadium with a herd of cows stickered with the logo of their party, a set of white scales against a blue background. They were bussed in by the local branch of the party to disrupt the rally and the cows were rented for a generous sum from a Sikh cowherd who lived nearby. The first few people arriving at the stadium weaved their way through the herd, patting the cows on their rumps. When the lines of people became longer and thicker and it was clear that the cows were more than a nuisance, a group of Onn supporters broke thick branches from the trees outside the stadium and beat the cows away. They threatened to do the same to the National Front members, who realised they were clearly outnumbered. They jumped back on the bus and left the rally. By the time Anil arrived the only signs of the confrontation were the heaps of dung left behind.

Wan Siti waves to the crowd. They wave back shouting, "Justice for Onn! Justice for Onn!" This woman in her sky-blue *tudung* has driven them wild without saying a word. She smiles brightly and says, "Yes, justice for Onn, justice for all." Her voice is thin but steady; there is no trace of weakness in it. She has the voice of a bird. "Truth for Onn, truth for all," she coos and chirps. The crowd responds more enthusiastically, as if truth were more important to it than anything else in the world.

"What do you think now?" Anil asks Sulaiman.

"She could have said anything and this lot would have cheered and shouted. Running a party is another matter."

"Why are you here?"

"I am a supporter of Datuk Onn. I don't believe the charges against him are true and I've had enough of the current lot."

"What about you?" Anil asks the teenager to his right.

"Party, that's what they told me, come for a party in the stadium," the boy says.

"I think they meant it as in political party," Anil says, laughing.

"Doesn't matter, this looks like fun. What else do I have to do?"

"How about you? You have not told us what you are doing here," Sulaiman asks Anil.

"Datuk Onn told me to come, so here I am."

"Sure, sure. You look like a reporter to me."

They go back to listening to Wan Siti. She talks about how the country needs to be cleaned up, how we need reformation, hope for the future. How we need to deny the government a two-thirds majority to stop them from passing any law they want to. Generalities, platitudes, the same things he has heard from many opposition parties. What did Onn think he would learn here?

Someone several rows ahead says, "Hey, I think the police are here. Someone said they've seen the FRU (Federal Reserve Unit)." The people around Anil grow nervous, several start heading for the exit. "Party over for me," says the teenager. Anil asks Sulaiman, "Why is everyone so scared? Surely they knew this was an illegal rally."

"The police were bound to show up at some point. The mention of the FRU is what is making everyone nervous. They are nasty. They must have sent a unit from Johor Bahru."

"What should we do?"

"Stay here and hope for the best."

A ripple of sound travels across the stadium as the news is passed from one row to the next. A man rushes onto the stage and whispers in Wan Siti's ear. She raises both hands, begging the crowd to stay silent. "I have just been told that the police and FRU are here. Stay calm. This is a peaceful rally. They cannot hurt us. Stay calm."

Before she can finish her sentence a line of federal unit officers storms into the stadium. They are in black riot gear and red helmets, their perspex shields held in front of them. Their leader shouts over a megaphone, "Leave the stadium immediately. This is an illegal rally. Leave the stadium immediately." Wan Siti says, "This is not an illegal rally, this is a rally for truth and justice." Loud, crackling noises fill the air and the microphone goes dead. The crowd sees Wan Siti speaking and tapping the microphone but they cannot hear her. "They must have cut the wires," Anil hears someone say. The officer with the megaphone repeats in a steady drone, "Leave the stadium immediately, leave the stadium immediately." Without Wan Siti's instructions and encouragement the crowd loses its sense of purpose and moves silently out of the stadium, crestfallen. Anil and Sulaiman leave together.

Outside, there is a group that refuses to be defeated. They face down the line of FRU officers guarding their trucks, hurling insults at them. "You monkeys," says one of them, "You stupid mothercunts," says someone braver. Anil walks up behind the group to see what is happening. Sulaiman tugs at his hand and says, "This is not a good place to be. Let's leave." Out of nowhere the leader with the megaphone appears and makes a sign with his right hand. The line of officers advances on the protesters, their batons raised. Most of the protesters step back but it is too late; the batons come crashing down on their heads and backs. Anil is pushed to the ground. Sulaiman reaches out to help him up. A canister lands a few inches away from Anil's face. An acrid smell hits his nose immediately and his eyes well up with tears. He struggles to breathe. "Teargas. The bastards are using teargas," someone shouts.

He stumbles to his feet. Arm in arm he and Sulaiman try to move away from the violence. But before they are clear a water cannon is turned on and they are knocked to the ground by the force of the jets hitting their backs. Anil tries to stand up but he keeps slipping. The water is turned off and the officers advance again. Anil feels the blows on his head and shoulders. He can taste the blood pooling in his mouth. The face of his assailant is hidden behind his helmet but Anil can see his eyes. There is no hint of malice in them; they belong to a boy who is hitting him out of duty, because he has been told to. He turns to look for Sulaiman, but he can't see him anywhere. Another blow lands on his head and he loses consciousness, crumpling onto the street.

He wakes up in a crowded cell. "So you're finally awake. I was worried about you." It is Sulaiman.

"I'm a little groggy," Anil says.

"Try to stand up. We have to see if those animals broke any bones."

Anil slowly gets to his feet, a hand on the wall for support. He takes a few unsteady steps.

"Are you in pain?" Sulaiman asks.

"I have a splitting headache and my right shoulder feels bruised. But I will survive. How are you?"

"They didn't beat me badly. I fell to the ground and stayed there until they dragged us into the trucks and brought us here. I was conscious all the time."

"Where are we?"

"The prison next to the courthouse. They must have taken the rest to another place. This prison is not big enough for the number of people they arrested. Look, there are ten of us in a cell for one."

Anil walks back to the bed and sits next to Sulaiman. There is another man huddled on the bed beside them, his head buried between his knees. Some of the others are standing, talking about what happened. The rest are sitting quietly with their backs against the walls. Blood and sweat, he smells both in the air, also the scent of stale urine. But there are no tears to be seen.

"Have they said anything?"

"No one has come round since they threw us in here. Not even to bring us some water."

Just as Sulaiman says this, a prison guard walks by. The guard and Anil recognise each other instantly.

"What are you doing here?" the guard asks.

"I don't know. I was at the rally minding my own business and the FRU started hitting us with their sticks. I was knocked unconscious and I woke up to find myself here. Don't start saying that this is not the truth and I am a known and violent criminal."

The guard is surprised that Anil remembers what he said to the girl in the waiting room a few days earlier. He gestures for Anil to come up close to him.

"Do you want me to call someone?"

"Tell the warden I am here. And call Mr. Ramalingam, please. Do you have his number?"

007 will have to come to his rescue again. The guard nods and says, "I know Mr. Ramalingam, so does the warden. We'll call him for you. Do you want some water, something to eat?"

"Only if you bring enough for all of them too."

When the guard is out of earshot Sulaiman asks, "Who are you really? How does the guard know you?"

"I came to visit someone here a few days ago. He remembered me from that visit."

"I don't think you're telling me the whole truth."

The guard returns with a jug of water and ten plastic cups. All ten rise and form a line and file past him for their share. The guard hands the cups to them through the iron bars. Each man gulps down the water thirstily. The guard says, "I can't find any food at the moment. I'll look in the kitchen cupboards and see if I can find some bread there." They thank him. "You are certainly not telling me the whole truth. You must have some power to drive a prison guard to kindness," Sulaiman says. Anil refuses to take his bait and smiles in reply.

An hour passes. He has slept fitfully during this time, his head resting against Sulaiman's shoulder. The warden arrives with 007 and the guard. He unlocks the door of the cell. The three men standing make their way to it but the warden shouts, pointing at

Anil, "Stay away from the door. I am here to get him." The men retreat and make way for Anil. He pats Sulaiman, his brother-in-arms, on the shoulder and says, "I will make sure you won't have to stay here for very long."

As they walk into the waiting room the warden snaps, "Mr. Ramalingam, I hope this is the last I will see of this young man. He has caused me enough bother already." 007 shakes his head from side to side with a sigh.

"What can you do with the youth of today? They are all so headstrong. But I will make sure he will not cause you any more trouble."

"Can you feed them and give them some more water? It was cruel to leave us without food and water for so long," Anil says to the warden. He and 007 leave the waiting room.

"Master Pillai, you should learn to be more careful. The warden did you a favour and you spat in his face," 007 says when they are outside the prison.

"I don't think it was a favour. He was saving himself any trouble for holding me in that cell."

"All the same, all the same. Mr. Pillai will not be happy when he hears about this."

"Leave that to me, I will tell my father about this."

"Not now though. Let's take you to your father's doctor so he can X-ray you and make sure nothing is wrong. Can I ask you why you went to that rally?"

"Onn asked me to go. He thought I would learn something there."

"What can you learn from these people? You have nothing to do with them. I hope you will understand before long that you are special because of your father. That is your position in the world. Nothing you do will change that."

"That is what I am afraid of."

They wait in the doctor's office while he goes to collect the X-rays. 007 reads a magazine taken from the pile on the coffee table, a publication on men's fashion. Anil walks around the room, afraid his muscles will go cold and start aching again if he stays still. "Who is this doctor? I have never seen him before," he says.

"This is the new Dr. Hoo. You probably remember the old Dr. Hoo. He retired last year and his son has taken over the business. Mr. Pillai says he is a good doctor, just like his father," 007 says.

The young doctor returns with the X-rays in hand.

"Nothing broken. They didn't crack your skull and there are no fractures anywhere on your back or shoulders. You were hit on the jaw too but it is not dislocated and none of your teeth are loose. You should be glad that the only marks they made are the bump at the back of your head and the bruises on your shoulders. Those will go away in a week or two. Just rest and make sure you come to see me if the headaches persist for more than two days or if you feel dizzy or nauseous."

007 claps and says, "That is good news, Mr. Pillai will be happy. This young man has a thick skull." The doctor laughs. "Thick skull or not, he is lucky not to have been more badly injured."

Outside the clinic, Anil tells 007 to go home. He doesn't want to face Acha or Aini right away.

"I need to take you home. You need to rest. Didn't you hear

what the doctor said?"

"I heard him loud and clear. But I want to be alone for a while. I'll be fine."

"You're an adult so you can do whatever you want."

"That's right. Thanks for your help."

Anil leaves 007 behind, looking dejected and staring at his feet. He goes in search of a drink. The first place that comes to mind is the *samsu* shop he was at a few days ago. He had thought of going back to buy a drink or two to make up for the one the owner served him for free. Didn't the man say that Acha went there to clear his head? That is what he needs to do now. But someone he knows may be there at the samsu shop. He wants to avoid Acha, Aini, everyone who knows him in this town; he wants to be alone with his thoughts and aches. After wandering into a few places he settles on the Lizard Lounge, next to the ice cream parlour on Jalan Abdullah. A new bar, this used to be an electrical goods shop when he left. He likes the atmosphere, lively yet relaxed, and there is live music playing. Better still there are no familiar faces. He struggles up the stairs to the balcony area, which is empty this early in the evening, and sits at a table facing the stage.

The audience appears to be enjoying the music the band is playing. From where he sits he can see most of them tapping their feet or fingers in time to the beat. Others are dancing close to the stage. The song is not to his taste yet he finds it pleasant. The girl sings about love, unrequited love, accompanied by a drummer, a guitarist and a keyboardist. They make up a typical Malaysian pop band: young Malay men with long hair, faded jeans and black T-shirts, making music to accompany lyrics sung by a pretty girl. The girl's face, clothes and voice all fit in with the song she sings, the men look like they should be playing hard rock or metal, music that is much less sentimental and more aggressive.

The music starts early here. In the city he would have had to wait until nine, ten before the show started. His body feels tired and battered but he wants to stay longer. The dizziness has gone; it has been replaced by a heavy head after three large beers. He shouldn't be drinking so much after what happened today. He doesn't want to get drunk but the alcohol helps him calm down, helps empty his head of the scenes at the stadium. Nothing, nothingness, is what he longs for.

He has felt like an observer, an onlooker, since coming home. A peeping tom who is curious to see everything but who wants to remain hidden, detached, who wants nothing to touch him too deeply. In the bar he sits perched above the rest, watching, listening. Does he find others repellent? He can safely say he doesn't but he has always felt a distance separating him from other human beings, even the ones he cares for the most. It is as if he was born in an invisible bubble, the thinnest of layers that keeps him disconnected and solitary at all times, even in the most intimate moments. Do others find him repellent because of this? He knows he has no trouble finding friends, talking to people, listening to them. He does not know if they sense his distance. There is a thin line between detachment and indifference, he thinks.

A group of men walk into the bar. They are loud and cheerful, they order soft drinks and crowd around the girls who are dancing. This is a place which doesn't serve Muslims alcohol, or the men are being careful. One of them is clearly the leader of the pack. His words and movements are forceful and the others seem to follow wherever he goes. There is something familiar about the man's face and body language; Anil is sure he has seen him before. He cannot take his eyes off the man. All of a sudden it dawns on him that this is the leader of the FRU unit at the stadium today; he is the officer with the megaphone. Anil realises that he was the only one without a helmet. He is sure of it. Names he loses easily, but it is hard for him to forget a face.

What should he do? If he were a man, if he had the balls, he would go downstairs and hit the officer. A punch in his face in retribution for what he did to him and all the others. Two hundred and forty five beaten and arrested, 007 had told him. How many broken bones and heads, how many teeth knocked loose, how many noses smashed, how many bruises? He gets up and walks down the stairs. As he makes his way to the group a girl grabs him by the shoulder and tries to pull him to her; she thinks he is here to dance. He winces in pain and pulls away. "What a spoilsport. Don't you want to dance?" she says. He ignores her and approaches the leader. The man is no taller than him but he is broad and muscular. Anil stands in front of him saying nothing, looking him in the eye. The man says to his group, "I think this boy wants to speak to me. Do you want to speak to me?" Anil remains silent, still looking at him while he speaks.

"Say something, or move away. You look like you have had too much to drink."

"Are you proud of what you did today?"

"What did I do today?"

"Ordering your unit to hit two hundred and forty-five harmless men," Anil shouts.

The band stops playing and everyone turns to look at him.

"Those men should not have been there. It was an illegal

gathering and they were threatening my officers."

"Threatening your officers? I heard two people shouting obscenities, two. Sticks and stones will break my bones but words will never hurt me."

The man laughs and says, "I guess they found out how true these words are." Anil thinks he should hit him now. He has never hit a person before, never hurt anyone physically. His arm feels heavy. Does he want to end up in jail again? 007 will not be able to help him if he gets arrested a second time.

"One day you will pay for this. You do not know who I am. I will make you pay for this," Anil says.

"I'm sure. Does anyone here know who this boy is? No? Neither do I. He thinks he will make me pay someday."

He looks at Anil threateningly and says, "I will give you some advice. I don't know if you were one of the people who were arrested today. I don't care. But you are threatening a senior officer of the FRU and I can arrest you for this. So my advice is that you walk away now and leave me in peace." Anil turns around and walks out of the bar. Half-hearted and pathetic, that's what he is, backing down as soon as the man flexed his muscles and power. The man will not lose a minute's sleep tonight, but he will toss and turn, thinking of how weak he was, how cowardly.

The next morning he sits at the foot of Acha's bed, explaining to him what had happened the day before. Acha listens to him without interrupting. "You should have come home straight after the doctor's visit to tell me about it. You punished me doubly by making me hear about the whole damn thing from 007. You can't imagine what torture that was. It almost made me reach for my morphine," Acha says when Anil has finished his story. Anil smiles and apologises. He has forgotten how charming and funny Acha can be when he wants to.

"It's not funny, it is really not that funny. What will Razak make of this? You are weakening your position even before I die. You don't know how much this hurts me. I won't be there to protect you for long. Do you think that Ramalingam can help you out without my backing?"

"I am sorry, it will not happen again."

"Who hurt you?"

"Some young officer, I wouldn't be able to recognise him. His face was hidden behind his helmet. But the man behind it all was the leader of the FRU unit. He was the one who ordered the men to start attacking us. No one was violent, just a few bad words from two people. That was enough for him to have anyone standing close by beaten and dragged to prison. He is the guilty one."

"Why did you have to go to the rally?"

"I wanted to learn something."

He will not tell Acha about his visit to see Onn in jail, he will not tell him about his confrontation with the FRU officer in the bar. Anil knows that 007 will not say a word about Onn either; he will be too afraid of the trouble it would cause for him.

"Learn what? That Wan Siti is now the leader of a party? You can read that in the newspapers."

He wants to say, "I went there to witness the consequences of your actions," but he does not answer Acha's question.

"What do you want me to do?"

"I want you to get the man who helped me at the stadium out

of prison as soon as you can. Sulaiman was in the same cell I was in. Middle-aged, with a goatee. He was a caring man. And I want the FRU leader punished somehow. I don't know what is the worst punishment you can inflict on him, but I am sure you can think of something. Demote him, send him to guard some remote highway in the north."

"Do you want me to do these things? I will show you how easily I can get your friend out of prison and make the FRU man pay. Maybe after that you will realise what I am leaving to you."

"Yes, I want him punished."

The officer must not get off free; Anil wants revenge. He would like to be there, a fly on the wall, when that man is told of his demotion and relocation to a distant village near the border. Why a fly on the wall? Anil wants to be in the room to witness the expression on his face when he recognises the boy and remembers his threat: 'You do not know who I am. I will make you pay for this.'

The Final Journey

"This is the first time in thirty years that Johor and Melaka have experienced such severe flooding," the reporter says. The camera shows people leaving their homes, grabbing anything they can before wading through water to get to higher land. Over twenty thousand people have been evacuated from Pagoh, Lenga, Kundang Ulu, Bukit Gambir, Sawah Ring, the low-lying areas in the district that are under ten feet of water. The report cuts to a shot of Muar from high up, from what looks like the top of the Umno building. It shows the river swollen and threatening to overflow its banks, monsoon drains filled to the brim, roads and streets flooded. There is almost no movement, no life. "The official advice is for everyone to stay at home unless it is absolutely necessary for you to go out," the reporter says with a smile, as if she were notifying the public of good news. "All schools and government offices are closed until further notice."

Heavy rain has fallen steadily without a pause for three days and nights, and the clouds have masked the sun, leaving the land in near darkness. Fresh water pumps and electric generators have been damaged, cutting off supply to some parts of the town and district. The palace on stilts has been spared, sitting above the flood waters like an island almost untouched by the troubles the rain has brought. Anil has been trapped in it for over two days now. He turns off the TV, goes to his room, puts on his green raincoat, and leaves the house through the Melakan wing. The water has risen above the second step. Dragging his feet along the ground for balance he heads towards Normah's house. The two-plank bridge is buried under water. He places his right foot on it, then his left, shuffling across to avoid falling into the drain.

Normah comes to the front door; she must have seen him from the window. She laughs and kisses him on the cheek.

"Your spaceman suit."

"You remember what I called it! I had to get out of the house."

"Come in, come in, I will make you some tea."

She leads him to the bedroom and tells him to get out of his wet clothes. He rubs his skin and hair vigorously with the towel she hands him, to bring some warmth back to his body. She wrings the water out of his shorts and T-shirt into a plastic pail and hangs them on a chair to dry; the raincoat she places on a hook behind the door.

"Do you want a sarong? I am sure I can find you one without flowers."

"Are you embarrassed seeing me like this? I am happy to stay this way."

She leaves the room and returns with a cup of tea. She has removed all her clothes. "Let's be equal in that case," she says. "I don't think I have ever been served tea by a naked woman before," he replies. "I shall call you my naked tea lady from now on."

They are no longer lovers but he still visits her to talk, to lie by her side. Their lovemaking came to an abrupt end when he gave her Amma's painting of them in the forest. He had stretched it over a board and mounted it in a wooden frame he found in Amma's studio. "Here is the painting you wanted," he had said as he handed it to her.

"Did you paint it for me?" she asked

"No, this was done by my mother. I could have never painted anything like it. I found it locked away in a cupboard. What do you think?"

"I wanted you to paint me, but this is beautiful, thank you. No cartoon?"

"I thought you deserved something better."

She led him by the hand to her bedroom, took off her clothes, undressed him. They kissed, he caressed her face and stroked her hair. He did not move his hands over her breasts, her body. His cock was half-erect; he could not say that he was aroused. What they were doing felt comfortable, comforting, not exciting. He had no desire to enter her. They held each other and fell asleep.

They woke up hours later; it was already dark outside. She asked, "It's all over, isn't it?" He touched her cheek and said, "Yes, I think so." She murmured in his ear, "I knew it would come to an end quickly. At least I have the painting as a reminder of our time together."

She lies now with her head on his chest as he tells her everything that has happened since they last met. She listens without saying a word. He is grateful for her understanding his need to speak, to tell his stories, without interruption. The rhythm of her breathing and her warmth help him to unburden himself. He feels pleasantly empty and tired when he finishes, as if he has just come inside her, and falls asleep on her bed.

Anil hears the soft, almost imperceptible, beat of tablas and other percussive instruments as he thinks about his song cycle. *Gamelan* drums to describe the pulse of the persistent rain, the gentle swishing of cymbals to capture the rising waters. He turns to his imaginary composition when he stops reading to Acha. He writes his monsoon cycle in his head with no rules binding his creativity. Or the rules are minimal, rudimentary, because he knows so little about music. Unlike with cartoons or paintings he can let his imagination run wild, with no fetters and no judgement. He can be a child at play again, the child he was before Amma taught him to think and talk about painting.

A worn copy of *One Hundred Years of Solitude* arrived in the post a few days earlier from Harish with a note that began, "The greatest rain-drenched novel ever written, perfect for your quiet moments during the monsoon season." Anil read two pages of the recollections of Colonel Aureliano Buendía out loud before he noticed Acha was no longer listening to him. Acha was staring at the wall, his eyes wide open, but they were vacant, dead. *He is fading away quickly.* His moments of lucidity have been rare since the heavy rain started, as if the floods were carrying him to the other side. The skin on his face and hands is dry and scaly and his colour is slowly draining away. He will be white as a ghost before long, Anil thinks. Only his voice is still of this earth.

Acha comes out of his trance. "You've stopped reading," he says.

"I thought you were asleep."

"I wasn't asleep, I just drifted away. I was thinking, not dreaming."

So his mind whirs and works even when his body shuts down. Will it be the last thing to go?

"What were you thinking about?" Anil asks.

"I was thinking about dying, what it means, what it feels like. The last moments, I mean. Why has no one tried to describe it? Someone who has gone through a near-death experience, someone who has escaped after being at death's door."

"I think some have tried. Haven't you heard of descriptions of the soul leaving the body, seeing a bright light at the end of a tunnel and such things?"

"Is that all? What about thoughts, emotions, surely there must be something else? The soul drifting away, the light, seem too cheap, too simple. You know what it reminds me of? Descriptions of aliens. They are almost always the same, they are always so boring and unimaginative. One of your revered authors should try. They try to explain everything else, including experiences they never had or can never have, yet they shy away from the most important thing of all."

There is some truth in what Acha has just said; he has never read anything convincing about death. His knowledge of literature is far from complete, perhaps Harish would know. A whole novel on death is needed, a long and sustained attempt to grasp what it is, what it means.

"Are you afraid of dying?"

"Most times I am not. I am not religious so I don't believe in an afterlife. If there is one, I think I stand as good a chance as the next man of getting into the better half of it. I have done bad things as well as good and if you ask me what my score is I wouldn't know how to answer. Positive, negative or zero? I have not had the time or the inclination to sum up my life. I have done many things. I have lived an active life and acted. Can I be blamed or punished for this? Am I better or worse than someone who has done nothing but who has not hurt even a fly by doing nothing? I have lived modestly, given the fortune I have. We have lived in this simple neighbourhood since I married your mother. The only luxury I have succumbed to is this house, but that cost a pittance compared to what I am worth. I have given much more money away than I have spent on myself. Does that count for something?

"But sometimes I become afraid, deeply terrified by the thought of death. This deep fear almost always comes to me when I am asleep. It grips me so tightly that I end up shaking, crying, sometimes screaming. Do you remember the first time you read to me, how I was howling, refusing to be pacified? Death came to me then as an enormous white cloud, slowly enveloping my body. I felt as if the cloud was eating me slowly, chewing and digesting me until I disappeared, disappeared completely into it."

Acha goes quiet and starts looking at the wall again. Anil knows they do not have many conversations left; this could be Acha's last day. He needs to talk about what Dr. Razak had told him.

"Dr. Razak mentioned your plans for me. That you wanted me to become prime minister some day. When did you tell him that?"

Acha does not look surprised, as if he was half-expecting the question.

"It was a long time ago, years ago, before your mother died, before you left for the city. I started thinking about my legacy and what I wanted you to do and become while talking to Razak about the future of the country. I was drinking, he was not. He never drinks. I wasn't drunk, not one bit, but it came to me with the aid of some whisky, a plan hatched over drinks. Remember I told you I worked behind the scenes for the day when one of us, an Indian, would come to power? But that strategy was vague and I had no control over what would happen after I died. I needed something, someone, more concrete, more immediate, that I could pin my hopes on. The thought came to me that you could be that person. Instead of a stranger, why not someone who shares my blood?"

"Did you tell anyone else?"

"No, I said it once to Razak and never again."

"Not to Amma?"

"She would never have understood. She was not interested in power, not of this kind."

"Dr. Razak remembered it so clearly."

"He remembers everything, that man. Wouldn't such a bold plan stick in your mind if you were a Malay?"

"He didn't think it was possible and told me to forget about it and just enjoy the money."

"Again, what do you expect a Malay politician to say? If someone plots to steal your power, would you encourage him? Don't listen to him."

"So you think it is possible."

"I don't waste my time on the impossible. It was not possible for me, not in my time. But if you start now, start acting slowly and carefully, the prize may be yours in twenty or thirty years."

"Were you ever going to tell me about my life's project?"

"Never, at least not in person. I have left a letter to be delivered to you after I die. In it I have laid out these plans for you."

"Why don't you tell me now? Why a letter?"

"It is too complex for me to explain everything to you now. The letter, my will and the notebooks are all you need. But it will take you months if not years to grasp everything in them and you will have to use your imagination to make my plans come alive. You have plenty of imagination, you just need to channel it in the right direction. The rest you will learn in time."

Acha closes his eyes, as if to signal that he has nothing more say about this. "Are the floods receding?" he asks.

"Not yet, it is still raining heavily."

"I regret not having the street paved when I had this house built. Half of it will be washed away. Do we have water and candles in case we get cut off?"

"Aini has put buckets and jars outside to collect water. We have many candles and torchlights."

"Check the candles again. I don't want to be alone in the dark."

The long, convoluted sentences of the book and the sound of the rain beating against the shutters and roof have dulled his mind; he struggles to keep awake. He forces himself to stay propped up on his bed reading. Two more pages of *One Hundred Years of Solitude* before he hits his quota for the day. Harish's note said, "Same rules as always," which meant that the book had to be returned within a month in the same condition it arrived in.

Aini rushes in just as he closes the book and reaches out to turn off the light. Her face is flushed and she gasps for breath; she has hurried here to tell him something. "Is something wrong with Acha?" he asks. "No, no, he is alright," she says.

"What is it then?"

"Santhia is here."

"Santhia? Are you sure?"

"I have never met her before but there is a young lady who just rang the doorbell who says she is Santhia and that she is here to see you."

Anil ties his sarong tightly around his waist and runs to the entrance. She is there, thoroughly soaked, a small suitcase next to her. Water drips from the hem of her dress onto the floor.

"Santhia, what are you doing here?"

"No kiss for me?"

"I'm sorry," he says as he kisses her, tasting the raindrops on her lips. "This is a surprise. I didn't expect you."

"I didn't plan it either. I woke up this morning and the first thought that came into my head was if you didn't want to come to me, or couldn't, I would go to you. You know, Muhammad and the mountain? So I caught the afternoon train and then a taxi from the train station. It took quite some time to get here from town because the roads are still very wet."

"You could have called me."

"For you to talk me out of it? I thought a surprise would be better. You can't turn a heavily pregnant woman away, can you?"

"No, I can't. Come, let's get you out of your wet clothes before you get sick."

They pass Aini on the way back to the bedroom. "Santhia, this is Aini," he says somewhat formally. "We've met," Santhia replies. "Can you boil some water and bring it up to the bathroom? Santhia should take a hot bath to warm up. Please make some hot Milo too," he says to Aini. She nods and walks away. When she reaches the stairs she turns round and says, "Should I tell your father?" Anil shakes his head and says, "No, don't disturb him. We'll go and see him first thing in the morning."

"The master of the house? You seem comfortable ordering her about."

"I am not the master of the house and I didn't order her about. She is paid to help and I have no qualms asking her to do things."

He helps her undress. He runs his hand over her belly as he towels her dry. Hard as stone, a belly to match Acha's. She puts on a yellow nightdress she pulls out of her suitcase.

"Look at the tents I have to wear these days."

"At least it is a pretty and bright tent. Your belly is low. Don't they say that a high belly means that it is going to be a boy and a low one carries a girl?"

"I've heard that before but I am not sure if it is true."

"I hope it is."

After her bath they lie side by side on the bed drinking the hot Milo Aini made. He studies her face as he did in the mornings soon after they first met. Her hair is longer, her face fuller. The extra weight she carries has softened her features. She will be a mother soon, the mother of his baby girl. He takes the cup out of her hand and places it on the side table next to the bed. He removes her nightdress and brushes his lips across her large, heavy breasts. A drop of milk drips out of her nipple when he sucks on it; it is warm and sweet. He runs his fingers over her pubic hair and touches her pussy. "Make me come, I haven't come in ages," she says. "Will it be OK?" he asks. "Don't worry, I promise not to pop."

Her large belly has slowed her down and it takes her a long while to turn around after she comes to take his cock in her mouth.

She jerks him off hard as she sucks his cockhead gently; it does not take long before he spurts his semen. She kisses his stomach, then his chest. She puts her tongue in his mouth and he tastes his bitter, sticky liquid, a sharp contrast to her milk. She falls asleep immediately with her head on his shoulder, her nose touching his cheek, her lips on his neck. Her right arm holds him tightly. Keeping perfectly still he waits to feel the baby moving in the stomach pressing against his side. There is a kick; a minute later another one comes. He stays awake listening to his baby playing, almost tasting Santhia's warm breath on his face and neck.

"How do I look in this?" Acha asks. Before Anil and Santhia can reply he says, "Aini couldn't find my cream suit so I had to settle for this gray one. She claims she looked everywhere. Either she is becoming as dotty as I am or it was lost at the cleaners." Anil turns away to hide his reddening face. He walks around the room, pretending to look for something.

"Have you lost something?"

"I think I left my book here."

"Is this forgetting bug infecting everyone? Santhia, have you forgotten something too?"

"Too many things for me to remember. Your suit looks perfect."

Acha smiles at her. His body appears to have grown overnight to fill his clothing. There is colour in his face and he is standing erect; he is such a picture of vitality that Anil half expects him to start whistling a tune. Perhaps there is life left in him yet.

What a different scene it was yesterday when I introduced Santhia to him, Anil thinks. Acha barely acknowledged her, closing his eyes soon after they walked into the room. Santhia said his name and touched his hand, but he did not respond. They left after a few minutes of painful silence; it was clear he had nothing to say and he didn't want them there. Now he talks to her, asking how she is and when the baby is due, touching her hand and face affectionately as if he has known her for years, as if she were his daughter. Anil can sense that she is uncomfortable with this sudden transformation, but she hides her discomfort well.

"What do you think? Shall we start the day?" Acha asks.

In the car Acha continues to be lively and charming. He rolls the window down to let some air in. "I am tired of stale air, tired of the same things. Don't be offended, Anil, but it is wonderful to have a new person around, new company."

Only high cirrus clouds dot the sky. The rain has stopped and the sun is shining brightly. Already the roads are dry and the water level in the monsoon drains has dropped several inches below the brim. Acha says, "I think the worst of the rainy season is over." Anil nods in agreement. In the rear view mirror he sees Santhia sitting where he used to, in the backseat next to Acha.

He asks Acha if they should stop at the office. "No, why should we bore Santhia to tears? There is nothing in the office that would interest her. Let's drive along the riverfront to the resthouse. We can show her the promenade and the sights along the way and have lunch there." Acha points out the new and old mosques to Santhia as they pass by them, and recites a short history of Muar.

"It's a nice town. I don't think Anil ever did it justice in his descriptions."

"What did he say? If I were running away from a place, I wouldn't paint it in the best light either. I've lived here for many years and I am not ashamed to say that I am proud of this town and its history, insignificant as it may seem to anyone who doesn't live here. I am proud of my history here too. You will understand some day that history becomes more and more important as you get older. All stories of the past become interesting. They somehow become as crucial to life as rice and water."

Lunch is uneventful apart from the surprised looks on the faces of the restaurant manager and the waiters. Acha doesn't notice their expressions, or pretends not to notice. A few people come by their table; he shakes their hands and makes polite conversation. After coffee Acha insists on walking along the river.

"Are you sure?" Anil asks.

"Don't suck the life out of me with your doubt. The cup of *Chai Kee 454* has given me added strength and I think I can manage the short walk I want to take. If I need help, I will lean on Santhia. You don't mind lending me a hand?"

Santhia holds his hand and says, "Let's go." They leave through the back entrance of the resthouse, which leads directly to the riverfront. The light off the water blinds them momentarily; it takes them a while to adjust to the glare. "Do you like this promenade?" Acha asks. "It looks like a pleasant place for a walk. What was here before?" Santhia replies. Anil interrupts, "I don't like it. It used to be a simple path lined with beautiful *angsanas*. They are all gone."

"Be careful that you don't succumb to nostalgia before you become middle-aged. It's not acceptable in a young man."

"It's not nostalgia. This used to be an interesting place, a place with some beauty and shade. What do you have now? A neat walkway, playgrounds and a hawker centre."

"I wasn't convinced when the town council came up with the

plans to transform this place. But you should see the number of people who use this every day after work and during the weekends. Compared to the handful of people who came here before, this has to be branded a success."

"What I hate most is I can't remember where I scattered Amma's ashes because of these changes."

"Let me take you there."

Acha walks briskly ahead of them and stops at a spot that looks like any other along the promenade. Santhia and Anil reach him a few moments later.

"Is this it? How can you be sure? There are no landmarks to distinguish this place."

"I was in the background when you waded out to scatter your mother's ashes. I remember very clearly that when I turned round from where I stood, I saw the front gate of that house over there. Directly behind me. You don't know this but that house is where my first girlfriend in this town lived. She lived there with her parents. I used to come and pick her up every day after work. This riverfront was wilder those days with thick trees and bushes everywhere."

"What happened to her?" Santhia asks.

"She moved away and we lost touch. I have not seen her since and I don't know who lives in that house now."

"I made a mark on the angsana that stood here. They cut it down so I lost my sign," Anil says.

Acha lights a cigarette and takes a long, deep drag. "Don't worry, it won't kill me," he says with a grin. After smoking the cigarette he says, "Scatter my ashes here too. Will you promise me that?" Anil nods. *Why does he want his ashes to be scattered here?*

He and Amma were so far apart when she died. Does he want to go looking for her after he dies to make amends? "One more stop before we go home. I think we deserve a drink after all this," Acha says.

They drive to the *samsu* shop. The owner greets them effusively and leads them to a table.

"Mr. Pillai, I have not seen you for a long time."

"I have not been well."

"I am glad to see that you are feeling better. The usual?"

"For me and for my son. As you can see, my daughter-in-law is pregnant so she can't drink. What will you have, Santhia?"

She is touched. Daughter-in-law; she didn't expect it, neither did Anil. "I'll just have a glass of water," she says. "Your son has already tasted the best," the owner says as he goes to the counter to pour the drinks. Acha turns to Anil and asks, "Really? When?"

"A week or two ago. I knew you used to come here so I wanted to see what it was like."

"How did you know? Did your mother tell you about this place?"

"I can't remember, it was probably Amma or Aini, but I have known this for a long time," Anil lies, not wanting to reveal that Abdul was the culprit. Acha looks puzzled but he does not pursue his line of questioning. The drinks arrive just in time to distract him. "A toast to the unborn, to the next generation," he says as he raises his glass. "May he or she arrive full of joy into this world." They clink their glasses.

"It is an acquired taste, samsu. I have always liked it more than whiskey and other more refined spirits. This shop has given me many hours of interesting conversation and solace. Everyone needs to get away sometimes and this was one of my escapes."

He has heard those words, or some minor variation of them, before. Was it when Goh Poh was talking about his Japanese garden?

The owner refuses to accept payment yet again. "It's on me, Mr. Pillai. It's an honour to have you back here again." Acha shakes his hand and thanks him. "Be careful you don't go out of business offering everyone a free drink," Anil says. "Don't worry, these people will pay my bills," the owner says, pointing at the other customers in his shop.

They walk back to the car. "Is there anywhere else you would like to go?" Acha asks. Anil and Santhia say no.

"Good, let's go home. I am feeling a little tired. I am not used to being up and about and the samsu has gone to my head."

Not a word is said during the drive back to the house. Acha retreats into his shell and shrinks steadily. By the time they reach the front gate he is again old and feeble. They lead him to his room and help him undress. He collapses on the bed and falls asleep immediately.

"It must have taken all his energy to put up that front today," Santhia says when they leave the room.

"I am not sure it was a front. I think he knew it was his last trip, his final journey out to see the world and he wanted to make it as his former self, the man he was before he got sick."

The End, and a Beginning

"Did you hear that? I think someone is knocking at the door," Santhia says as she shakes him awake. Anil struggles to open his eyes. "It must be Aini. Don't worry, go back to sleep. I'll see what she wants." Before he finishes his sentence she is out cold. Her head is turned towards the wall and her breathing is deep and steady. He rubs his eyes and forehead, trying to banish the dream he was in the middle of. The only image he remembers clearly is that of Acha being swallowed by a cloud as he struggles to save him. He had his hands around Acha's legs, he pulled with all his might, but the cloud was too powerful and Acha was sucked in.

He gets up and gropes in the dark for his sarong. He sleeps without any clothes on beside her, as he used to when they were in the city. Before she arrived he slept in his sarong or shorts, as if he was ashamed of his nakedness when he did not have a woman next to him.

The light in the corridor is on; he closes the door behind him. From Aini's face he can tell something is wrong.

"Your father is not well. I went to check on him before I went to sleep and he was sitting up in bed. I could see he was in pain. He was groaning quietly. I asked him what was wrong but he did not answer, he could not answer. I think he did too much today. He shouldn't have gone out."

They walk to Acha's room, Anil still replaying the dream in his mind. When he sees Acha he knows the end is near. He is in bed without any clothes on, sitting up with his back resting against the headboard as Aini left him, but he is no longer here. Anil sits beside him and pulls the blanket up to his waist. He lowers his head so it rests on the pillow. His hair and face are damp. Anil asks Aini to hand him a towel; he wipes Acha's face and chest dry.

Suddenly, as if someone has switched him on, Acha comes alive. He opens his mouth but no words come out, only strange sounds. He tries to move his arms but they remain limp. Tears flow down his cheeks, a torrent of pain and grief. After struggling for what seem like minutes, Acha moves the little finger of his left hand up and down. The sign, is this the sign? He may have made this gesture by mistake. Anil turns to Aini and says, "Can you leave us alone? I think I can take care of him." Aini shakes her head, refusing to go. He goes up to her and says, "I need to be alone with him. He will be fine with me." He leads her by the hand past the study and almost pushes her out of the room, closing the door when she is gone.

He sits down at the edge of the bed. "Can you hear me?" Acha's head moves, almost imperceptibly. "Can you hear me?" he shouts. Anil is sure Acha understands what he is saying when he sees his head move again. "Was that the sign?" Another nod. "Are you ready to die?" Acha moves his lips as if to smile and nods once more. His tears have dried up. This is the answer Anil fears. He opens the drawer, takes out three syringes and the morphine vials. How many did he say, six? He fills the syringes with fluid from nine vials, three more than needed to be safe. He places them on the table and looks in the drawer for the tourniquet. If it were bigger it could be a hangman's noose. He ties the tourniquet tightly around Acha's arm, just above his elbow, and pulls on it until he sees a vein bulge. Steeling himself he stabs the first needle into the vein and presses the head of the syringe until all the liquid disappears. He repeats this with the other syringes, moving along the vein so he does not puncture it at the same spot. He unties the tourniquet and puts it back in the drawer.

He puts the empty vials and used syringes in a plastic bag he finds in a cupboard. Not once did he look at Acha's face, not once did he look in his eyes, while he pumped him with morphine. He turns around now to face his father. His eyes are closed. Anil would like to think Acha is at peace, at rest. Trickles of dried blood trail from where the needles punctured his skin. Anil rubs the blood off with fingers he wets with saliva. He presses an ear to Acha's chest; it moves up and down in shallow breaths but his heartbeat is still strong. How long will it take the morphine to work its way through his body and stop his heart? He places his hand on the small of Acha's back, lowers his body until he lies flat on the bed, and pulls the blanket up to his chest to keep him warm and comfortable. With the plastic bag in hand he switches off the bedside lamp and leaves the room. He will not stay with Acha while he dies; Acha is no longer conscious and he feels he has done more than his duty as a son requires. Acha will have to take his last steps alone.

*

Anil is in Amma's studio, studying her paintings again, and drawing cartoons. His subjects are varied: scenes from the recent floods, factory workers in Tanjung Agas, the night market, Santhia's arrival.

He is not afraid he will be found out. There are so many vials and syringes in the drawer beside Acha's bed that no one will notice that some are missing. He is sure that even Aini doesn't count them. And what are three more needle marks on arms covered with them? An autopsy will never be done on a man who everyone knows was close to death. A word to Dr. Hoo will be enough to ensure that.

Aini was not waiting outside the door when he left Acha's room. He walked by her bedroom to see if she was awake. There were no sounds from within and the light was off. The plastic bag he found in Acha's room was clear, so he walked to the kitchen to find a black bag to hide the vials and syringes in. He moved the day's rubbish in the bin to one side and placed the bag at the very bottom, then covered it until it was hidden from view. He washed his arms and hands with soap, dried them with the kitchen towel and went to the studio.

He grows tired of Amma's paintings and his cartoons, so he turns to Acha's notebooks which he takes out of the drawer he had placed them in. He had moved them here from the office a few days earlier. I want all the things that bind me to be in one place, he had said to himself. *Sleeping numbers, names, dates, but they can rise from their deep slumber in a flash and rule my life if I allow them to.* He is unable to concentrate hard enough to find anything new in them. He puts the notebooks away and starts exercising. Jumping jacks, push ups, sit ups, choreographed movements to get his blood flowing and to stay awake. *I can't fall asleep now.* He keeps this up for as long as he can, until he grows weary. He picks up a book at random from the pile on the desk, opens it at page 155 and starts reading aloud. The words enter him; they reverberate in his body. But they mean nothing, signify nothing. They are mere sounds, voices speaking in a language he does not understand.

I need to leave this house for a while, I am going crazy here. He was calm, almost numb, as he filled the syringes and plunged the needles into Acha. Empty of emotion, his only thought was to keep his hand as steady as when he picked up a pencil to draw. A cold-blooded exercise, the end result unimportant, as long as it was done well. *Why are my palms sweating, why am I trembling with agitation now?* This anxiety started at his feet and is rising like a flood threatening to drown him. No rain, there is no rain falling on the roof to soothe him. He drops the book to the floor and walks to the window, throwing the shutters open. The air is clear, the sky cloudless. He sees the big dipper, its little brother, Orion's belt. Is that Venus sitting low in the heavens?

He goes back to his room, opens the door slowly, looks for his clothes. By the light of the corridor lamp he finds a pair of jeans, a T-shirt, his shoes, his raincoat. It is cool outside and the raincoat will keep him warm. He remembers to pick up his keys from the bedside table. Santhia is asleep. He risks a kiss on her neck before he leaves; she does not stir.

He dresses in the studio, leaving his sarong on the chair. He places a torchlight in the pocket of his raincoat. The streetlamps and the moon might not be enough to light his way. He does not know where he is going, only that he needs to flee to lessen the pain and pounding in his head.

The street to the main road is easy enough to navigate in the dark; he has no need for his torchlight. He takes the road to town, not knowing where else to go. After walking briskly for twenty minutes he reaches the turning to the stadium. *If I take this road I will find the shortcut to the banyans. They will give me the solace I need.* He meets no one on the way, and no car or lorry passes him in this dead of night.

He arrives at the cluster of *kampung* houses where the path to the river begins. He points the torchlight to the ground as he passes the houses, worried that he may be mistaken for a burglar if someone sees the light. The path continues through a secondary forest. Take a left whenever there is a fork in the road, he reminds himself, or you will end up at a dead end. Fighting through the undergrowth and bushes encroaching on the trail he gets to the clearing where the banyans are. He and Amma spent a lot of time here; they were her favourite trees. She used to say banyans were eternal and pointed beyond this life.

There are scratches on his hands and face. He sits under the roots of the tree in the middle and shines his light upwards. The illumined tree looks like a giant cave with needles pointing down from its roof and reaching up from its floor, wooden stalactites and stalagmites. He stays like this for a long while, a Buddha crouched under a banyan tree. But there is no illumination, no awakening, for him. The best he can hope for is the throbbing in his head to go away. He turns off the light and envelops himself in darkness. The canopies of the trees hide the moon and stars and he cannot see the roots all around him. He reaches out to touch and caress the skin of the figs. He listens to the chirping of crickets. A melody for four voices: calling, courting, repelling, mating.

Do they have a voice for death and dying, or is that too painful for them also? Acha wanted to die, it's not murder, he reminds himself. Mercy killing, mercy killing, he repeats again and again like a calming mantra.

He gets up to stretch his legs once he realises they are numb. He does not know how long he has been sitting and chanting. His headache has subsided, he feels better, calmer. He walks to the river.

A whole night has passed; it is already first light. He sits on the dead tree trunk waiting for the monkeys to come and beg. Two arrive out of nowhere, one on each side, looking at him without making a sound. They tug gently on the sleeves of his raincoat. The raincoat and torchlight are too heavy and will hold him back, so he leaves them with the monkeys as presents. They grin in delight as they play with their new toys, hiding underneath his spaceman suit, shining the torchlight that he has left on in each other's eyes. He must hurry, he must get home before Aini wakes up and finds Acha dead.

A flock of birds flies over the mangroves out to the river, rising and falling without pattern, gliding in formation a few feet above the water like an airborne stingray. This is the first time he has seen so many birds at once since coming home. They have been in hiding from the rain and are now out in numbers, celebrating the end of the monsoon season.

He arrives at the house sweating, out of breath. He has run all the way home and his heart is beating fast, his head light. Entering the house through the Melakan wing he goes to the studio to change.

Aini must not know he abandoned Acha and left the house in the middle of the night. He wipes his hair and face and body with his T-shirt, waiting until his sweat dries before putting on his sarong. He wraps his muddied shoes in the clothes on the floor and throws the bundle into the cupboard where Amma's paintings are.

If he is lucky Aini will still be asleep after a bad night. He checks the kitchen; she is not there. He goes to Acha's room and opens the door, half expecting him to be awake and looking out the window. But he is lying as he left him, alone and still. His eyes and mouth are closed, his face serene. So unlike the hideous expression on Amma's face when he found her dead. Acha's body is cold. No breath, no pulse, no heartbeat. Anil takes a deep breath; he is relieved that he has fulfilled Acha's last wish without slipping up.

He wakes Aini up and takes her to Acha's room. As they walk through the door he says, "He is dead. He is gone." She goes to the bed, throws her arms around Acha and starts sobbing. She kisses his forehead, his lips. Anil leaves her to a private moment of grieving and goes into the study. *Let her cry all she wants now. She will not be able to mourn in public; she is the maid, the mistress, the hidden woman.* He hears her saying, "I am all by myself now. You have left me all alone." From the study he says, "Aini, stay as long as you want. I have to go and make arrangements. But I need Acha's phone book." She comes out, takes a leather-bound diary from the bottom drawer of the desk and hands it to him. "All the numbers are in here."

He calls for help; he does not know what to do. First Uncle Ravi, asking him to come over immediately, then 007. "Don't worry Master Pillai, I will be there as quickly as I can. I have helped with many funerals, so leave everything to me."

All decorations have to be removed, all paintings and drawings covered with white cloth or taken down, that much he remembers. He starts with the living room near the main entrance; this is where people will first enter. It takes him more than half an hour to strip the room bare of adornment and he realises that the house is too big for him to do this by himself. There will be others to help later.

He goes to tell Santhia the news. "I was wondering where you were," she says. "Acha is dead. He died in the middle of the night." She touches his hand. "I am sorry," she says. *Are you? Am I sorry?*

Uncle Ravi and Aunty Shanti arrive an hour later, their children in tow. "I am sorry we couldn't come earlier," Uncle Ravi says. "We had to get the children ready and you know how long that takes." Aunty Shanti throws her plump arms around him, kissing his cheeks and forehead.

"Poor boy. First your mother, now your father so soon after. I have to take you to see a priest I know after the funeral. He can read your palm and your astrological chart. This must be your dark period. *Sanniasi* is attacking you. There are things the priest can do to help."

Shaking his head Uncle Ravi says, "Why do you always have to say the silliest things? Leave the boy alone. He knows nothing about Sanniasi and I don't think he cares."

"I'm only trying to help. You're not angry, Anil?"

"No Aunty. I need all the help I can get. Does your priest also tell the future? I need someone to tell me what to expect."

Uncle Ravi raises his hand to stop her from replying.

"Enough of this. We have more important things to talk about".

"Uncle, can you talk to Mr. Ramalingam and help with the arrangements? I have no idea what needs to be done."

"We'll take care of everything. I do not know who should be invited but Mr. Ramalingam will know or he will be able to find out. That man knows everything and everyone. Your aunty will take charge of what needs to be done here in the house, with Aini's help."

Leading the children to Anil, Aunty Shanti says, "What should you say?" In unison they almost sing their rehearsed sentence, "*Chetta*, we are very sorry about Uncle Sankaran." They wrap their arms around his legs and waist. He pats their heads and tousles their hair.

Santhia walks in holding her stomach. Uncle Ravi, Aunty Shanti and the kids look at the stranger, wondering who she is. "This is Santhia," he says. He is about to add my girlfriend, my wife, but he stops himself. There will be time later to explain. "Santhia, my uncle and aunty and my cousins," he completes his introduction.

"I am sorry to interrupt," she says calmly. "My water has broken, and the contractions are strong. I think I am going to have the baby soon." Aunty Shanti clutches her face and gestures dramatically. "We should rush her to the hospital," she screams.

"We should have the baby here. I'll call Dr. Hoo and ask him to come immediately with everything he needs. Santhia?"

"As you wish, Anil. My doctor in KL expected no complications with the birth so I'm sure it will be alright. It will be much nicer than being in the hospital."

"Aunty, can you please take Santhia to the bedroom and make

her comfortable? I'll call the doctor. Uncle Ravi and the children can wait here for Mr. Ramalingam."

The machinery of birth and death has been set in motion. If reincarnation exists, would the possibility of Acha's soul entering the body of his child increase because they are in the same house? A law of inverse proportion with distance that most forces obey. It would be a fitting punishment for his crime. The son who murders his father is haunted for the rest of his life by his child who has been possessed by the restless soul of his father. Absurd thoughts. His head has been full of them since last night, thoughts of duty, fate and punishment.

He hears Santhia wailing, screaming with all her might. She is dying, she will die in childbirth because of my stupid decision, he thinks. He rushes into the room. Dr. Hoo is standing next to the bed and the other doctor has his hands between Santhia's legs. The old midwife is in the background with her hands clasped behind her back. She casts a disapproving look at Anil. In her world men should appear only after the baby is born and cleaned and the mother made presentable. Santhia is panting, her face and hair drenched with sweat, her eyes wide open. She does not realise he is in the room with her. "Push, one last push," the doctor urges. Santhia draws a deep breath and lets a sound out that does not belong to this world, a cross between a grunt, a shout, a cry for help. "There we go, there we go," the doctor says soothingly, "it's all over." Anil sees a tiny, wet and slimy creature emerge. The doctor cuts the umbilical cord and places it in a stainless steel pan the midwife hands him. He turns the baby upside down and slaps its back a few times. The baby spits and splutters and starts crying. The midwife wraps the baby in a large white sheet and cleans its face and hair. She hands the bundle to Santhia, saying, "It's a baby boy." Santhia holds the baby and sobs quietly. There are smiles all around. Dr. Hoo pats Anil on his back. "Congratulations. Everything went well but if you choose to do this again, make sure it is in a hospital," he says with a laugh.

"Thank you, thank you," Anil says.

He sits on the bed next to Santhia and strokes her hair and face. She does not turn to look at him. Who does the baby look like? More a little rat than anything else, but he thinks he will soon resemble his mother. He had hoped for a girl, he had wanted a baby girl. He will have to hide his disappointment and learn to love his son. He feels nothing for the child lying in Santhia's arms.

He has been here before. The priest sits next to him, chanting. It is the same little man who conducted the funeral rites for Amma three years ago, the priest with the melodious voice who propped him up when his legs went weak at the funeral pyre. Aunty Shanti whispers in his ear, "Say Siva, Siva, Siva, every time the priest finishes a line. You have to say that." Now he realises it was she who had instructed him to repeat those words in front of Amma's coffin. This time he ignores her.

"Should we dress him in a suit or a *munda*?" the elders had asked Uncle Ravi while washing Acha's body. When Uncle Ravi turned to him he said, "A munda." If Acha were dressed formally he would have to be laid out in the cream linen suit, his favourite one that Anil had taken from his wardrobe, and he did not want to give it up. The man who was always careful to look his best in public lies half-naked in his coffin, lines of grey and red *basmam* drawn across his chest and forehead, surrounded by jasmine flowers. No roses for him, but the priest sprinkles rosewater and burns sandalwood incense. Anil makes the elders lay a piece of white cloth across Acha's swollen stomach and cover his marked arms with flowers. He should not be made to suffer the shame of baring the evidence of his disease and his only relief from it. At least Acha's face looks stately and imposing even in death; he would have liked that.

There are many more people today than at Amma's funeral, many faces he does not recognise or has only seen on TV. Colleagues, politicians, businessman, dignitaries come to pay their last respects. He is relieved that he, as the chief mourner, does not have to greet them and make small talk. His place is by the side of the coffin, away from the spectators. 007 darts in and out, making everyone feel welcome, directing them to their places. He sees Tom holding on to a wall for support, barely able to stand up straight. Dr. Razak waves to him; Anil raises his hand to acknowledge his presence. Would he have come to the funeral if he was not already in town? He was not there when Amma died. *Datuk* Velappan and Mr. Lim are here. Normah is hiding in a corner, Aini close to her. Uncle Ravi and Aunty Shanti are by his side.

Santhia is missing; she is with the baby. Harish, Goh Poh and Aris are with her. He had called Aris, told him about the birth and death, and asked him to come with whoever could spare the time to keep Santhia company. He was pleased to see them again. The first words that came out of Harish's mouth after they arrived were, "Have you finished the book I sent you?" Aris shook his head and said, "What an idiot! Do you think he has nothing better to do than read your stupid books?" Anil laughed, glad to be part of their banter again. He will gather them tonight at the house, when everyone is gone, to drink and talk and laugh.

The priest stands up, a signal that the procession to the crematorium is about to begin. Anil walks out of the room, out of the house, to where Abdul stands. "Let's go," he says. "Don't you have to lead the coffin to the hearse and walk behind it like you did the last time?" Abdul asks.

"I don't have to do anything. Let them play along with rules and rites no one seems to know or understand. I am tired of having to do everything because I am the only son."

He gets into the car and tells Abdul to drive to the crematorium.

"Why didn't you turn left back there?" he asks Abdul.

"The old cremation place doesn't exist anymore. It was shut down two years after you left. There is now a different one further down this road. It's a big, new building. Your uncle told me to drive there."

They walk from the parking lot of the crematorium towards the main building. It is a large, open structure with wide columns, painted light blue, like a temple with benches, its idols missing. Gardens with flowers and manicured lawns, willows and jasmine trees, worlds away from the plot of land with pits dug out. "I am Mr. Pillai's son, Anil," he says to the well-dressed man who comes up to greet them. The man looks surprised.

"Are you here alone?"

"For the moment, yes. The hearse and the others will be arriving soon. I would like to walk around for a little while if you don't mind."

"Feel free, make yourself comfortable. When you are ready, take a seat on the first bench in front on the right. I have to go and make some final arrangements."

Anil feels like he is in an upmarket shop or office in the city where service is courteous and professional and the surroundings immaculate. Death dressed up and made more palatable. He explores the grounds with Abdul. Too clean, too clinical, even the flower he picks up by the jasmine tree seems to have been stripped of its scent. What will Goh Poh make of it? He will say that the gardener has lost his way, confusing order and perfection with beauty.

They hear the sound of cars approaching; they walk to the first bench on the right, as instructed, and take their seats. "I don't think I belong here," Abdul says. "I should sit at the back." Anil grabs his arm and says, "Nonsense, you can sit here if I want you to. I don't want to go looking for you when I am ready to leave."

The coffin is brought in on the shoulders of six men, two more than for Amma. Is this because of Acha's weight or importance? They place the coffin on a stand a few feet away from where he and Abdul sit; he can see Acha's face from here. The benches fill up quickly. He turns around to see women seated in the back rows. The rules have changed in three years. Perhaps women are now allowed because this place is not too brutal for them. Uncle Ravi sits beside him. "You shouldn't have gone away like that. You were supposed to walk the coffin to the hearse," he says sternly. Anil says, "I promise to be a good boy from now on."

The priest takes him by the hand and walks him around the coffin three times. Each time they pass Acha's head the priest stops and chants for a while. He hands a stainless steel cup filled with rosewater to Anil and tells him to sprinkle a few drops on his father's face. The ritual has changed too; he has always suspected that the priest and elders make up the rules and rites as they go along, or they are adjusted to match the whims and wishes of the people involved and the surroundings. After the circling is over the priest begins a long, uninterrupted prayer.

The journey from the house to the crematorium has not shaken the blissful look off Acha's face. Does the face mirror the soul in death? Did Acha find peace in his last moments or did he die frightened? His expression is probably the handiwork of the morphine in his body. If this is true he too would want to die like this, floating away on a sea of tranquillity, or at least appearing to do so.

He hears sobbing in the crowd behind him; he thinks he recognises the sound of Aini's crying. *Please, please, let this end before it all starts to crumble.* As if hearing his plea, the priest stops praying and nods to the coffin bearers. They surround the coffin and lift it off the stand onto their shoulders. The priest leads Anil through an archway. He turns round to see if there is anyone behind him but only the bearers follow them. They proceed along a passageway lined with square metal covers in two rows. The well-dressed man appears out of nowhere. "It's further down this way. Just a few yards more," he says. It is very warm here; Anil feels beads of sweat trickling down his face and chest. "It's this one," the man says when they reach the end of the passageway, pointing to the cover on the top row.

The priest asks Anil to sprinkle more rosewater on Acha's face and he says one last set of prayers. He tells Anil to step aside to let the bearers pass by. The man opens the cover; he feels a rush of hot air out the hole in the wall. Through the hole he sees fire. He realises these are ovens, large ovens to burn human bodies. The bearers slide the coffin into the hole until only the last foot sticks out. The priest takes Anil's hands and places them on the coffin. "Push," he says, "you must push." He obeys and pushes with all his strength. He hears a loud crash as the coffin disappears through the hole. The man closes the cover and says, "We can go now."

The pits are replaced by ovens but the ritual is as cruel to him as it was the last time. The new crematorium and the scab around his spirit from going through the funeral rites for Amma do nothing to help make it easier the second time around. He feels his legs starting to buckle and again the priest has to hold him up. As they pass through the archway back into the light he sees faces and bodies in front of him but he does not seem to recognise any of them. The priest and the man are on either side of him, holding his arms to prevent him from falling to the ground. Uncle Ravi and Abdul take their places and walk him back to the car.

There are no bones, not a single one in the earthen tray the priest prays over. The fire in the oven was strong enough to turn a whole skeleton to ash. He will not have to consult his book of bones, he will not have to decipher which ones were left behind. The priest pours the ash and flowers into an urn. They walk to the car and drive to the river, the urn in Anil's lap. Only four of them this time: Uncle Ravi, Abdul, the priest and Anil. "Tell the elders and whoever else needs to be told that I want to scatter Acha's ashes without a crowd," he had said to Uncle Ravi after the funeral.

The priest suggests they go further along the river, towards the mangroves, to perform the final rites. "My father wanted his ashes scattered in exactly the same spot as Amma's. I know where it is." He leads them to the place Acha had pointed out three days earlier, turning around to check if the large house with the two elephants on the front gate pillars is directly behind him. "How are we going to climb over this wall?" the priest asks. "That's why I said to go further up where it is easier to get to the water." Anil says, "I'll get over the wall and you hand me the urn when I am on the other side. The rest will be the same, I know what to do." He folds his munda at the knees and jumps over the low wall. The priest stretches his short arms out to give Anil the urn. He walks out into the river until the water reaches his shoulders, then starts swimming with the urn balanced in his left hand. He wants to make sure that Acha's ashes and the urn float out to the straits and don't return to land. The water gets deep and he begins to feel afraid; he is not a good swimmer and he does not want to drown. He dives in and releases the urn, and quickly swims back to shore.

He sits on the low wall to catch his breath. The swim has cleared his head; he had spent the whole night drinking and playing cards with Goh Poh and Aris, breaking off only when Abdul and Uncle Ravi arrived to take him to the crematorium. Turning towards the river he sees that the urn has been dragged down to the riverbed by the currents; Acha will not return. He feels the warmth of the sun on his back. The coconut trees near the mangroves dance in the light breeze. Pulau Besar is visible in the distance. All this is a distorted image in a mirror or a window of what happened three years ago.

He asks Abdul for a cigarette. "But you don't smoke," Abdul says. "I was here three days ago with Acha. He smoked a cigarette before we walked back to the car. It was his final cigarette. Let me smoke one as a gesture of remembrance." A cigarette in place of tears.

"Does this have to be done now?" he asks the man sitting in front of him in the living room. The man is no more than forty, with a handsome face and a thin moustache above his plump, red lips. He is dressed in dark blue trousers, a striped light blue shirt, and a yellow tie. Anil notices the gold watch against the dark skin of his wrist and hand. "I have strict instructions. I have to pass all this to you within a week of your father's death," the man says.

"I don't understand. Why would my father need a lawyer when he was a lawyer himself? Didn't he have enough lawyers working for him?"

The man had introduced himself as Mr. Sivakumar, his father's lawyer.

"Precisely for moments like this. And lawyers are like doctors in a way, they don't like working on themselves. Your father had many lawyers working for him but he used me and my firm for all personal matters."

"Couldn't he have found a firm here in Muar? Why all the way in KL?"

"I don't want to blow my own trumpet, but we represent many prestigious people. How do I put it? We are professional and discreet."

It sounds like an advertisement, a slogan, to him, but he likes this Mr. Sivakumar, he likes his smile and his informal manner. He decides he will keep him on as his own lawyer.

"Do I need to know anything special?"

"Only that your father amended his will two weeks ago."

Two weeks ago, that was after the incident with 007 and the dowry for his daughter but before his conversation with Acha about Dr. Razak. What could have happened to make him change his will?

"How did he do that?"

"He called me and had someone pick up an envelope with handwritten notes to serve as part of his will, and another envelope, sealed and only to be opened by you."

"Did he cut me off? I wouldn't be surprised if he did as a cruel joke."

The man laughs and slaps his thigh.

"No, no, not at all. The notes were merely very detailed information about where everything is. He told me that you had his notebooks which would give you a good picture of your inheritance but he wanted to make it clearer, more precise, so you would not have to struggle with the numbers. That's what he said to me, struggle with the numbers."

"I am not a genius with numbers but I understand them well enough."

"I'm sure you do. Like everything else they just take getting used to. But your father did make one change to his will."

"What was that?"

"He has left a million *ringgit* to Aini. It was two hundred thousand in the original will, quite a difference. The girl will be set up for life if she is careful with her money. She must be quite a maid. You can contest this if you are prepared to state in a court of law that he was not of sound mind when he made the change. It would not be hard for me to arrange it."

"I have no wish to do that. My father's mind was perfectly sound till the end. He must have been worried for her future. This will allow her to do whatever she wants. You must understand that Aini was not only the maid but his mistress too."

"You needn't have told me that."

"I know, but if I am to keep you on as my personal lawyer, I don't want there to be too many secrets."

Mr. Sivakumar looks at his watch and says, "I have to go soon. There is a meeting I have to be at in KL late afternoon."

"Don't let me keep you. I think I have all I need. Acha told me that he had written a letter to me. This sealed envelope must contain it."

"He did not say what the envelope contained. Don't you want to know what you are worth?"

"I am not sure I care. Don't tell me now, maybe another time."

He shows Anil the notes and the original will. Next to each entry is an estimate of what the asset is worth.

"You can total it up if you wish. Let me just say that you are one of the richest men in the country. Your father's personal accountant will be able to give you a more precise number. Here is his card."

Acha had said there was nothing he couldn't do with the money left to him, Dr. Razak that he could move mountains with it. The numbers next to the entries must add up to some staggering total that makes these words true.

"Can you tell me what is happening with the Onn Rahim trial? I have not been following it," Anil says.

"The trial is in its early stages but the sodomy charges look very weak. All the evidence is highly questionable. The witness, the alleged victim, changed his story a dozen times when Onn's lawyers quizzed him. But I think the corruption charges will stick. There appears to be no way for him to escape a long sentence."

All his money will not be able to save Onn from spending years in a prison cell, Anil thinks. But it could help his wife's newly-formed party and it could help Onn start again after he gets out.

The smell of *puttu* reaches him as he walks into the kitchen. The gentlest of smells, steaming flour and grated coconut. He loves the special utensil it is cooked in: a metal steamer with cylindrical shells sticking out of the main body, like a space probe. Aini is crumbling molasses into a bowl. She turns to him and says, "I thought we should eat something filling after starving for two days."

"Good idea. Santhia loves puttu as much as I do, so she will be happy too."

"How is she? How is the child?"

"They are both fine. I am glad that our friends are here to keep her company. I'm afraid I have neglected her and my son. The gang goes back to KL today so I must make sure to be with her as much as I can."

"I'm making plenty of puttu so it should be enough for all of us. If your friends don't like it there is bread and jam and fruits. I'm sure Santhia will understand that you have a lot to do."

"I'm not sure. You should know what women are like, they

can't bear to be neglected. That is the biggest sin in their books."

Aini laughs. "You're right. We need a lot of attention."

"I have something to tell you."

She stops working and turns to him, a worried look on her face.

"It's good news. Acha has left you a million ringgit in his will. I'll have the money transferred to you as soon as I have your bank details."

"He told me about it. I don't care about the money. You can keep it if you want."

"It's your money Aini. Why would I keep it? I have more than enough. It means that you can do whatever you want. You can leave if you wish."

She drops the molasses on the floor and starts crying. Anil puts his arms around her; she rests her head on his shoulders.

"What will I do, live on my own? I can't go back to my family with this child. They won't accept me. What do you want me to do?"

He steps back and touches her belly.

"I want you to stay. My half-sister is in here. I hope it is a girl. I wanted Santhia to have a girl but I have a son. It would be nice to have a baby sister."

"I will make sure it is a girl for you."

After the funeral these words were said about Acha, among others:

Dr. Razak: Your father was a special man, a great man. You should be proud that he did so much for his country. Always behind the scenes, not wanting any attention for himself. That is rare. I hope you will follow in his footsteps. If you need any help, anything at all, you can always call me.

007: I will miss Mr. Pillai. He was kind to me. I hope I will be able to serve you the same way I served your father. It was an honour to work for such a great man.

The Straits News: Mr. Pillai died peacefully today at home in Muar, Johor. An important entrepreneur and business leader, he will be missed by his colleagues and friends. He leaves behind a son.

The Daily Planet: What can we make of this? A businessman dies and half of the capital city empties to attend his funeral. Politicians, business leaders and dignitaries galore. How important was this man to the workings of our government, what did he do behind the scenes? An enigmatic character for sure. He never held an official post but he was always there in the mix. Another example of the murky waters of our political scene. We will never know who this man really was.

A man he does not recognise: Your father was a good man. He found me a job when I lost mine many years ago. I was too old to find another one on my own. One of his friends hired me to work in his office. He got my son a scholarship to study at the university. My son is now a lawyer in Singapore. There are some people who will tell you that he was like any other businessman and politician working just to become richer and more powerful. Don't believe them. I can find you many people he helped over the years.

Abdul-the-driver: Your father is gone but he will be remembered. I am not a clever man but I know the company he kept from all the years of driving him around. The most important people in the country made time for him wherever he went. That should tell you something.

Aini: Don't hate your father for what he did with me. He didn't want to hurt your mother, I know that was never his intention.

Tom: He beat me to the grave.

What would he say about Acha? The words used to describe him — special, great, important — mean little to Anil. He would have to agree with the *Daily Planet*; Acha was an enigmatic man. The man he did not recognise at the bus station said, "Your father was a good man." No one else used those words. Was he a good man? Acha did not seem to care if he was a good man or not, it didn't matter to him. What was the true sum of his life, positive, zero or negative? He will have to make a list, like the will Acha has left behind, placing values next to each entry, adding up his father's life. How will Acha be remembered a year from now, ten years on, when a generation has passed? He wanted to be remembered without distortion. But everything fades with time, memories turn into unrecognisable forms, a man is reduced to a line or two which has little to do with his true essence when he was alive.

Santhia and the baby are sleeping, Aini is in town shopping for food and other things they need. He uses these moments alone to wander through the house, reacquainting himself with its structure and layout. This is the first chance he has had since coming home to explore all nine wings and their interconnecting passageways. There are some things he has forgotten altogether or has the vaguest memories of: the formal dining area in a hidden part of the Minangkabau wing, the numerous ornamental objects collected from all over Malaysia housed in glass cases in the Terengganu wing, the opulent guest rooms in the kampung house from Kedah. White cloth still covers the paintings and decorations; one more day before he can have them removed.

Now that the house is his, he can do as he pleases. The Melakan wing he will keep as his studio; he will work on his cartoons and store Amma's paintings there. Amma's bedroom he will leave as it is, hanging Tom's portrait of her there when he buys it off him. Most of Acha's possessions in his bedroom and study will be removed and given away or destroyed. He will keep only his sarong and cream linen suit. Aini will protest but he will allow her to keep what she wants and remind her of the fate of Amma's things after she died. The study next to Acha's bedroom will become his study, where he will work on his inheritance, his business affairs if he can call it that. He and Santhia and the baby will need more room. The Minangkabau wing, with its ample space and light, will suit them best. The Johor wing he finds the least inspiring. It surprises him that Acha chose it as the entrance to the complex and the location of the main living room. He believes it was Acha's only mistake when having the house built. He will have to find some way of using a more attractive wing to greet visitors. Aini will continue to be the sultana of the Pahang wing, where her bedroom is. The two extra bedrooms there will be enough when her baby is born. Once he has brought about all these changes Santhia will have full reign over how the house should be furnished and decorated. It will help make her feel at home.

The wandering has turned into something altogether different; he is marking his territory, putting his stamp on it.

*

"When can we go home?" Santhia asks. Anil is holding the baby, making funny sounds and trying to make him smile. "We are staying," he says.

"Staying? This was never part of the bargain."

"I don't think there ever was a bargain. There is so much for me to sort out that I need to stay, at least for a while. But you can go back to KL if you want to."

"That's cruel. We have a baby together and I have to go home alone and take care of him."

"What I meant was you could go to KL if you really can't stand it here. I'll make arrangements to buy as big a house as you want there, and for you to have as many servants as you wish. I'll come and visit as often as I can."

"The rich man speaking. What kind of life would that be?"

"I am richer than you can imagine. But it's not about that. I don't want to make you do anything. There are so many things you don't know about."

"Like?"

"Aini is pregnant with my father's child. It will be my half brother or sister. I can't abandon her, not now."

She looks at him with her eyes and mouth wide open. "What, your father made her pregnant when he was dying?" she shouts.

"It was probably a mistake or Aini stopped taking precautions, I don't know which. She was his mistress for many years."

"You can't abandon your father's mistress but you can abandon me."

"I wouldn't be abandoning you. KL is not that far away by car, I could see you a few days a week. And Aini is not as independent and strong as you are."

"How I wish I was weak and helpless."

"What about my work?" she asks after a while. "I need to go back to work in eleven weeks, otherwise I will lose my job."

"That won't happen."

"How can you be so sure? My boss is not the most understanding person in the world."

"I control a majority stake in the newspaper. Acha did and now it's mine."

Santhia sits on the bed, silent.

"Now you know why your chief editor did not want my work anymore. All it took was a call from Acha or one of his men. Your newspaper is not as independent as you think it is. The owners sold stakes to various companies, all owned by Acha as subsidiaries. Who knows what else he got your editor to do? But I wouldn't despair if I were you. Did you see the column on Acha's death? It wasn't the most flattering but it was not blocked. Maybe it was your editor's revenge."

The baby has fallen asleep in his arms. He puts him in the cot and sits beside Santhia.

"Will you marry me?"

"So you're keeping your promise."

"Will you marry me?"

"Who will I be marrying? After what you have told me, I am not so sure."

"Me, it's still me."

Is it still me? Anil looks in the mirror in Amma's bedroom. He has lost weight; his face is drawn and haggard and his body leaner.

The past month has aged him. He looked eighteen when he came home but now he appears at least his age, if not older. It is time that he learns to act like a man; after all he is a father. And he is the emperor of the vast kingdom Acha has left him. His money has countless consequences. Shouldn't he feel responsible for them, the same way he feels responsible for Santhia, his son and Aini? His circle has expanded and the things that concern him are no longer limited to his work, cartoons, Santhia, his friends. His life is bigger, even though he only senses this abstractly; he does not yet feel or grasp its size. Has it really grown? Does a man who inhabits a small world but inhabits it fully have a smaller life than one who has many possessions and cares, one who is spread, through his connections, over so much space and time that he appears to be everywhere?

He goes to the studio. Acha's will and notes lie on the desk unread, the sealed envelope with his letter unopened, the notebooks hidden away safely. Amma's paintings are still in the cupboard. His cartoons are stacked neatly on a table in a corner. The three points of a triangle which encloses him, traps him inside. He has the sudden urge to build a pyre outside the Melakan wing with everything in the studio, to cremate all that binds him. He could leave with Santhia and his baby and go back to their flat in the city, return to his old life or start something new. Music perhaps, or he could try his hand at writing. But he knows that a clean slate is an illusion.

Notes and Acknowledgements

A word on italicisation. Foreign words, meaning those used in Malaysia in Malay, Indian and Chinese, are italicised when they first appear in any given passage but not again for the rest of that passage. Commonly used words like tabla and mahjong have not been italicised.

The two main towns in the book, Muar and KL, exist but street names and other 'facts' have been invented in many cases. For example, there is a Jalan Abdullah in Muar, but the train from KL does not stop in the town. In fact, Muar is not on any train line!

Rehman Rashid's description of Tunku Abdul Rahman and the independence ceremony in *A Malaysian Journey* (pages 53–55) influenced the writing in Acha's speech to Anil towards the end of the chapter *The Palace on Stilts* (pages 23–24).

Harish's brief biography of Borges in *Cartoons* (pages 111–112) relies on the version found on www.kirjasto.sci.fi/jborges.htm (the author is identified as Petri Liukkonen and the material there is under a CCL). Harish goes on to read from *Funes the Memorius* and *Tlön, Uqbar, Orbis Tertius* (pages 112–113). This, together with Anil's reading of a passage from *The Garden of Forking Paths* and his quote of a line from *Tlön, Uqbar, Orbis Tertius* in the chapter *Father and Son* (pages 140 and 144), are all reproduced from *Labyrinths* (Jorge Luis Borges, Penguin).

Tom gets a few facts wrong (pedants often do!) when describing Prinzhorn in *Illuminations*. Prinzhorn extended the Heidelberg collection significantly but it had already been there for some time, and he did so from 1919–1921.

There are probably some unacknowledged influences, phrases and quotes. I apologise in advance for any omissions.

Tita, my wife, inspired the trick Anil has to perform to get the TV to work in *The City*. She ingeniously discovered it when trying to get the first TV set we owned to come alive again when it suddenly went dead. More crucially, I thank her for all her love and support.

Thanks to Jacob Ross, whose insightful interpretation and comments upon reading the first draft have greatly improved the book, to Lee Mei Lin (my editor at Marshall Cavendish), and to Tara Dhar, who did such a fine editing job. I also thank Neil Katz, who read the initial chapters many years ago when I first began turning this story into a novel.

Needless to say, this is a work of fiction. Any similarities between characters in the novel and the quick and the dead are coincidental. The same holds for events in the novel and those in the real world.

About the Author

Sunil Nair was born in Malaysia. He moved to the United States to obtain his undergraduate and post-graduate degrees. After two years as a post-doctoral fellow in Trieste, Italy, he began a new career in academic publishing in London. He still lives there with his wife and is now a publisher. *When All the Lights Are Stripped Away* is his first novel.